"Kit, do not go.
The danger is too great."

Damaris turned to face him, and in spite of the modish gown and the preposterous array of jewels, it was a child who spoke, a child lost and frightened, crying in the dark for the comfort he had never failed to give her.

"Why, what is this?" He came towards her through the dimness, for the only light now in the room was that which found its way through the half-open door. "It is not like you, Damaris, to shrink from the thought of a blow against Spain."

"I am afraid," she said, her voice catching on a sob, "and you have been home so short a time. Oh, Kit, let it go! What use is gold if it costs your life to win it?" Her voice broke. "Do not go! Something tells me that this venture is ill-fated."

He caught her to him, crushing her in a merciless grip so that she could scarcely breathe, and buried his face against her shining hair.

"I will come back," he said fiercely in a whisper, and his tone made a vow of the simple words. "I will come back!"

The
GOLDEN PANTHER

Sylvia Thorpe

A FAWCETT CREST BOOK

Fawcett Publications, Inc., Greenwich, Connecticut

THE GOLDEN PANTHER

THIS BOOK CONTAINS THE COMPLETE TEXT OF
THE ORIGINAL HARDCOVER EDITION.

A Fawcett Crest Book reprinted by arrangement with
Hutchinson Publishing Group, Ltd.

ISBN 0-449-23006-6

Printed in Canada

PROLOGUE

The moon was at the full, and the countryside, held fast in the iron grip of frost, lay silent and glittering beneath it. Everything was still and sharply defined, with no softness, or kindly blurring of harsh outlines. The trees in the valley lifted their branches starkly against the sky, and, on the ground below, the black filigree of their shadows lay as motionless as though drawn in ink; the road, a mere track which climbed and coiled along the floor of the valley, had every rut and pitfall clearly revealed, while, far off, the rugged horizon of the moors etched a hard line against the stars.

The silence and cold brilliance of the night, as much as the ardently desired but totally unexpected change in his fortunes, were exhilarating as a draught of strong wine to young Kit Brandon as he strode along, following the twists and turns of that abominable road. After dreary months spent in plying a quill in a dark and musty shop, under the eye of a merchant whose thoughts never strayed far beyond his profits, simply to be walking thus was to feel like a prisoner enlarged. To be doing so with no prospect of a return to that clerkly drudgery filled him with an exultation which rendered him heedless of fatigue.

He walked briskly, at a steady pace which had scarcely faltered since he set out from his master's house in Tavistock some two hours before. A stout staff

was in his hand, carried rather as a protection against
any chance-met danger than because he needed its
assistance, and his cloak of thick, rough cloth hung
loose from his shoulders over a doublet and breeches
of the same coarse stuff. His dress was poor, and of
the sober pattern common to gentle and simple alike
in this, the fourth year of the Commonwealth, but there
was nothing lowly in his features or bearing. He looked
as though he would have been more at home with a
good horse beneath him and a sword at his side, than
going humbly on foot, armed only with a staff.

Not that Kit had ever had the opportunity, in all his
sixteen years, of riding thus gallantly equipped, for during the course of the Civil War his father, an ardent
Royalist, had given wealth and blood alike in the Stuart
cause. Their beautiful home, Fallowmead, had gone
early in the struggle, captured by Parliamentary troops
and by them reduced to a blackened, smoking ruin,
and thereafter had followed, for Kit and his young
mother, years of hardship, of fear and uncertainty and
harsh, grinding poverty. He had seen his father for the
last time on the eve of the Royalist defeat at Naseby,
for though the elder Christopher Brandon survived the
battle, it had never been possible for him to rejoin his
wife and son. For six years they cherished the hope of
a reunion, and then had come certain news of his death
on the field of Worcester.

Their material circumstances were unchanged by
their loss, for Colonel Brandon had nothing left to bequeath to his son but a burning loyalty to the Royal
cause. These were days, however, when such loyalty
was best hidden under a superficial obedience to the
new masters of England; some day the sword might
be unsheathed once more, but meanwhile the mere

business of making a living occupied all the energies of Jane Brandon and her son.

Matters had grown desperate when Jane succeeded in obtaining for herself a post as lady's maid to the wife of a Parliamentary officer, and for Kit a lowly place in the Colonel's stables. The boy, willing enough to perform menial tasks himself, seethed with helpless rage at the thought of his mother's humiliation, but, young as he was, he had already learned patience and self-command. It was a lesson which was to stand him in good stead in the years to come.

The Colonel's duties brought him to Devon, and in Tavistock Kit had the good fortune to find work as a clerk to a merchant whose fanatical Puritan zeal concealed the grasping nature of a miser. It was a galling life to a spirited lad with three generations of soldiers behind him, but to be a clerk was better than to be a stable-boy, for it meant that he could provide his mother with a home. This was a tiny, tumbledown cottage so remote from all other habitation that it had long stood empty, but it was a home of her own, where she was no longer at the mercy of a peevish mistress. It was the first step towards the goal he had set himself when he learned of his father's death—the rebuilding of the Brandon fortune.

The second step had been made possible far sooner than he had dared to hope, and was the cause of his present excitement. A week earlier, a kinsman of his master had come to Tavistock on some matter of family business, and had since been lodged in the merchant's house. Josiah Barrow was a native of Plymouth, a ship's captain and owner of the vessel he sailed. He was a big, bluff, hearty man, with features which seemed to be carved from some dark, weather-

beaten wood, and a voice accustomed to making itself
heard above the roaring of Atlantic gales, and he came
into his cousin's dark, narrow house like one of those
same gales, with a burst of genial laughter which rang
strangely through the sombre rooms.

Kit liked him from the first, and Master Barrow's
curiosity was immediately roused by this dark, handsome boy whose proud bearing accorded so ill with
his present occupation. He fell into the habit of talking
to him whenever the opportunity occurred, and the
end of it was that when his visit was drawing to a
close he asked him if he would like to sail with him on
his next voyage, adding scornfully that a lad of his
spirit and muscle was wasted scribbling figures for a
niggardly, Psalm-singing shop-keeper.

Kit stared at him in astonishment, and as though the
words were an incantation to conjure up visions, he
saw unimaginable vistas opening before him; action
and adventure and, above all, escape from this England
where all that he had been taught to love and reverence
lay in the dust. He saw blue seas breaking on tropic
shores, and heard the unfamiliar cadence of foreign
tongues. The vision of a whole new world seemed to
flash before his dazzled eyes in the fraction of time
between one heartbeat and the next, and then the voice
of duty spoke coldly to check his exultation. The vision
faded, and he shook his head.

"I—I cannot, Master Barrow," he stammered. "God
knows I would like nothing better, but my mother is a
widow and looks to me for support. I could not leave
her."

"Aye, lad, you told me, and I've thought of that.
There's a house in Plymouth that sorely needs a
woman's care, for it's stood empty these two years

past, ever since my own old mother died, and 'tis a poor welcome after long months at sea, to come back to shuttered windows and a cold hearth. I'd be grateful if your mother would bide there, and make a home for you and me to return to at the end of a voyage."

Overcome by the sailor's generosity, Kit tried to express his gratitude, but at once Barrow cut him short.

"I want no thanks, lad. I'd not suggest it unless I thought you could be useful to me, and mind, 'tis no easy life I offer you. There'll be hardship and danger a-plenty, and ye need expect no favours above your fellows, but there's freedom on the seas such as ye'll not find in England for many a day to come." He paused, and then added in a lower tone: "There was Royalists fell at Worcester as well as Roundheads, and as to that I ask no questions, but many a loyal King's man finds it well to feign sympathy wi' Cromwell and his like while they have the power. Remember that, Kit Brandon."

So Kit accepted the offer, subject to his mother's approval, and that same evening, Master Barrow having obtained from his kinsman the necessary leave, he set off to bear the news to her at the little cottage on the edge of the moors. Barrow had promised to ride out the following day to speak with Mistress Brandon, and Kit beguiled the tedium of his solitary tramp with roseate dreams of the future, and happy musings upon the chance which had placed it within his reach. He still thought of it as no more than a stroke of good luck; it needed the later events of the night to suggest to him that here was no chance, but the first workings of some mysterious pattern of destiny.

So absorbed was he in his thoughts that the hoofbeats coming up behind him had drawn quite close before he

became aware of them, although sounds carried far in
that echoing silence. Even then it was their strangely
irregular rhythm which caught his attention, and
brought him swinging round to stare with a puzzled
frown along the winding road he had just traversed.

At length the rider came into view, and the bright
moonlight showed only too clearly the reason for his
mount's stumbling gait, for the poor brute had been
ridden almost to a standstill. It was in a lather of sweat,
its sides heaving, its flanks streaked with blood from the
pitiless spurs; from its distended nostrils the breath rose
smoking on the frosty air, and the bridle was flecked
with foam. Its rider was muffled in an ample cloak, his
high-crowned hat pulled low over his brows, but Kit
could see that he carried some bulky object in the crook
of his arm. At sight of the lone wayfarer he checked as
though to speak with him, then, apparently changing
his mind, urged the horse onward again.

Kit remained where he was, startled and oddly disturbed by the encounter, and as he stared after the
reeling horse and its muffled rider he saw the man look
back over his shoulder, but the glance did not seem to
be directed towards him. It was then, for the first time,
that he became aware that there was another traveller
abroad that night, for the steady, purposeful beat of
galloping hoofs, faint as yet but growing louder each
moment, came echoing out of the black and silver
stillness behind him.

In no way reassured by the sound, he went on his
way, and only a few hundred yards further on came
upon a sight which occasioned him little surprise. In a
hollow where the road ran down to ford a brawling
brook, the man who had passed him stood helplessly
beside the dark mass of his fallen mount, looking about

him in a hunted way. Kit quickened his pace, and as he reached the unfortunate wayfarer the bundle the man still held stirred and whimpered, and the boy realized with astonishment that it was a child.

"Young man," the stranger greeted him urgently, "do you know these parts? Is there a house or an inn at hand where I may find me a fresh horse?"

"No, sir, I fear not," Kit replied courteously. "The nearest house is my mother's cottage, a mile or so further on. We have no horse, but if you will come with me I know that she will gladly offer you shelter, and care for the little one."

The man shook his head. His hat lay now upon the road, and the moonlight disclosed a young, haggard face, grey with fatigue and wasted as though by sickness; his sunken eyes seemed unnaturally bright, and from time to time a violent shudder shook him from head to foot. The child in his arms was so muffled in wraps as to be invisible, and only its plaintive, whimpering cries betrayed its presence.

Kit was conscious of the liveliest curiosity. After years of civil war, the roads of England swarmed with half-starved vagrants of all ages, but this man was clearly not of their kind. His speech and manner were not uncouth, and though he was plainly, even poorly dressed, there was something of authority in his bearing.

"A mile!" he muttered now, in answer to Kit's words. "Too far, too far! We could never reach it before—" he broke off, and clutched Kit's arm with his free hand. "Listen! Do you not hear him?"

Kit listened. The hoofbeats were nearer now and growing rapidly louder, a steady drumming relentless as fate, a pursuit that neither faltered nor turned aside, and the menacing rhythm of them sent an unreasoning chill of fear through his whole being. He conquered it with an effort, and turned to his companion.

"There is but one horseman there," he said, and the other nodded.

"Aye, he rides alone, as always! None share his secrets." Another convulsive shudder shook him, and he added under his breath: "None save the Devil, his master!"

Once more Kit felt his spine prickle with inexplicable dread. In those days the supernatural world came very close to that of reality, and men who had a profound faith in God believed with equal conviction in Satan. Witches and wizards were the earthly servants of the forces of evil, and few doubted their ability to harm or the source whence they derived that power. The loneliness of the place and the hour, and the wild aspect of this stranger with the burning eyes, wrought so strongly upon him that he found himself trembling, and in spite of the cold there was sweat upon his brow.

It was the child which checked his ebbing courage. It was still uttering small, sobbing cries, and the sound roused him to the fact that whatever was approaching, were it man or devil, some attempt must be made to shield this helpless little creature. He took a fresh grip on his staff, and spoke with more assurance than he felt.

"If he who follows you brings danger, sir, at least he comes alone. You have a sword and I my staff, and between us we can surely account for one man. Set the babe down for a moment—'twill be safe enough between the roots of the great tree yonder."

"Safe?" the other repeated wildly. "She will never be safe while that devil lives! If she falls into his hands he will destroy her very soul." He bowed his head over the muffled infant, and a groan burst from his lips: "My sweet babe, my little Damaris! Better she had been laid with her mother in the grave than be spared for such fate as that."

He was swaying on his feet as he spoke, and as Kit gripped his arm to steady him he realized suddenly that the stranger was in the grip of a raging fever, and barely responsible for words or actions. And all the while the hoofbeats were drawing closer. It could be a matter of moments only before the rider topped the rise and saw his quarry before him.

Kit cast a frantic glance about him. Concealment would be easy enough, for the tree he had mentioned was but the outpost of a fair-sized copse thick with undergrowth, but the carcase of the horse could not be hidden and must inevitably betray them. Nor could he, burdened with the sick man and the child, hope to evade the unknown enemy.

"Sir!" He spoke urgently, forcing into his voice every ounce of authority he could muster. "In a moment your pursuer will be upon us. De we stand or fly?"

The other stared at him, and seemed to make a tremendous effort to achieve coherent thought. Apparently he was at least partially successful, for a calmer look descended upon his face, and when he replied his voice was quieter and more decisive.

"I will stand, young man. Do you take the babe and conceal yourself in yonder thicket, nor let her utter a sound while he is within hearing. It may be that I can trick him into following a false trail."

This was little to Kit's liking, for he would have preferred to stand his ground at the stranger's side, but he was given no chance to protest. The child was thrust into his arms, and as the pursuing hoofbeats thundered

up the far side of the little rise he plunged into the
dense black shadows beneath the trees. Glancing back
as he gained their shelter, he saw the young father
standing erect and motionless beside the dark mass of
the dead horse; he had drawn his sword, and now
waited with its point resting lightly on the ground and
its blade a blue-white flame in the moonlight.

On the crest of the rise, in the gap where the road
cut through the trees that crowned it, a horseman appeared, and checked as he saw what the hollow held,
his mount rearing with the suddenness of that abrupt
halt. Then he came on again, but slowly now, the horse
held in to a deliberate, almost mincing gait as it picked
its way down the slope towards the waiting man. Finally
it was reined in again close beside him, and its rider
sat looking down at him in silence.

Kit, watching intently from his hiding place, saw
that here was a very different figure from the first. The
fugitive, with his cropped hair and homely garb of
leather and homespun, was of Puritan severity, but the
newcomer had all the elegance his quarry lacked. Here
were long curls flowing from beneath a broad hat
pulled so low that it completely shadowed his face, and
the hat itself carried a curling plume. His cloak swept
down in graceful folds from arrogantly poised shoulders, and the hand which held the chafing horse was
clad in a fringed and laced gauntlet. There were few
men bold enough to risk apparel so blatantly reminiscent
of the Royalist cause, but Kit felt a sudden conviction
that this man, whoever he might be, did not waste an
instant's thought upon the opinions of others. His
whole figure, as he swayed easily to the movements of
his stamping, sidling mount, spoke of an arrogance
which followed its own paths with a self-sufficient ruth-

lessness that nothing could restrain.

"So we meet at last!" he said, and his voice was clear and cold and as arrogant as his bearing. There was a slight pause, while his glance swept the moonlit hollow, and then the tone changed to one of sharp, imperious command. "Where is the child?"

The other man laughed shortly.

"Safe beyond your reach, my lord," he said, and the watcher's eyes widened as he noted the title. "You were in such haste to catch me that you never paused to wonder if I still bore her with me."

"While she lives, she will never be beyond my reach," replied my lord coldly. "Were she in the care of Cromwell himself I would have her out of it. She is of my blood, and she shall be reared in my faith."

"Never!" The distraught note was creeping again into the first man's voice. "My child shall never learn to bow down to Rome. Rather would I see her dead, my lord, and so I say again, she is safe beyond your reach."

The mounted man shook his head, and when he spoke his cold voice held a sneering note. Kit could imagine how, in the shadow of the concealing hat, his lips must be writhing with a matching mockery.

"A clumsy device, my friend. Fanatical Puritan though you be, you would not stain your hands with your own child's blood. She was with you when you came ashore, therefore she must be hidden somewhere betwixt that point and this, for I have been too hard upon your heels for you to turn aside. I shall find her, rest assured of that."

Kit felt a surge of jubilation. The ruse was working it seemed, and if my lord could be persuaded to turn back in search of the missing child, the fugitives might well make their escape. His sympathies were entirely with the young father, in spite of his hatred of all Puritans, for there was something about the haughty figure on the fretting horse, something in the sound of his level voice, which roused in him a depth of aversion as uncontrollable as it was inexplicable. Whatever story lay behind the present meeting, he felt sure that my lord's part in it was evil.

The fugitive was speaking again.

"Can you search each house along the road, my lord? This is Puritan England, not papist France, and were your identity suspected the people would rend you limb from limb."

A low laugh came from beneath the broad-brimmed hat, a hateful sound of infinite mockery.

"Why then did you not arouse your heretic rabble against me as you rode? But of course, you, too, have something to fear, have you not? An officer who deserts in time of war goes in some danger if he be foolish enough to return to his own land."

He paused there, and the other man, as though spurred by an anger beyond his control, started forward with shortened sword. My lord did not move a muscle, and his very immobility seemed to set a curb on the other's fury. He checked, and drew back a pace, and spoke in a shaking voice.

"I am still soldier enough to deal with you. Light down, my lord, and let us settle our quarrel here and now."

"Mother of God!" The cold voice had changed again; it was now that of a master addressing a lackey. "Am I to cross swords with a renegade dog who could not be true even to the false cause he served? I have but one more word to say to you. I know not by what damnable arts you seduced my sister from loyalty to her Church and to her King, but this child bears noble blood in her veins, and she shall be reared as befits a niece of mine, as a Catholic and a Royalist. And now farewell."

He reined his horse back a pace or two as though to turn back the way he had come, and then his right hand came at last from beneath the flowing cloak, there was a sharp report and a tongue of yellow flame, and the Puritan stiffened and dropped where he stood. The horse reared and whinnied, but my lord curbed it with an iron hand and sat looking down at the fallen man, the pistol still smoking in his grasp.

In the shadows of the copse, Kit stood rigid with horror. Beneath the wrappings, his hand was clapped tight across the mouth of the writhing, terrified child, and he had the wit to keep it there throughout the interminable moments while my lord slowly replaced the pistol in his belt and looked keenly all about him. Kit could guess what he was waiting and hoping to hear. If the child had been hidden, sleeping, amid the undergrowth, the sound of the shot would have awakened her, and her frightened cries would betray her presence.

At last, after what seemed an eternity to the watching boy, the cloaked figure moved. The horse was turned, and urged up the slope it had descended so short a time before. Horse and rider vanished again through the gap in the trees, and the hoofbeats quickened as they receded. The little hollow lay vacant and placid under the moon, with only the sprawling corpses of horse and man to tell of the crime which had been wrought there.

When at last the sound of my lord's going had died away in the distance, Kit moved stiffly from the hiding-

place which had served him so well. Setting his wailing
burden down in a leafy hollow between the tree-roots,
he went quickly towards the fallen man. It needed only
a glance to confirm that he was dead, for the bullet
had taken him between the eyes, and for perhaps a
minute Kit stood there, knowing what must be done
and trying to nerve himself to do it.

At length, not without a feeling of nausea, he went
down on his knees beside the dead man and searched
methodically through his pockets. The search was not
rewarding, for it yielded, apart from a very small
amount of money, only such oddments as any man
might carry with him, and nothing which furnished a
clue to his identity. The saddle-bags, to which he next
turned his attention, proved equally barren, for they
contained only a few spare garments belonging to both
father and child.

After a few minutes' deliberation, Kit took everything which belonged to the little girl and made a rough
bundle which he secured to his belt. The rest he returned to the saddle-bags. Then, satisfied that he had
removed all trace of the child's presence, he went back
to where she lay. Her screams of terror had subsided
into long, shuddering sobs, and since she had flung off
most of the coverings, her small face and hands were
as cold as ice; he wrapped her up again as well as he
could, and, picking her up, set off with what speed he
could muster towards the cottage.

A light shone from its window to tell him that his
mother was not yet a-bed, and when he rapped on the
door her voice responded at once, inquiring, on a
startled note, who it was that knocked.

" 'Tis I, Mother. Kit!" he replied, and in a moment
a bolt scraped and the door swung open.

"Kit!" she exclaimed. "My dear son, what brings you here?" Then, as she reached out to embrace him and draw him in, she became aware of his burden. "Why, what have you there?"

He entered the cottage and moved quickly to the fire, saying over his shoulder:

"Bar the door again, Mother. I will explain all, but first, here is a task to which you will be more apt than I."

There was a note of urgency in his voice, and Jane Brandon obeyed without question, moving quietly and without fuss to do his bidding. She was a graceful woman, tall, and still neat of figure despite her poor attire, and with a sweet, worn face lit by beautiful eyes of an unusually deep blue. Those eyes, and her dark hair, were all of her looks she had bequeathed to her son, for Kit's aquiline cast of feature was inherited from his father. As she shot the bolt again and came back to the fire, her face was puzzled and a trifle anxious, but when she discovered the nature of the burden he held, all other emotions were overwhelmed by compassion.

"Ah, poor babe!" she exclaimed, and gathered the whimpering child into her arms. "Where did you find her, Kit? Who is she?"

He told her what he could, while she set the child on her lap beside the fire, and rubbed warmth into the tiny hands and feet that were blue with cold. Presently she interrupted him to bid him set milk to heat above the embers, and he went on with his story as he did so, describing in a voice which held still an echo of the horror and fury he had felt then, those moments of drama in the hollow by the brook, and the brutal murder which had made an orphan of the little girl.

By the time the tale was told, the waif, warmed and fed, was drowsing in Mistress Brandon's arms. She was a pretty child between two and three years old, with a mass of shining, golden hair, and big, long-lashed eyes of a strange colour that was neither blue nor green. Her clothes were plain and poor, but one of the coverings in which she had been wrapped was a woman's velvet cloak, faded and threadbare but lined with costly fur.

"So there you have it," Kit concluded soberly. "Her name is Damaris. Her father was an officer in Cromwell's army, her mother the sister of a Catholic, Royalist lord; and that is all we know, save that her uncle seeks her that she may be bred a papist." He paused, regarding his mother with troubled eyes. "Did I do right, madam, to bring her away as I did?"

Without hesitation Mistress Brandon nodded.

"Assuredly, my son," she replied quietly. "Could you have left her to the mercy of a man whose hands are stained with her father's blood? I pray God that she may never fall into his hands."

"Small fear of that, I fancy." Kit was moving about the room as he spoke, setting food and drink upon the table, for his long walk had made him hungry. "He knew nothing of my presence, and so will not seek the babe beyond the place where he killed her father. If what I heard be truth, he will need to go warily in his search for her. Whoever he may be, it seems he is not unknown in this part of England."

He pulled a stool up to the table and attacked his supper with a hearty appetite. His mother waited patiently until his hunger was appeased, and then she said quietly:

"You have not yet told me, Kit, what brings you here

tonight. You are not—" there was a hint of anxiety in her voice "—not in any trouble with your master?"

"Dolt that I am!" Kit smote the table with his hand, then, thrusting mug and platter aside, leaned forward eagerly. "This other matter had driven it out of my head. No, Mother, 'tis good news I bring, not ill."

Without more delay he told her of his meeting with Josiah Barrow, and the offer the mariner had made him. He spoke eagerly, his face alight with enthusiasm, and wistfulness deepened in his mother's eyes as she watched him. She had seen that look before, on her husband's face when he rode away to offer his sword to his King; and she knew that the time had come when she must let the younger Kit go from her also.

"You mean to accept this offer, my son?" she said with difficulty when he paused for an answer, and he nodded.

"With your permission, Mother," he said, and came to kneel beside the low stool on which she sat, "but you will give it, will you not? This is the opportunity I have prayed for! I cannot, I dare not stay in England while I must feign sympathy with those who killed my father and my King. God knows how I have curbed my feelings so long! There is freedom on the seas, Master Barrow says—aye, and there are fortunes to be made there also!"

Jane frowned.

"I would not have you influenced by the greed for gold, Kit," she rebuked him gently.

"Is it greed, Mother, to wish to give you again the life you once knew? This is the first step towards it, for you may leave this hovel for a house where you will have comfort, and neighbours about you instead of this loneliness. One day I will build you a new Fallowmead to replace the one that the Roundheads destroyed, but until then Master Barrow's house will serve. Oh, Mother, we must accept this offer! It means security for you, and freedom for me, and—" he broke off, looking down at the child now sleeping in his mother's arms, and added more slowly: "And safety for her."

"For her?" Mistress Brandon's voice was startled. "What mean you?"

"I mean that we have at hand the means to shield her for ever from her murderous uncle. In Plymouth we are known to none. If you say that the child is yours, that she is my sister, no one will question it. We may even teach her to believe it herself." He rose to his feet, and after a moment's hesitation gave voice for the first time to a thought which was to become a conviction in the years ahead. "This was no chance, Mother. These two meetings, first with Master Barrow, and then with this babe's father, do they not seem to you to be the very workings of destiny?"

She shook her head.

"This talk of destiny has a heathen ring to it, Kit, and I like it not. Rather should you see in this matter, as I do, the hand of God. This child has been sent to us as a sacred trust, that she may be saved alike from the dominion of Rome and the sin of disloyalty to her rightful King. It is a charge we must do our utmost to fulfil."

Kit accepted the correction meekly, for Jane Brandon was as devout a believer in the Established Church as she was an ardent Royalist, and he knew that his thoughtless words had both grieved and displeased her.

"So be it, then," he said after a moment. "Whatever her true name may be, henceforth she shall bear that of Brandon. Once we have left these parts, no one will question it."

"What of Master Barrow?" Jane asked suddenly. "Must we deceive him also?"

Kit frowned.

"I like it not," he said slowly. "We could do so, I have no doubt, since he knows so little of us, but if we are to accept his generosity we had best be frank with him. I am sure he is to be trusted."

" 'Tis what I would wish," she agreed in a tone of some relief. "Now, Kit, it grows late, and we were best a-bed."

He nodded his agreement, and knelt again to tend the fire, while his mother began to prepare the little girl for the night. Suddenly a startled exclamation brought him to his feet once more.

"What have we here?" she said in surprise. "See, 'twas pinned inside her dress."

She held a brooch out to him as she spoke, and he took it from her and carried close to the candle to examine it. It was a magnificent example of the gold-smith's art, an oval of onyx framed in gold, and bearing, in the same metal, the exquisitely wrought image of a fearsome heraldic beast with flames issuing from its mouth. It lay in his palm, gleaming and beautiful and utterly baffling, for while so unusual a trinket must have some extraordinary significance, what its meaning was he could not even guess.

"I have never seen such a thing before," he said at length, and held it out again for his mother's inspection. "What beast is it, Mother? A lion?"

"I believe it is a panther," she replied doubtfully, "for I can recall seeing pictures of such in a book of heraldry when I was a girl."

"A golden panther!" Kit said slowly. "I'll warrant 'tis some clue to her identity, could we but read its message."

The child had wakened again, and now the gleaming ornament caught her attention. She snatched at it, as though aware of its true ownership; Kit laughed and shook his head.

"No, no, little Damaris," he said. "Whatever secret this beast guards, 'twere better for you, perhaps, if we never learn it." Gently he unclasped the baby fingers, and restored the golden panther to his mother's keeping. "Bestow it safely, madam, where none may see it. 'Tis her only patrimony and we must guard it for her, but after what befell tonight 'twould be unwise, I think, to probe the mystery of her parentage. Who can tell what more of violence we might discover?"

Jane Brandon sighed and nodded.

"Hers is indeed a dark heritage, poor babe," she said softly. "I pray that it will be in our power to shield her from it."

Kit made no reply. The child, deprived of the brooch, had instead clasped his hand in both her own, looking up at him with a·sudden, enchanting smile, and in the same moment, although he knew it not, she took a hold upon his heart which while he lived would never again be loosed.

Chapter I

CAPTAIN LUCIFER

Sir Jocelyn Wade, of Frayne Manor in the county of Sussex, and, more recently, of Whitehall and the Court, stood very erect despite his bonds, and stared across the cabin at his captor with the utmost disdain. It was not easy for features cast in so boyish and ingenuous a mould to appear haughty, but so outraged was Sir Jocelyn by recent events and the present situation that for once his usual amiability of expression was entirely lacking. The lips below the almost imperceptible line of moustache were tightly compressed, the grey eyes bright with indignation, while the very curls of his periwig seemed to quiver with suppressed fury, for at that moment Sir Jocelyn Wade was an exceedingly angry young man.

The effect of all this aristocratic wrath, however, was wholly wasted upon the man whose actions had called it forth, for he appeared completely indifferent to it. He was a swarthy-skinned mulatto, a giant of a man sadly inclined to corpulence, and clad in a fashion which, to anyone familiar with the Indies, proclaimed his calling at a glance. Below the loose, rawhide breeches which reached midway down his calves, his legs and feet were bare; his shirt, stained with sweat and blood, hung open to the waist; and a brilliantly coloured kerchief was swathed about his head. Heavy gold rings dangled from his ears, and into the wide sash girt about his waist a brace of pistols was thrust, while a sword-belt crossed his broad chest. The formidable cutlass this should have supported lay now on the grimy table before him, and he lounged at his ease, one leg hooked over the arm of his chair.

Sir Jocelyn was not familiar with the Indies. He had but recently arrived in the Caribbean, aboard the ship which could even now be seen through the open stern-ports, its blazing hull and rigging sending a tall pillar of smoke aloft towards the cloudless sky, but he was in no doubt whatsoever concerning the trade of the man confronting him. He referred to it now, in terms which showed more courage than prudence.

"Will you explain what you intend by me, you damned pirate?"

The dark eyes in that broad, unprepossessing face regarded him with a kind of ominous amusement, as though their owner was prepared, for the present at least, to be tolerant. A similar expression was in his voice as he answered.

"That depends on the length o' your purse, my bully. From the look of ye, 'tis a deep one." His gaze roved over the prisoner's elegant, if somewhat disordered, person, and his grin broadened. "Still, I'm a reasonable man, I hope! I'll not price ye at more than five thousand pounds."

"Five thousand pounds?" Sir Jocelyn repeated blankly. Then astonishment gave way to renewed indignation. "Not five thousand pence, you cursed scoundrel! I'll see you in hell before I pay you so much as a groat!"

"Have a care 'tis not t'other way about," the other replied grimly. " 'Tis not my custom to take prisoners, and those I do take must pay for the privilege. I've set your ransom at five thousand pounds, and that's what you'll pay if you want to go free."

"And if I refuse?"

The pirate grinned again, and reached out for the can of rum which stood within easy reach. He swallowed a generous measure of it and wiped his mouth on the back of his hand before he replied.

"Why, then, you'll be of no more use to us than the scurvy rogues who manned yon ship we've just taken, and ye'll go the same road as them. Only, since ye're so disobliging, we'll maybe have ye dance and sing a bit first, just to amuse the lads."

"Dance and sing? I?" Wade stared as though his captor had suddenly taken leave of his senses. "You must be mad!"

"Nay, I've seen unlikelier folk than you do it, my lad, if the tune be right. A knotted cord about the brow, or a candle-flame between the fingers, can be mighty persuasive at times. Or if those fail, there's other ways!" He paused, watching his captive's suddenly blanched countenance. "Were ye a bit hasty-like in refusing, d'ye think?"

Sir Jocelyn stared at him for a moment or two in silence. He was by no means a coward, but during the voyage from England he had heard something of the ways of the pirates who infested the Caribbean, and these tales were stirring now in his memory. Stories of inhuman cruelties, which he had regarded with a certain scepticism, seemed hideously probable in the presence of this hulking, evil brute who looked capable of any infamy.

"But, damn you, how can I pay?" he burst out at length. "Do you suppose I carry such a sum with me?"

A guffaw of derisive laughter greeted the question.

"If ye did, my lad, we'd have emptied your pockets of it long since, but ye've a family, I suppose, or friends who will send that sum when they learn how urgently you need it. Meanwhile, I'll house and feed ye at my own expense. As I've said, I'm a reasonable man."

Sir Jocelyn cast a glance of extreme distaste around the filthy cabin, but whatever answer he would have made was forestalled, perhaps fortunately, by the arrival of another of the pirates, a stocky, grey-bearded ruffian lacking an eye, and with his face hideously disfigured by a tremendous scar. He seemed perturbed.

"Ye'd best leave this, Marayte," he announced. "There's other matters to deal with first." He jerked his head expressively towards the door. "While you've been haggling here, the *Loyalist* has come up, and she's lying hove-to not a quarter of a mile away. I don't like it, and that's a fact! She's got twice our armament and three times the number o' men."

"Ye cursed lily-livered rat!" Marayte growled, unmoved by the other's disquiet. "She's been in sight an hour or more, and what of it? If she's come for pickings, she's out o' luck! Let her take her own prizes."

The other man glowered at him.

"Cap'n Lucifer's not the man to take your leavings, Marayte, and well you know it. Aye, and he a'nt got such a fondness for us that he'll alter course just for the pleasure o' bidding us good-day."

"And there, my friend, you are quite mistaken," a new voice put in from the doorway. It was a quiet, pleasant voice, speaking a precise and cultured English that was so unexpected in those surroundings that Jocelyn's head jerked round in astonishment. "A boat has just put off from the *Loyalist* towards us, and in it is Lucifer himself."

The speaker advanced into the cabin, revealing himself as a slight, soberly clad young man who, at first glance, appeared to have nothing in common with his two ruffianly shipmates. His straight, fair hair framed a pallid face whose original good looks had been marred at some time by the ravages of smallpox, and his dress might have been that of a tutor or a prosperous merchant. Only his eyes, which were pale blue and singularly cold and calculating in expression, were at odds with the rest of his appearance, but they struck a note as sharply incongruous as the long cutlass that swung at his side.

His words did nothing to soothe his comrade's anxiety; rather did it seem to increase it. He hooked his thumbs into his belt and rolled his single eye truculently from one to the other.

"Then 'tis no good as brings him, I'll be bound," he declared. "Since when has he troubled himself to be civil to the likes of us? Too plaguey proud to notice us, he is! Lucifer! Bah!" He spat copiously in token of his profound disgust, and the young man shrugged.

"He is well named, certainly," he agreed indifferently. "For pride, there is not his equal in all the Indies."

"As you know to your cost, eh, Renard?" Marayte put in slyly. Renard turned his head to look at him, and though no word was spoken, the mulatto's grin faded, and in some disorder he buried his face again in the drinking-can. A faint, unpleasant smile touched the younger man's lips, and he turned his attention once more to the grey-bearded pessimist.

"If Lucifer's intentions towards us were unfriendly, Ben," he pointed out, "he would not now be coming aboard. He is no fool."

"Nay, and who's to tell what trick he may be planning?" Ben demanded belligerently. "Look'ee, Renard, if a man join the Brethren, let him do it in earnest, say I! Let him fill his pockets at sea and empty 'em ashore, same as we do, and to the devil wi' tomorrow! Who's Lucifer, for all his airs and graces and pimpish fine manners, to be setting himself above you and me? He's no better than the rest of us."

Renard's smile broadened a trifle, but it lent no warmth to his pale, pock-marked countenance; rather did it deepen his expression of cold mockery. He said softly:

"Say as much to his face, then, when he comes aboard."

Marayte, glad of a victim upon whom to avenge his own discomfiture, loosed a guffaw of scornful laughter.

"What, and get a foot o' cold steel through his vitals? Ben Gribben's not the lad to risk so much! He'll snarl at Lucifer behind his back, and fawn on him when he comes aboard." He drained the last of the rum from the can, and launched the empty vessel at his henchman's head. "Get out o' my sight, ye lousy, whining cur!"

Ben dodged the missile with the agility of long experience, and departed, muttering dire prophecies in his beard. Marayte glared ill-humouredly after him.

"Plague take him, he grows old and timorous," he grumbled, and then, as though Gribben's words had weighed with him in spite of his denials, he added abruptly: "What does Lucifer want with us?"

Renard looked at him contemptuously.

"Can I read his thoughts, you fool? We shall know soon enough." He dropped into a chair by the table, and turned his cold glance upon Sir Jocelyn. "How goes this matter?"

"Well enough," Marayte replied sullenly. "At first the gentleman weren't over-willing to loosen his purse-strings, but now he knows the alternative he's disposed to be reasonable, a'nt ye, my cockerel?"

During the respite afforded by Gribben's interruption, Sir Jocelyn had had time to consider his situation. It was not encouraging. Obviously his present immunity from harm would continue only as long as the pirates saw a profit to themselves in treating him well, and he must resign himself to paying a substantial price to preserve his life, though the sum named by Marayte would come near to ruining him. He said so.

Appearances were against him, and he was not at first believed. He stood his ground, however, in the face of all Marayte's threats, and they were still haggling over the exact amount of the ransom when brisk footsteps sounded in the gangway and a tall gentleman entered the cabin.

A gentleman! That was the astounding fact which Jocelyn's bemused mind at first refused to accept, for here was no swaggering ruffian tricked out in a vulgar ostentation of finery, but a man who would not have looked out of place at Whitehall itself. From the sweeping plume in his broad black hat to the soles of his elegant shoes, there was not a single detail to betray the fact that he had come straight from the deck of one pirate ship to the cabin of another.

He paused just within the door, and Jocelyn, recovering from the impact of such modishness in so unlikely a spot, had time to take stock of the man himself. He was tall and finely proportioned, with a look of strength about him which had nothing in common with Mar-

ayte's mere bulk, but which suggested rather the lithe
toughness of tempered steel. His dark hair, which he
wore long in place of a periwig, fell in curls over his
shoulders, and between the curls was a handsome,
aquiline face, with a resolute chin, and eyes of an exceedingly dark blue. It was the face of a man who had
learned to command himself as well as others, and that
early in life, for he could not be much more than
thirty years old.

A sudden silence marked his entry into the cabin,
and Jocelyn became aware of a certain increase of
tension. Then Renard came slowly to his feet and
bowed with exaggerated courtesy.

"Captain Lucifer, this is indeed an honour!" There
was the same ironical emphasis in his precise voice,
but Wade had the impression that no jest was intended.
"Behold us utterly overwhelmed. A chair, Captain,
and a glass of wine."

The newcomer advanced into the cabin, but made
no move to avail himself of the invitation. There were
two other men at his heels, one young, with fair hair
and laughing, hazel eyes, and the other a tall, lean
fellow of middle age, his dark, cadaverous countenance
wearing an expression of settled melancholy. They, too,
advanced, the younger slamming the door with a back-
ward thrust of his foot. Captain Lucifer paused by the
table and rested one hand lightly upon it.

"Do you command the *Albatross* now, Renard, in
name as in all else?" he inquired pleasantly.

The fair boy laughed, and Renard's pale eyes narrowed to mere glittering slits, but it was Marayte who
answered, heaving himself up out of his chair with a
violence which sent it scraping a yard or more across
the grimy floor.

"Plague take ye, Lucifer, I command this ship, and I'll slit the throat of any as says otherwise! Whatever ye want here, ye'll settle it wi' me."

"So be it!" There was a fine edge of steel now to Lucifer's voice. "Then since you are captain, Marayte, perhaps you will tell me what the devil you mean by attacking an English ship."

The pirate's jaw dropped, and he gaped ludicrously before the unexpectedness of that swift attack; then, before anger could come to drive away surprise, Lucifer went on:

"And as if 'twere not enough to plunder an English ship, you must needs take prisoner a gentleman of the Court. God preserve us! Where are your wits?" He broke off to say over his shoulder: "Alex, release the gentleman, if you please."

With no lightening of the gloom of his expression, the dark man moved to do his bidding, and as Renard's hand went swiftly to his sword, the movement was forestalled by the pistol which had appeared suddenly in the fair boy's grasp.

"Easy, my friend, easy!" he adjured him with a grin. "Don't put me to the trouble of blowing your brains out."

The tone was light, but the unwavering barrel of the pistol held a command it would be death to disobey, and Renard released the hilt of his sword as though it had suddenly become red-hot. In a silence charged with a variety of emotions, the man called Alex plied a knife, and the cords dropped from Sir Jocelyn's cramped arms. He was turning to express his gratitude to his deliverers when Marayte came out of the stupor of astonishment which had hitherto held him silent and motionless. He loosed a crashing oath, and flung himself at the leader of these high-handed intruders.

Captain Lucifer fell back a pace, and the slim rapier seemed to leap of its own accord into his hand, so swiftly did he draw it. Marayte was brought up short with its keen point against the base of his throat, and saw the other man's arm drawn back for the thrust.

"Keep your distance, Marayte! Your person offends me!" Lucifer said coldly, with a hauteur which accorded well with his name. "It offends me almost as much as your dull-wittedness, and that is saying a deal. God's light! Are there not Spanish ships enough in the Caribbean, that you must take and burn an English merchantman?"

The pirate, cheated by the rapier pricking his throat of the physical violence he craved, fell back instead upon verbal abuse. His face working with fury, his great hands clenching and unclenching in uncontrollable rage, he spewed forth a torrent of obscene invective culled from the lowest haunts of the pirate-ports of the Caribbean. Captain Lucifer continued to hold him off at the length of the sword, regarding him with a faint, disdainful lift of his level brows, and when at last sheer lack of breath brought the mulatto's foulness to a close, he said in a voice of ice:

"If you've quite done, I've a word more to say. There is a ship burned and English lads murdered, and no way of mending that, more's the pity, but you will restore to this gentleman every last farthing you have stolen from him, or, by Heaven! I'll see a rope set about your neck if you venture to show your face again in Port Royal."

"Ye lousy pimp! Ye damned, fleering jackanapes!" Marayte was beginning again, but Renard's voice cut suddenly through the start of that fresh stream of lewdness.

"How long, may I ask, have the Brethren of the Coast preyed upon one another, or Captain Lucifer played catch-poll for the Governor of Jamaica?"

The blue eyes flicked him with a glance of open contempt, and the firm lips curled to a deeper disdain.

"As long, Renard, as such as you have styled themselves Brethren of the Coast. You are no buccaneers, you and Marayte, but dirty pirates with every man's hand against you. I hold the King's commission, as Morgan does, and many others, but how long will the Brethren sail under that protection if they tolerate such as you in their ranks?" He broke off, and made an impatient gesture with his free hand. "But why waste words upon you? Alex, Nick, let us make an end of this business."

The melancholy Alex, who, after releasing Sir Jocelyn, had also drawn and cocked a pistol, came forward and jabbed the barrel of the weapon against Marayte's side. Captain Lucifer sheathed his rapier and spoke briskly.

"You will go with us on deck, and there you will order your men to restore Sir Jocelyn's property to him. If there is the least sign of treachery from you or your crew, there will be two scoundrels less upon the earth, and two more in hell. You understand me, I hope."

The sullen, impotent anger in their faces showed that they did. They were disarmed, and then his two lieutenants urged them out of the cabin. Captain Lucifer turned to Sir Jocelyn, and with a graceful wave of his hand invited him to follow.

Wade, passing from surprise to surprise, and uncertain whether the Captain was his rescuer or his captor, obeyed in bewildered silence, and so they came on deck, and into the presence of the staring, muttering pirate crew. A short way off, across the pellucid, blue-green water, lay a fine, powerful ship with a row of wicked-looking cannon gleaming along her white flank, and it was the threat of those guns, rather than the danger to their own leaders, which wrung from Marayte's men a reluctant obedience to Captain Lucifer's demands. The *Loyalist* was not likely to open fire upon a ship which held her own commander, but it was common knowledge that Lucifer's men held him in an esteem amounting almost to reverence, and it was certain that if any harm befell him they would wreak a terrible vengeance upon those responsible.

So, grumbling and snarling like so many curs, they disgorged that part of their plunder which had been stolen from Sir Jocelyn Wade. Under the still slightly bemused eye of its owner, and the keen, contemptuous regard of Captain Lucifer, it was gathered together and transferred to the waiting boat, while Marayte and Renard stood, furious but helpless, beside their watchful guards. At length they, too, were ordered into the boat, and the tall, elegant buccaneer turned to address the puzzled crew.

"Those two come with me as hostages for your good behaviour. No doubt Marayte could well be spared, but Renard has the keenest wits among you, and you would fare ill without him. Once we reach the *Loyalist* you may put off a boat to fetch them back. If you disobey, not only will those two rogues hang, but my gunners will blow this hulk and every man aboard her into hell."

He paused, but remained for a moment or two facing them, watchful for any sign of defiance. None came, and with a faint, scornful smile he turned his back upon them and, signing to Wade to precede him, climbed down to the boat. The oarsmen pushed off, and the little craft slipped through the sparkling water towards the big white ship whence she had come.

Boarding his own vessel again, Captain Lucifer left the prisoners in his lieutenants' charge and led Sir Jocelyn at once to the great cabin, the elegance and comfort of which made the young courtier open his eyes very wide indeed. The ship in which he had crossed the Atlantic had been considered well appointed, but it lagged far behind the almost sybaritic luxury of the *Loyalist*. To find such magnificence aboard any ship, particularly a fighting craft such as this, was something for which Sir Jocelyn had been totally unprepared.

"Pray be seated, sir!" The Captain waved him to a chair, and proceeded to divest himself of his sword, and the silver-encrusted baldrick which supported it. A soft-footed negro servant appeared from somewhere as he spoke, and set upon the polished table a heavy silver tray bearing a flask of wine and four delicate glasses. Lucifer handed him the sword and dismissed him, bidding him see that quarters were prepared for the newcomer.

"You are bound for Jamaica, I believe, Sir Jocelyn?" he remarked as he poured the wine. "Fortunately, your recent misadventure, unpleasant though it was, need not occasion you any delay. We are bound for Port Royal, and should arrive there early tomorrow. Until then pray consider yourself my guest."

He handed him one of the glasses of wine, and Sir Jocelyn, accepting it with a word of thanks, swallowed a generous portion of it. He felt he needed it. Thus

fortified, he made a determined effort to collect his
wits and get to the bottom of an affair which was
beginning to savour of the miraculous.

"Captain Lucifer," he began, but the other checked
him with a smile and a shake of his head.

"My name is Brandon, Sir Jocelyn. Christopher
Brandon, at your service. The other—" he shrugged
and laughed "—a sobriquet bestowed upon me, I fear
in no very flattering sense, by the Brethren of the
Coast. But I interrupt you, sir. Pray go on."

"Captain Brandon," Jocelyn began again, "I am,
believe me, profoundly grateful to you for delivering
me from a devilish uncomfortable situation, but I am
at a loss to understand how it came about. One might
almost suppose you gifted with second sight."

"Nothing so remarkable, sir," Brandon replied with a
laugh, and sat down in the chair at the head of the
table. "The explanation is simple. When we first
sighted you, Marayte was already in pursuit, steering
athwart your course. I know him of old, and I knew,
too, that the English flag would afford you no protection against him. We were too far off to intervene,
and by the time we arrived on the scene some accident
of battle had set your ship ablaze. We picked up one
of the crew who had evaded both the flames and
Marayte's cut-throats, and from him we learned that
an English gentleman had been taken prisoner. The
rest you know."

"And, knowing it, I can find no words to express
my thanks. To put yourself to such trouble, to court
danger for the sake of one wholly unknown to you—
upon my soul, sir! I do not know what to say."

"As to the danger, Sir Jocelyn, 'twas slight enough,
and for the rest, my motive was not wholly unselfish.

Marayte is a pirate, who preys, as you have seen, upon any ship unlucky enough to come within his reach. I, on the other hand, am a buccaneer, and though to you in England there may seem little to choose between us, I assure you that the difference does exist."

Sir Jocelyn nodded, regarding him with considerable interest.

"You said something of the sort, I remember, to Marayte, but I am new to the Indies, and ignorant of such matters."

"Permit me, then, to explain. The buccaneers have a certain official standing, for they are the only force at present in the Caribbean capable of keeping in check the inordinate greed of Spain. Therefore the Governor of Jamaica bestows commissions upon leaders such as Harry Morgan—of whom even in England you may have heard—and myself, and others whom he can trust. I was with Morgan when he took Puerto Principe and Porto Bello, but latterly, for reasons of my own, I have confined my attentions to Spanish ships rather than Spanish cities." His gaze lifted suddenly to his guest's face, and Jocelyn hurriedly composed his features into an expression which he hoped betrayed none of his misgivings. A smile glinted in Brandon's eyes, and he added softly: "The Dons give us ample provocation, you know."

Sir Jocelyn said hurriedly that he felt sure they did, and lapsed into an uncomfortable silence, which Brandon broke presently to ask:

"Are you expected in Jamaica, sir?"

For some reason this civil inquiry, far from setting Wade at his ease, seemed to cast him into even deeper confusion. The colour rose in his fair, ingenuous countenance, and he stammered a little in his reply.

"No—that is, I have acquaintances there whom I met in England and—and hope to see again. You may perhaps have heard, sir, of a family named Charnwood? I believe they are of some standing in the colony."

"James Charnwood, the planter, you mean?" Kit agreed with a nod. "Yes, I have some acquaintance with him. A man of solid worth, though somewhat hasty in his temper."

"I believe that to be the case, Captain Brandon, though I have not yet had the pleasure of meeting him." Wade hesitated for a moment, then, as though realizing that courtesy demanded some further explanation, added airily: "In point of fact, it is his two daughters with whom I am acquainted. They were brought up in England, and only recently returned to Jamaica."

"I see!" The buccaneer's voice was non-committal, but Jocelyn saw amused comprehension in the blue eyes which, as he now discovered, could be extremely penetrating. No more was said on the subject, however, Captain Lucifer merely adding: "In that case, sir, I may hope that you will continue my guest, ashore as well as afloat."

Jocelyn returned some civil answer and the topic was abandoned. After a little, Brandon excused himself and went on deck again, and when he returned it was to sit down to the ample supper laid before them by the servant. With him this time came the two men whom Sir Jocelyn had seen aboard the *Albatross,* and whom the Captain now introduced, more formally, as Nicholas Halthrop and Dr. Alexander Blair. It was obvious that these two were his friends as well as his lieutenants, and as the meal was eaten and the wine went round, Jocelyn reflected with growing wonderment that in

London itself he had often dined worse and in far less agreeable company.

Perhaps because he was fatigued by the excitement and adventures of the day, perhaps because of the comfort of his quarters, he slept late next morning, and when he came on deck the mountains of Jamaica could already be seen, lifting their blue peaks a short distance ahead. By the time he had eaten a leisurely breakfast and returned again to the poop-deck, the *Loyalist,* with her guns thundering a curious triple salute, was gliding past the guardian fort and into the broad harbour of Port Royal.

Sir Jocelyn leaned upon the bulwarks and looked eagerly across the bay at the little town, its red roofs climbing a gentle slope, and backed by the vivid green of a range of hills. He had not been entirely frank with Captain Brandon the previous day. His acquaintance with the Misses Charnwood, to which he had so casually referred, was, where Miss Regina was concerned, far more intimate than he had disclosed. He came, in fact, to seek her hand in marriage, for her father had removed her and her sister so abruptly from England that Jocelyn had had no chance to propose to her. He was not sure of the reason behind that abrupt departure, but he hoped that if he were the cause, the long journey he had undertaken would convince Mr. Charnwood of the sincerity of his regard.

When at length the ship had come safely to anchor, and all was satisfactorily bestowed, Kit Brandon joined his guest upon the poop. Taking for granted Sir Jocelyn's acceptance of his invitation, he came to tell him that all was in readiness for them to go ashore, and to warn him that since their destination lay a little

distance from the town, it was desirable that he should
go prepared for riding.

Sir Jocelyn's curiosity, already piqued by the little
he had seen of this most unusual buccaneer, was increased by that matter-of-fact suggestion, and he made
haste to fall in with it. A boat manned by members
of the *Loyalist's* crew took them ashore, and there on
the mole, amid the bustle of a busy port, and the
colourful crowd of idlers which marked it as one of the
greatest buccaneer strongholds of the Caribbean, they
were met by a negro groom in green and silver livery,
who led two spirited horses by the bridle. He bowed
almost to the ground as Brandon approached, and then
looked up with a beaming, white-toothed grin which
seemed in danger of splitting his face in two. The
Captain glanced at him with a smile.

"You are prompt, Samuel," he said pleasantly. "Is
all well at Fallowmead?" The negro nodded happy
assurance, and he went on: "This gentleman rides with
me. Give him your horse, hire another for yourself,
and follow us."

He tossed him a coin and swung lightly into the
saddle; Sir Jocelyn, wondering what manner of free-
booter this was who kept liveried servants to do his
bidding, followed suit, and the horses moved forward.
As they left the waterfront a group of hard-bitten men
and gaudy women about the door of a tavern raised a
cheer for Captain Lucifer, and he acknowledged it with
a faint smile and a lifted hand.

Their way led them through the town and to the
green hills beyond. Once free of the streets, Brandon
rode fast and spoke little, as though he had forgotten
his companion in an overmastering desire to reach the
journey's end, and Sir Jocelyn, more intrigued than

ever, respected his silence, and kept to himself the many questions he would have liked to ask.

They turned at length from the road, and, passing between a pair of tall gates, came by way of a short avenue to a big, white house set in the midst of a garden blazing with all the gorgeous colours of the tropics. It was built in the style prevalent in the colony, its rooms opening on to tiers of arched verandahs, and a short flight of shallow steps leading up to an imposing door. Another groom appeared to take charge of the horses, and as they dismounted, Wade, looking about him in astonishment, felt that there was little cause for wonder in his companion's eagerness to return to such a home as this after long months at sea.

A slight sound behind him made him turn. The door had opened, and framed in the archway was a vision more likely to be the real cause of that eagerness; a young girl, vivid and lovely, with a great crown of shining, golden hair. A moment she paused there, and then she came skimming down the steps to cast herself into Brandon's arms.

"Kit!" she exclaimed. "Dear, dear Kit, home at last! Oh, how happy I am to see you!"

He had held her for a moment as though here was his dearest treasure, but then he kissed her cheek and let her go, and his voice was light as he answered.

"Lord save us, child! Will you never learn decorum? What kind of a welcome is this to show to a guest? I bring you Sir Jocelyn Wade, whom I had the good fortune to meet with on my travels. Sir Jocelyn, allow me to present Miss Damaris Brandon—my sister."

Chapter II

THE LADY OF FALLOWMEAD

Sir Jocelyn checked in the midst of his bow, stared for an instant, and then went on with it, wondering why the simple words had startled him. Somehow he had expected Kit Brandon to introduce this radiant girl as his wife. The scarcely veiled impatience with which he had ridden from Port Royal, the expression which for a moment had softened his face as he held her, had suggested to Wade a man fathoms deep in love. Then, with an inward laugh against himself, he decided that he had imagined it; that his own ardent impatience to see Regina again had distorted his judgment.

Miss Brandon curtsied and bade him welcome with pretty grace, but next moment she was turning again to her brother, demanding to be told the whereabouts of Alex and Nicholas, and the reason for their absence. Kit drew her hand through the crook of his arm and led the way into the house, saying as he did so:

"They will be here directly. There were certain matters to be looked to which I left in their hands, that I might bring Sir Jocelyn here without delay. He is new come from England, and weary, I'll warrant me, of ships and the sea."

"From England!" Damaris turned impulsively to Jocelyn. Her eyes were shining, her voice a trifle breathless. "Oh, sir, have you been to Court? Have you seen the King?"

"I have had that honour upon many occasions, madam," he replied, a little amused at her eagerness. "His Majesty has been gracious enough to number me among his friends."

It was clear that she was profoundly impressed by this, for her eyes widened, and she regarded him with something akin to awe. Her brother turned upon him a keen, searching look, but after a moment said gravely:

"You are fortunate indeed, Sir Jocelyn, and we who are less favoured must account it an honour to entertain one of His Majesty's friends."

"The honour," declared Sir Jocelyn gallantly, sketching a bow towards Miss Brandon, "is wholly mine, but His Majesty, I feel sure, would be gratified to know that he commands such loyalty, even in this distant part of his realm."

By this time they had passed through a spacious hall into a cool, lofty room with a vista of similar apartments beyond, for all the rooms opened into one another. On the table, wine and glasses were already set out, and Damaris went at once to pour it. As he watched her fill the delicate goblets, Kit said quietly:

"As to that, sir, the Brandons have always been true to their King. My father fought beneath the Royal standard until he died on Worcester field, and had opportunity occurred I, too, should have offered my sword in His Majesty's service."

There was a faint trace of bitterness in the last words. Damaris looked up quickly.

"Do you not serve him here, Kit, guarding his colonies against the arrogance of Spain?" she said firmly. "Why, among the Brethren you stand second only to Morgan himself."

"And, like Morgan, serve myself at the same time," Kit replied with a wry smile, "buccaneering being a prosperous trade."

"That, Captain Brandon, is the way of the world," Jocelyn said with a laugh. "Indeed, were I indiscreet, I could name you many who, while professing to serve His Majesty, are intent upon nothing but lining their own pockets."

"We shall not tempt you to indiscretion, Sir Jocelyn!" Damaris's smile was roguish as she handed him his wine. "But tell us, if you please, if the Court is as gay as we have heard. Oh, how I long to see it for myself!"

Sir Jocelyn, eyeing her appreciatively, reflected that if ever her wish were granted there was no doubt that she would find favour in the roving eye of her sovereign. Miss Brandon was exremely personable. Her face, with its high cheekbones, wilful mouth, and eyes that were the blue-green of tropic seas, was perhaps more arresting than strictly beautiful, but her hair was of a gold so bright that even in this cool, dim room it seemed to glow with a radiance of its own, and she had a complexion which the fierce sunshine of the Antilles had done nothing to impair. From the filmy lace topping her low-cut bodice rose a neck and shoulders of dazzling whiteness, and though only moderately tall she bore herself with incomparable grace. When to these physical charms was added a sparkling gaiety, and a vivacity of manner as beguiling as it was unaffected, the sum total was such that it seemed to Sir Jocelyn a thousand pities that it should be wasted in an out-of-the-way spot like Jamaica. Miss Brandon would have graced a palace.

So, too, would Miss Brandon's jewels. Magnificent diamonds hung from her ears and flashed on her slender fingers, while a gold chain about her throat supported a cross of the same precious metal literally ablaze with gems. Sir Jocelyn, regarding it, wondered if the Brandons were papists, not knowing that it had been taken from a captured Spanish galleon by Nick Halthrop, who later bestowed it upon Damaris as a token of his regard.

His thoughts were diverted by Kit inquiring of his sister whether she had yet made the acquaintance of the Misses Charnwood, whom he believed had recently arrived in Jamaica. Damaris shook her head.

"No, I have not yet seen them," she replied. "They have been here barely a week, for I believe they stayed for a time in Barbados, where they have kinsfolk." She broke off, looking puzzled. "How were you aware of their arrival?"

"Sir Jocelyn was my informant." There was a glimmer of friendly mockery in Kit's eyes as they rested upon his guest. "He knew the ladies in London, and has come hither in the hope of renewing the acquaintance."

"Indeed?" Miss Brandon, it seemed, was as quick-witted as her brother. "May I ask, sir, whether you are a Catholic?"

"Not I, madam," Jocelyn replied, with another uneasy glance at the jewelled cross, but she seemed in no way put out by the denial, merely remarking brightly:

"Then you cannot be he!"

He was bewildered, and showed it. Brandon said patiently:

"You talk in riddles, my dear. Who can Sir Jocelyn not be?"

Damaris laughed.

"He cannot be the reason for Mr. Charnwood removing his daughters from England. Rumour has it that he did so because one of them was being courted by a Catholic gentleman, and her father feared that his persuasiveness might lead her to forsake the Church of England for the Church of Rome." Her bright glance flashed to Wade. "What say you to that, sir?"

"I say, madam, that you are singularly well informed, but that Mr. Charnwood's fears are without foundation."

"And naturally, sir, you are in a position to speak with certain knowledge?" Both voice and expression were mischievous as she came to replenish his glass, but Jocelyn met her eyes with an answering gleam of laughter in his own.

"I venture to think so, madam. The gentleman in question is one of my closest friends."

"Your friend!" It was clear that his words had taken her by surprise. "But I thought 'twas Miss Charnwood who——"

His lips twitched.

"I must remind you, Miss Brandon, that James Charnwood has two daughters."

For an instant she stared beneath knit brows, and then, with a comical little grimace, turned aside to refill her brother's glass.

"I suppose I deserved that," she told him confidentially. "I feel very foolish."

"The just reward of pertness," Kit replied gravely. "I should like to think that you would profit by the lesson, but experience has taught me the futility of such hopes. Now will you have the goodness to see that a room is prepared for our guest?"

She set down the wine and went submissively towards the door, and there turned to face them again. Her satin skirts billowed as she curtsied; her eyes were downcast, the corners of her red lips drooped a little.

"I cry your pardon," she said in a small voice. "I had no thought to offend, and pray believe, Sir Jocelyn, that it shall be my duty to make your visit here all you would wish it to be. Tomorrow I will seek out the Misses Charnwood, and make myself known to them." A tiny pause, and then the long lashes lifted, the roguish smile flashed out again. "Both of them," she added, and was gone with a ripple of stifled laughter before her brother could make any comment. Kit looked ruefully at Sir Jocelyn.

"I fear my sister has been too much indulged," he said. "Her life has of necessity been less circumscribed than if we had remained in England, and she has been mistress of this house since my mother's death four years ago. I am a great deal from home, and so——" he shrugged, leaving the sentence unfinished.

"You have been long in the Indies, sir?" asked Jocelyn tentatively. He was still extremely curious concerning the Brandons, but in view of his obligation to the Captain he did not like to pry too closely into this seemingly fantastic situation.

"For close upon nine years, Sir Jocelyn. I brought my mother and sister here in '60."

"The year of His Majesty's return?" Wade was more puzzled than ever. "Surely, sir, that event should have kept a man of your sympathies in England?"

For a moment he thought that Brandon was not going to reply. He stood looking down at the glass in his hand, his keen, bronzed face wearing an expression withdrawn and a trifle cold, as though he resented

the question implicit in Sir Jocelyn's remark. At last he
said slowly:

"No one rejoiced in His Majesty's return more
sincerely than I, but I had little hope from it of worldly
gain. My home had been lost nearly twenty years
before, the house plundered and burned, the estate
shared among strangers. On the other hand, I was
master of my own ship, and I knew the Indies, and
the opportunities they held for men with the ambition
and the ability to grasp them." He paused, and cast an
expressive glance about the handsome room. "I have
never regretted the choice I made."

"That I can believe, and yet, when all is said, 'tis still
a life of exile, is it not?"

Kit shrugged.

"My memories of England are not so pleasant, Sir
Jocelyn, that I have any desire to return."

"But your sister, sir? An I mistake not, she is less
resigned to her exile."

"Damaris is but a child," Kit replied with a wry
smile. "She dreams of the Court, and sees London as
some city of legend, all gaiety and gladness. I shall be
grateful if you, who know both so well, will picture
them for her in truer colours."

"If by doing so I may discharge some part of my
debt to you, I will do it gladly," Jocelyn replied with a
smile. "God knows, such dreams are a far cry from
reality. I tell you, Captain Brandon, I have had a sur-
feit of the lying and intrigue that cling about the throne!
Let me but win my lady, and 'tis to Sussex I'll take her,
never London."

"Convince Damaris of that, and I will be your
debtor," Kit assured him, and raised his glass. "I drink
to the success of your wooing, Sir Jocelyn."

Wade bowed his thanks, but seemed a trifle doubtful of the outcome of his courtship. In a suddenly expansive mood, he disclosed the cause of his uneasiness.

"I would be a deal easier in my mind if I could be certain that the rumour Miss Brandon spoke of were well founded," he admitted gloomily. " 'Tis likely enough, I own, but it is possible also that a word against me has been dropped in the old gentleman's ear. He may well suspect me of trifling with his daugher, if I have been named to him as a rake and a libertine."

"And are you?" Kit inquired, regarding him with some amusement. Sir Jocelyn cocked a humorous eyebrow.

"My dear sir, I have been one of His Majesty's intimates. That honour is not lightly accorded." He sighed deeply and tossed off the remainder of his wine. "The Royal favour is a very fine thing, but it makes it damnably difficult to convince a father of one's honest intentions."

"I think you may set your mind at rest," Kit said with a laugh. "James Charnwood is no Puritan. Oh, he is sober enough now, but his fortune, like my own, is founded upon Spanish gold. Moreover, who could have set him against you, and with what purpose?"

"The same person, no doubt, who informed Mr. Charnwood that my friend, Martin Farrancourt, is endeavouring to persuade Miss Olivia to embrace the Romish faith. As for his purpose, 'tis common enough —self-interest."

"You are aware, then, of his identity?"

"I have my suspicions, Captain Brandon. There is a cousin of sorts, one Ingram Fletcher, a step-son of the aunt with whom the young ladies lived while they were in England. Unless I am much mistaken, Mr. Fletcher has an eye to the Charnwood fortune, and takes this path to ward off any rivals. At all events, he escorted the sisters on their journey hither."

Kit's brows lifted.

"Does he then propose to take both ladies to wife?"

"I know not what he proposes," Jocelyn said darkly, "but he is assiduous in his attentions to both. No doubt Olivia, being the elder, would be his choice, but if she will have none of him he may hope to win Regina."

"We must hope, then, that Miss Olivia will smile upon him," Kit replied, "for I fear your friend has little chance of winning her. James Charnwood has seen too much of Spanish ways to look kindly upon any papist."

"To be frank with you, sir, I fancy it would never come to that," Jocelyn confided, "for Martin's family most certainly would oppose such a marriage as bitterly as the lady's. He is brother to the Earl of Chelsham, and his lordship is a man who likes to be obeyed. There are not many who would care to cross him. His influence is too far-reaching."

"Influence?" Kit was surprised. "And he a papist?"

"A papist, yes," Jocelyn agreed with a shrug; "but, like so many of his religion, he fought loyally for his King during the late wars, and three of his brothers died in the Royal cause. Then, too, he has stood for years high in the esteem of the Queen-Mother. Of course, there are those who declare he intrigues with France and Spain, but such suspicions fall readily upon a man of his faith. For my part, I believe he intrigues nearer home, and thus maintains his power at Court, but if he does, he moves so deviously that no one knows how or with whom. 'Tis said of him in London that the Golden Panther always hunts alone."

Kit had been lounging easily against the side of one of the long windows, but now he stiffened as though he had been struck. His face went white, and he stared at the speaker with eyes grown suddenly bleak.

"What was that?" he demanded, and it was Captain Lucifer who spoke, in a voice of icy command. Sir Jocelyn blinked.

"An idle jest, sir, no more," he stammered, taken aback by the change in his host's manner. "The golden panther of Chelsham is part of the Farrancourt arms, and my lord is sometimes called by that name."

"Indeed?" This time Kit spoke slowly, as though his thoughts were elsewhere, and as slowly came back to the table and sat down. "You interest me, Sir Jocelyn. Do you know his lordship well?"

"No one knows him well, Captain Brandon. As I have said, I am a close friend of his brother, but Martin Farrancourt is a man easy to like. Not so the Earl. He is civil to all, but admits no one, not even Martin, to his confidence. None share his secrets."

Kit stared at him. As though the words had been a spell, in a flash fifteen years had rolled away, and he stood once more in a Devon lane under a winter's moon, hearing those same words from a haggard, wild-eyed man who clutched a whimpering child in his arms.

"None share his secrets," he repeated under his breath, and dropped his head upon his hands. "None save the Devil, his master."

Sir Jocelyn, who had failed to catch the sense of the muttered words, regarded him with growing uneasiness. He could not imagine what he had said so gravely to discompose one whom he had begun to suppose imperturbable, but before he could make any attempt at apology or inquiry, Miss Brandon came back into the room. On the whole, Sir Jocelyn was glad of the interruption. He was a simple soul, and had begun to feel out of his depth.

Kit got up rather abruptly and returned to the window, where he stood with his back to the room while Damaris informed their guest that a bedchamber was being made ready for him. Wade saw her cast one or two anxious glances towards her brother, and, supposing that after a long separation they would have much to say to each other, he begged the lady's leave to withdraw. It was given gladly, with a look of gratitude for his tactfulness, and a servant was summoned to conduct him to his apartment.

As soon as they were alone, Damaris went quickly to the silent figure by the window, setting a hand on his arm and looking up anxiously at his face.

"Kit," she said, "what has happened? Have you quarrelled with Sir Jocelyn?"

"Quarrelled with him?" he repeated, not looking at her, but forcing himself to speak naturally. "Is that likely, when he is a guest in my house?"

"No," she said slowly, "it is not likely, but you seem suddenly so strange, and if 'tis not Sir Jocelyn's fault, what can it be?" Her eyes widened; her grip on his arm tightened and a sharper note of anxiety rang in her voice. "You did not tell me the truth just now! Some harm has come to Nicholas—or to Alex!"

"I told you no lie, child. They are both hale and well, and will be here soon." Now at length he turned and looked at her, his eyes searching her face as he added in a low voice: "Is this concern for them both, or for Nicholas alone?"

The colour deepened in her cheeks, and her hand went involuntarily to the jewelled cross she wore, but she answered lightly enough.

"Why, for them both, of course! If Nick chooses to deal in folly, must you tease me therefore?" She gave him no chance to reply, but continued hurriedly: "This is to divert me, sir, but it will not serve. I must and shall know what is troubling you. Did you fare ill, this last voyage?"

He smiled, and, thrusting a hand into his pocket, drew out some object wrapped about in silk, and put it into her hands.

"Judge for yourself," he said. "Here is a fresh toy for you."

Eagerly she unwrapped the gift, and caught her breath in a gasp of delight as she saw what the package contained.

"Pearls!" she exclaimed, her voice hushed with ecstasy. "The most beautiful I have ever seen!" The wrappings fluttered to the floor as she held up the creamy, iridescent rope, a thing of infinite, shimmering loveliness. "Oh, Kit!"

For a moment or two she stood thus, gazing at the precious thing swinging between her hands, and then she flew to a mirror on the other side of the room. Kit stayed where he was, watching her, and smiled a little to see how, where all else had failed, the gift had diverted her thoughts from his own strange behaviour; and not from that alone, for the jewelled cross lay, discarded now, upon the table. On that score at least he need not torment himself; she was a child still, with a child's delight in the gifts showered upon her.

She turned at last to face him, her cheeks flushed, and the pearls, wound twice about her throat yet still

falling to her waist, no whiter than the skin against
which they lay. She already possessed gems worth a
fortune, for both Kit and his two friends always brought
her some choice part of their plunder, but each fresh
gift gave her as much pleasure as though it were the
first she had ever received. She danced across the
room again, and caught both his hands in hers, laughing up at him with the unshadowed affection in which
he found at one time torment and delight.

"Each gift you bring me is lovelier than the last!"
she declared. "I am sure that the Queen herself would
envy me my jewels, could she but see them." She tilted
her head, regarding him with an expression at once
rueful and cajoling. "Dear Kit, is there no hope that,
one day, she may see them?"

He did not reply at once, but stood looking down
at her with a frown in his eyes. It was by no means
the first time that she had tried to coax him into taking
her to England, but now, coming so soon after Sir
Jocelyn's unwitting disclosure, the suggestion seemed
to acquire an ominous significance.

It was a wish he meant never to grant, for it was to
avoid all chance of contact with the Court that he
had brought her so far away from England when King
Charles returned in triumph to the throne. With the
wide ocean between Damaris and a land where a Royalist lord might once more move at will, he had ac-
counted the secret safe, and now that chance had
revealed the identity of the man whom hitherto he
had known only as "my lord", his determination that
she should not leave the Indies was increased a hun-
dredfold. He shook his head, and answered as he had
often answered in the past.

"Captain Lucifer can never take you to Court,

Damaris. You should know that as well as I do, but, if you doubt it, ask Sir Jocelyn how I would fare in London." He smiled at her crestfallen look, and gently pinched her chin. "However, if you are weary of jewels, I'll bring you none from my next voyage."

For once his teasing brought forth no answering smile. Her lips quivered, and her eyes, lifted to meet his, were wide and serious, with no glimmer of mischief in their blue-green depths.

"Come safe home yourself," she said in a low voice, "and what shall I care for jewels? Do you not know how I fear for you while you are at sea?" She flung herself into his arms and hid her face against his breast. "So many dangers, of storm and battle and sickness! Oh, Kit, I wish you would bide here at home with me!"

He held her close without speaking, and stroked her hair as he had always done when she was in any way grieved or frightened, but above the bowed, golden head, his face was the face of a man in torment. For many months now he had been struggling against the knowledge that to him she was no longer the cherished young sister, but his love, his life, the very heart and spirit of his world. The truth had broken upon him suddenly, in a blinding, horrifying flash of revelation, and ever since he had been fighting against the temptation to tell her of that night so long ago when she had been thrust into his care, fighting because he could not foresee what effect upon her such a disclosure might have. Never by word or look had it been hinted to her that she was not the child of Jane and Christopher Brandon, and how could be tell her the truth without shattering for ever the love and trust with which she regarded him? It was a risk he dared not take, and yet he did not know how long he could maintain the role of brother without betraying himself.

Suddenly he remembered what Sir Jocelyn had told him of the Catholic Earl whose crest was a golden panther, and with remembrance came the thought that here again, perhaps, was the hand of that destiny which years before had chosen him as the protector of an orphaned waif. Was not his meeting with Wade as strange a chance as that other meeting long ago, and might it not betoken that the decision he had tried to make would be taken out of his hands? Wearied and shaken by a conflict too cruel to be long endured, Kit found himself hoping with all his heart that it might be so.

Chapter III

UNDERCURRENTS

Sir Jocelyn, prompted by courtesy to leave Miss Brandon and her brother alone, found plenty with which to occupy his thoughts. He had stumbled upon a mystery, and since he possessed his fair share of curiosity, it was natural that he should wonder why the mere mention of the Golden Panther should so seriously discompose the Captain. He would have liked very much to probe deeper into this intriguing problem, but he was restrained as much by gratitude and a sense of obligation towards his host as by the scarcely acknowledged thought that it might be imprudent to provoke Captain Lucifer too far. There was fire and steel beneath those courtly manners, and he must tread warily.

Curiosity of another kind presently took him forth into the garden. He was, after all, in a new, strange land, and the prospect from his window was like no other that he had ever seen, while the warm breeze carried an exotic fragrance at once mysterious and alluring. He made his way out of the house, and spent perhaps half-an-hour wandering along the shaded walks and terraces of that spacious pleasance, admiring the flowers and trees, both known and unknown, which grew in lush, tropic profusion, and amid which fluttered butterflies he could scarcely have covered with his hand.

The house was built on a level plateau, and from certain, cunningly placed points of vantage a fine view to seaward was disclosed. He was admiring the prospect from one such spot, where a stone seat was placed in the shade of a great tree, when Miss Brandon joined him. He turned, bowing his greetings, and wondering how she contrived to look so cool and untroubled in this infernal climate; then his attention was caught and held by the fabulous rope of pearls about her neck, and the polite phrases withered on his lips.

Damaris perceived the source of his astonishment, and laughed with unselfconscious pleasure. She took the hanging coils of the necklace between her fingers and lifted them, shimmering and glowing in the sunlight.

"You are admiring my pearls, Sir Jocelyn?" she said gaily. "They are a gift from my brother, a token of a successful cruise." She let the necklace fall, and laughed again. "Some proud Spanish lady will weep for the loss of this pretty trinket."

Sir Jocelyn looked at her and frowned. Willing though he was to admit that he knew nothing of West Indian politics, this light-hearted acceptance of what seemed to him the most barefaced piracy was something he could not quite accept. What kind of society was this where buccaneer captains were apparently respected citizens, yet decked their womenfolk with plundered gems?

"Madam," he said with a hint of austerity, "I am, as you know, unfamiliar with conditions here, but surely, if England is not at war with Spain—"

Damaris interrupted him. She was no longer laughing, but spoke gravely and with some feeling.

"In the Indies, sir, there is always war with Spain. Who, think you, are the buccaneers but men of other nations whom Spain has wronged and persecuted? In all the New World she admits no rights save her own, and upholds those rights with fire and sword and the horrors of the Inquisition. By her own greed and injustice she created the Brethren of the Coast, and now the weapon she forged threatens her with destruction. England captured Jamaica from Spain, but could she hold it, think you, were it not for men like my brother and Captain Morgan and the rest?" She paused, and a gleam of humour peeped again in her eyes. "Come, Sir Jocelyn, were we in England 'tis you who could speak with authority, but I have grown up in the Indies, and what I tell you is true. For your own sake you must believe it."

"For my own sake?"

She chuckled.

"Yes, indeed, for Mr. Charnwood himself followed the black flag in his youth, and you will not commend yourself to him by showing disapproval of the buccaneers." She came closer and took his arm and looked up mischievously into his face. " 'Tis a mistake which I hear this self-important cousin has already made."

Sir Jocelyn was only too ready to abandon the wider topic of West Indian politics in favour of his own affairs, and he soon discovered that Damaris had taken upon herself the part of match-maker. She asked a great many searching questions concerning himself and Miss Regina, but with so obvious and sincere a desire to help that resentment was impossible, and he found himself telling her even more than he had already confided to her brother. He favoured her also with his frank opinion of Mr. Ingram Fletcher, which made her laugh, but say that if Mr. Fletcher were indeed so ill-disposed it would perhaps be prudent to keep Sir Jocelyn's arrival in Jamaica a secret for the present.

"Because," she pointed out, "if Mr. Fletcher has already tried his fortune with Miss Olivia, and failed, his hopes will be pinned now upon Miss Regina, and news of your arrival will prompt him to discredit you as much as he can in her father's opinion."

Sir Jocelyn, much amused by the air of worldly wisdom with which this colonial child was preparing to take command of his wooing of Regina Charnwood, inquired with outward gravity how she proposed to assist him. Damaris met his quizzical glance with a look of limpid innocence, and smiled enchantingly.

"I shall make friends of the young ladies," she explained. "Kit shall take me to visit them tomorrow, for luckily we know Mr. Charnwood well, and when I see a little more clearly how matters stand I shall invite them here. I think—yes, I think I will give a party—to mark my brother's safe return, you understand—and you shall meet Mr. Charnwood then. He has a great respect for Kit, and some kindness for me, and even if he has already been prejudiced against you, he will not be uncivil to a fellow-guest in our house. I will exert myself a little to distract Mr. Fletcher—" a naughty twinkle in her eyes accompanied this remark "—and meanwhile it will be for you to convince Mr. Charnwood that whatever has been said to your discredit is false. Now, sir, has that scheme your approval?"

"I am all admiration, Miss Brandon," Jocelyn admitted with a laugh. "I trust, however, that my mere presence in Jamaica will convince Mr. Charnwood of the sincerity of my regard, and my intention to quit the Court if I marry Regina of the fact that whatever fol-

The Golden Panther 63

lies I have committed in the past are over and done with."

"To quit the Court?" There was frank incredulity in Miss Brandon's voice. "You, who are a friend of the King himself? You do not mean it!"

Sir Jocelyn smiled at her evident disbelief.

"I assure you, madam, that I do. Perhaps, viewed from this distance, and, if you forgive me, with the eyes of imagination rather than experience, the Court may seem a very desirable place, but even the friendship of a King is a mixed blessing. A Royal favourite is for ever beset by the ambitious, who seek to climb to similar heights, and the envious, who desire only to drag him down. He may trust no one, depend on no one, for everyone at Court has some private end to serve, whether it be mere personal gain, or the advancement of the faction to which they belong, and very few have any scruples concerning the means they use to attain it. Having once broken away from that life, I have no wish to return to it."

For a moment or two Damaris was silent; then she said wistfully:

"It sounds very exciting."

Sir Jocelyn, perceiving that his well-meant effort to paint an uninviting picture of the Court had most dismally failed, made haste to change the subject. He asked Miss Brandon what her own recollections of England were like, and learned with quickening interest—for the Farrancourts were a Devon family—that as far as she could remember she had always lived in Plymouth.

"My mother kept house for Captain Josiah Barrow, with whom Kit used to sail," she explained, "and when Captain Josiah died he left everything to Kit. But my brother had already resolved to settle in Jamaica, so he sold the house and brought my mother and me to Port Royal."

By this time they had moved to the seat beneath the tree. Sir Jocelyn, fanning himself with his broad, plumed hat, said curiously:

"Was your brother at that time sailing with the buccaneers, madam?"

"Oh, no!" Damaris shook her head. "He was the master of a merchantman, but soon after we came here his ship was attacked and sunk by Spaniards, and Kit and a few others barely escaped with their lives. He swore then that Spain should repay his loss a hundred-fold, and indeed, he has fulfilled his vow many times over. Today he is one of the richest men in Port Royal, and the Dons hate and fear him as much as they hate and fear Morgan."

Sir Jocelyn, his curiosity piqued by the constant recurrence of this latter name in conversation relating to the buccaneers, confessed his total ignorance concerning its owner, and thus earned a look of pitying surprise from his fair companion. She owned to an acquaintance with Captain Morgan, at present absent from Port Royal upon the delectable and profitable business of plundering the Spanish Main, and went on to relate to Wade some of the more colourful exploits of the Welshman whose name in recent years had blazed across the Caribbean, striking fury and terror into Spanish hearts and bringing triumph—and fabulous booty—to the city he had made peculiarly his own.

It was not until the evening that Nick Halthrop and Alex Blair arrived at Fallowmead, and by that time Sir Jocelyn was upon excellent terms with his young hostess. He thought her fascinating, for though she was undoubtedly well versed in feminine wiles, there was a directness about her which suggested that such blandishments were used only in order to get her own way. He had learned, too, that she was as capable as she was attractive, for it appeared that not only the management of the house, but, during her brother's frequent absences, of the whole plantation, was left in her hands. Decidedly, thought Sir Jocelyn admiringly, a most unusual young woman.

It soon became apparent to him that his high opinion of Miss Brandon was shared by Nick Halthrop. There was no difficulty at all in perceiving the depth of the young man's regard for her, but the lady's emotions were less easy to read. She was certainly not averse to flirting with Halthrop, but Sir Jocelyn had the impression that she treated the whole matter as a game. Her brother, he thought, occupied too prominent a place in her affections for her to give her heart as yet to any other man.

He wondered what Brandon thought of it all, and stole a covert glance at him as they lingered over supper. It was not easy to read that calm, resolute countenance, but Wade thought to detect a faint frown in the blue eyes as they rested for a moment upon Damaris and Nicholas. He was not surprised. Miss Brandon could look higher than that for a husband.

At this point in his reflections, and somewhat to his discomfiture, Damaris broke off her conversation to inform her other two guests, with a touch of severity, that she wanted no one to know of Sir Jocelyn's presence at Fallowmead.

"For he is here upon a very delicate matter," she concluded. "I have promised to help him, but we do not want all our plans overset by unthinking clumsiness on your part."

Nicholas immediately signified his willingness to obey this or any other command, but Dr. Blair, who appeared to exert a sort of avuncular authority, said with the dry humour which belied his melancholy expression:

"If 'tis a delicate matter, lassie, and you're to have a hand in it, there is no more to be said, except that Sir Jocelyn has my sympathy."

"Oh, unjust!" she exclaimed with assumed indignation. "Pay no heed to him, Sir Jocelyn, I beg of you. He knows nothing of the matter at all. You will see how fortunate it was for you that you fell in with Kit." She paused, a frown wrinkling her white brow. "Do you know, you have not yet told me how your meeting came about?"

Thankful for the change of subject, Wade plunged immediately into an account of his capture by Marayte, and his subsequent deliverance from the pirate's hands. He was lavish in his praise of Captain Brandon's prompt action, but as the story progressed he became aware that the captain's sister was not sharing his satisfaction. There was growing dismay in her eyes, and when the tale was done she turned anxiously to her brother.

"Renard again!" she exclaimed. "Oh, Kit, is it wise to provoke him so constantly?"

Kit's brows lifted.

"I think you are discourteous, child," he rebuked her gently. "Your words imply that Sir Jocelyn should have been left to his fate."

"You know I did not mean that!" she cried, and turned to Wade. "I ask your pardon, sir, but this man,

Renard, bears my brother no goodwill, and Kit knows it, but he will pay no heed to any warnings."

"I do not fear Renard," Kit replied contemptuously.

"Then you should!" The interruption came unexpectedly from Blair. " 'Od rot it, Kit, your sister is right! Renard hates you as he hates no other man, and his hatred is none the less dangerous because it is dissembled. More dangerous on that account, say I! Remember, 'tis not for nothing he is called the Fox."

Kit looked down the table with an amused smile. It was clear that he was unmoved by the elder man's words.

"Cease croaking, you old raven!" he said good-humouredly. "God's light! What harm can Renard do me, unless it were to slip a knife into my back some dark night, and I am not fool enough to give him the opportunity for that. I'll bear with warnings from Damaris, for a girl's fears can be understood, but sink me if I'll listen to your prophecies of doom!"

Dr. Blair shook his head.

"You treat the matter too lightly, Kit," he replied. "I said yesterday, and I say it again, that you are storing up trouble for yourself in that quarter. Now don't misunderstand me, Sir Jocelyn! I am not saying we should have left you to Marayte. He and his devil-begotten crew stood in need of a sharp lesson, and I am glad we were at hand to give it, but I maintain 'twas not sharp enough. Kit should have strung the two scurvy rogues from their own yard-arm while he had the chance. The seas would have been the cleaner, and he would have two enemies the less."

For a second or two longer Kit's gaze rested upon Blair; then it shifted to Halthrop, who as yet had taken no part in the argument.

"Well, Nick?" he said amiably. "Have you nothing to say on this matter?"

Nicholas looked troubled.

"I agree with Alex," he said slowly. "Renard can be dangerous, and better to crush a snake before it can do harm. There's not another buccaneer afloat who would have let him go free."

The smile still lingered about Brandon's lips, but the amusement in it had given place to a somewhat saturnine mockery.

"Perhaps," he said pensively, "there is not another buccaneer afloat who shares my aversion to the rôle of hangman."

"So that's the truth of it!" Nick's voice was scornful. "By God! They spoke truly who named you Lucifer. But your hands need not have been soiled, Kit. I would have hanged Renard for you, just I would have run him through a year ago, when you were too damnably proud to cross swords with him."

There was a moment's silence. Sir Jocelyn, who had seen more than one mortal quarrel blow up out of skies as clear as these, shot a swift glance at Alex, and saw him tense and watchful. Damaris was looking from her brother to Nicholas with anxious, bewildered eyes.

"I do not doubt it," Kit said at length, and the quiet, deadly tone was like the sudden unsheathing of a sword, "but his quarrel, then as now, was with me, and not with you."

A dark flush swept over the boy's face, and he started up, sliding his chair backwards across the polished floor, but before he could speak he was forestalled by Alex. The Doctor had risen also, as quickly as Halthrop yet somehow contriving to give an impression of leisureliness.

"Damaris, my dear," he said quietly, "since we have all done with supper, will you not sing for us?"

"Yes! Yes, of course!" Swift to take the hint, she rose and turned to Sir Jocelyn. "Shall we go into the next room, sir? I trust you have a taste for music?" She went to her brother, and slipped her hand into his. "Come, Kit! I have learned some new songs while you were away, and you must tell me whether or not they please you."

With Alex and Nicholas following, they moved into the adjoining room, and the moment of tension passed. Miss Brandon went to the virginal which stood in one corner, and for the next half-hour entertained them with old English songs, and some haunting Scottish airs which Alex had taught her. She had a beautiful voice, clear and true and effortless, but Sir Jocelyn, his mind preoccupied by the incident with which supper had ended, found himself unable to give his full attention to the music. Brief though his stay in Kit Brandon's house had been, he was already aware that beneath the pleasant, placid surface of its life there were dark undercurrents, treacherous and sinister.

He looked at Brandon, sitting now a little withdrawn from the candle-light with his gaze fixed upon the singer, and wondered at the strange, complex character of the man. What had provoked that sudden, bitter anger against Nick Halthrop, which had seemed to Sir Jocelyn, for one startled moment, the blind, involuntary desire to wound of a man tortured beyond endurance by—what? Hatred? Nicholas was his trusted friend. Jealousy, perhaps, yet what had the boy done but display a romantic devotion to Brandon's beautiful sister? Then, too, there was the mysterious business of the Golden Panther. Clearly Kit Brandon was a man of many secrets, and Sir Jocelyn, his curiosity tinged now with uneasiness, had the uncomfortable sensation of being borne along by forces beyond his power to control.

So strong was the impression that later, finding himself alone with Dr. Blair, he sought reassurance from that level-headed Scot. It was his hope, he said tentatively, that Captain Brandon's generous gesture in coming to his rescue the previous day would not prove to have placed him in any danger from the thwarted pirates.

"The blame is not yours, Sir Jocelyn," Alex told him gravely. "There are some men destined to be enemies from the moment they meet, and so it was with Kit and Renard. There has always been bad blood between them, but a year ago something happened which brought matters to a head. 'Tis a thousand pities it did not end then. Renard would be better for a foot or so of steel through his black heart."

"What was the nature of their quarrel, sir?" Wade asked curiously. "Unless," he hastened to add, " 'twould be a breach of confidence to tell me."

Alex shook his head, smiling a trifle grimly.

"Nay, sir, all Port Royal knew of it, and there is no reason why you should not hear the tale. 'Twill help you to a better understanding of the situation. Renard had the damnable impudence to raise his eyes to Damaris. He waited till we were away at sea, and then came fawning round her with his damned French gallantries, but she's a sensible little maid for all her chatter, and told him in no uncertain terms that she would have none of him. He has a high opinion of himself, has Master Renard, and the rebuff roused all the nastiness in him. He lay in wait for her when she rode out, with what evil purpose you may guess, and struck down the groom attending her, but by the mercy of God the lassie herself was armed, and knew how to use her weapon. She put a bullet through his leg and made her escape, and by the morrow all Port Royal was laughing to hear how Renard had been worsted by a girl scarce out of the schoolroom."

Sir Jocelyn laughed, too, in amused appreciation.

"Miss Brandon is a remarkable young woman, sir, stab me if she is not! But what followed?"

"When we returned, and Kit heard the story from his sister, he called at once for his horse and rode down into the town to look for Renard. Nick and I went with him, expecting to see murder done, for if ever I saw the devil looking out of a man's eyes, I saw it then. Renard was whole by that time, and amusing himself in a tavern with others of his kind. Kit kept his sword in its sheath, but he took his riding-whip and flogged Renard until he couldn't stand. Then he flung the whip away as though 'twere a thing defiled, and walked out of the tavern through a silence one could almost feel," Alex paused, and regarded his companion sardonically. "Well, Sir Jocelyn, do you wonder now that Damaris is anxious?"

Wade slowly shook his head.

"I am in entire agreement with you, Dr. Blair. This man Renard would be better dead. Yet I should not have guessed, from his bearing yesterday, that his hatred of Captain Brandon is so great."

" 'Tis as I said earlier, Sir Jocelyn—Renard is not called the Fox for nothing. That is what he is, a sly, cold fox who will bide his time and await the opportunity for a vengeance that will match his hatred. I confess I am uneasy. The whole crew of the *Albatross* have a grudge against Kit now, for depriving them of a large part of their plunder, and while Renard leads them—"

"But surely," Jocelyn broke in, " 'tis Marayte who leads them? I had the impression that he was master of the ship."

"Captain he may be," Alex replied with a short laugh, "but Renard commands the *Albatross,* have no doubt of that. He has sailed aboard her under no less than three captains, all figureheads chosen by him to take the blame when things go awry. There is only one man, ashore or afloat, who believes that Marayte is master, and that is Marayte himself."

"A dangerous man, indeed," Jocelyn said reflectively. "He is a Frenchman, you say? He speaks English with remarkable fluency."

"And Spanish or Dutch with the same ease, but he is French for all that. 'Tis the one sure thing known of him, for even his real name he keeps secret. There is a rumour that he was trained for the priesthood, and 'tis certain he is cunning enough to be a cursed Jesuit." Alex rose to his feet, laying aside the long, clay pipe he had been smoking. "Ah well, it grows late and I am growing old. I will bid you goodnight, Sir Jocelyn."

"Just one more question, Dr. Blair," Jocelyn said quietly as he, too, stood up. "Have you ever heard Captain Brandon speak of a golden panther?"

"A golden panther?" The Doctor's blank stare was answer enough. "No, sir, I fear I have not. It sounds an unlikely sort of beast."

" 'Tis a heraldic emblem," Jocelyn replied with a smile. "Part of the arms of the Earls of Chelsham, one of England's great Catholic families."

Alex chuckled.

"I'll not dispute it, sir, but what have the arms of an English Earl—and a Catholic one at that—to do with a Protestant buccaneer who has not set foot in England these many years?" He nodded, and went towards the door. "Goodnight to you, Sir Jocelyn."

"A pertinent question, Dr. Blair," Jocelyn said to himself when he was alone. "What, indeed? Devil take it I wish I knew the answer!"

Chapter IV

JEALOUSY

James Charnwood's plantation was situated only a short distance from Fallowmead, and during the following forenoon Kit and Damaris rode thither together. They had dispensed with attendants, and during the ride Miss Brandon was able to acquaint her brother with the plans she had made to further Sir Jocelyn's wooing. Kit, listening with amused indulgence, promised to make no mention of his guest, and also engaged himself to do all in his power to help Damaris to have a private talk with Miss Regina. It was his opinion that Sir Jocelyn was well able to manage his own affairs, but Damaris was obviously deriving immense enjoyment from her schemes, and if Wade had no objection to her quite unwarranted interference, Kit saw no reason to spoil her pleasure.

The Charnwood house, though built on similar lines to their own, was smaller and of a style less eloquent of taste and refinement. For ten years it had lacked a mistress, and though it was comfortable enough, it was essentially a masculine abode, reflecting the somewhat rude taste of its owner. Kit wondered with some amusement what the two young ladies from England thought of the home and the parent they had not seen for so long.

A coloured servant in shirt and loose breeches of coarse linen met them at the door, and left them to

wait in a cool, rather bare room while he went in search
of his master. He found him on the wide piazza at the
back of the house, in company with his daughters and
Mr. Ingram Fletcher, and informed him that Captain
Brandon and his sister had come a-visiting.

The news had a revivifying effect upon the somewhat
languid group, for although to the three younger people the name of Brandon meant nothing, the prospect
of fresh faces was a welcome diversion in a life which,
after the bustle of London, seemed tedious in the
extreme. As for Mr. Charnwood, he started up out of
his chair, his rubicund face wreathed in smiles, and
roared at the slave to bring the visitors to him without
delay. Then he turned to his companions, rubbing his
hands together with undisguised satisfaction.

"So Kit Brandon's home again, is he?" he said jovially, and bent a not altogether kindly eye upon Mr.
Fletcher. "Now, my lad, you may see for yourself one
o' the buccaneers you've been so high and mighty
about, and maybe you will learn something from
the encounter."

Mr. Fletcher inclined his head with a slight, incredulous smile, but made no reply. He was a lanky young
man, with a long, bony countenance framed by the
flaxen curls of a monstrous periwig, and wearing an
expression of long-suffering boredom which did nothing to render it more attractive. He was almost ridicu-
lously over-dressed, but he prided himself upon the
elegance of his appearance, and looked down his nose
at the colonial planters he had encountered since his
arrival in the Indies. Mr. Charnwood, a blunt man,
had disliked him at first sight.

Miss Regina, who was less careful of her dignity,

looked up at her father's words, her piquant face alive with curiosity.

"Are we to understand, sir, that this Captain Brandon is actually a buccaneer?"

"One o' the greatest," Charnwood assured her. "Captain Lucifer, he's called by the Brethren, and to the Dons, he's the devil incarnate. They would pay as much to get him into their hands as they would for Harry Morgan. 'Twas an ill day for Spain when those two chose to join the buccaneers." He paused, regarding his daughters benevolently. "A stroke of good fortune, this visit. I'd been meaning to take you to see Miss Brandon, for you will be feeling the need of friends of your own age."

Mr. Fletcher's eyebrows lifted superciliously, but instead of making any comment to his host, he addressed the remark to Olivia, as though she were the only person present capable of sharing his sentiments. It was a trick calculated to express the depth of his regard for her, but it did nothing to endear him to Mr. Charnwood.

" 'Pon honour, cousin!" he said languidly. "Your good father has a somewhat curious notion of the sort of company you affect. However, 'twill no doubt be an interesting experience for us to see this filibuster and his sister."

Charnwood glared at him, but the sound of footsteps heralded the visitors' approach and he had no time to reply. As Kit and Damaris emerged from the house, he had the satisfaction of seeing Fletcher's air of superiority perish in mortification, and smiled a trifle grimly as he went forward to meet his guests.

During the round of greetings and introductions which followed, Damaris took swift stock of the sisters. Save in their brunette colouring they were not much alike, for while Regina was obliged to depend for her looks upon the liveliness of her countenance and a certain rich duskiness of complexion, Olivia was undeniably beautiful, with the face of a Madonna and a remote serenity to match her looks. Mr. Fletcher Damaris dismissed at once as a conceited, ill-natured popinjay, but she gave him her hand, and a limpid smile which effectively concealed her thoughts.

He kissed the hand absently. He was not usually indifferent to a pretty woman, but on this occasion he was too full of aggrieved surprise at Captain Brandon to pay much heed to the Captain's sister. No buccaneer, Mr. Fletcher thought resentfully, had any right to be so devilish handsome or so courtly of manner. He had fondly imagined that in Jamaica he would be safe from any rivals, but with the advent of Kit Brandon that happy certainty deserted him.

He was fated, it seemed, to find the path to affluence beset with rivals whose attractions he could not hope to match. In England there had been the cultured and eloquent Martin Farrancourt, brother to the splendid, sinister Earl of Chelsham, and Sir Jocelyn Wade, about whom clung all the glamour of the Court. He had succeeded in removing the sisters from the vicinity of these dangerous suitors, and now, when he had begun to breathe freely again, there appeared on the scene this infernal sea-robber, who would undoubtedly be a dangerous fellow to cross. Mr. Fletcher, no hero, took gloomy stock of the Captain's intrepid, aquiline face and masterful air, and decided that the fates were working against him.

Mr. Charnwood was eager to bear a detailed account of his guest's latest venture against Spain, but Kit, mindful of his promise to Damaris, turned his questions aside with a laugh and exerted himself to engage Olivia and Mr. Fletcher in conversation. Damaris bestowed upon him a look of warm approval, and lost no time in persuading Regina to stroll with her in the garden. They were gone for some time, and when they returned Miss Charnwood was flushed and starry-eyed and Damaris wearing an expression of benevolent satisfaction. Kit concluded that her schemes were thriving, and Sir Jocelyn's wooing likely to prosper.

Later, as they rode back to Fallowmead, he inquired with some curiosity how she had broken to Miss Charnwood the news of Wade's presence in Jamaica. Damaris gave a gurgle of laughter.

"I think I was very clever," she said candidly. "I told her a little about Marayte, and how he is said to torture his prisoners, and then I added, quite casually, that Sir Jocelyn had fallen into his hands. That gave her such a fright that she betrayed herself at once, and after that 'twas the simplest thing in the world to persuade her to confide in me."

His lips twitched.

"You, my child, are a heartless baggage," he told her roundly. "Where was the need to alarm her so?"

"But, Kit, she would not otherwise have confided so much to a stranger! Besides, a deal of trouble has been prevented, for that hateful cousin had convinced her that Sir Jocelyn was merely amusing himself at her expense. Now she knows the truth, and all Sir Jocelyn needs to do is to gain her father's consent to their marriage." A hint of anxiety crept into her voice. "Will he give it, do you think? Perhaps I should tell him that anything Mr. Fletcher may have said against Sir Jocelyn was prompted by malice."

Captain Brandon perceived that she was in danger of being carried away by the success of her plotting, and that the time had come to put an end to it. He said, quite quietly, but with a note of authority in his voice which made her jump:

"You will not mention the matter to him. Now understand me, Damaris! Sir Jocelyn is very well able to manage his own affairs, and you will leave him to do so henceforth. Give a party if you wish, and invite Charnwood and his daughters, but let us have no more meddling."

Indulged Damaris most certainly had been, but she had heard that note in Kit's voice before. She stole a speculative glance at his face, decided that argument would be fruitless, and rode on for a while in philosophical silence. Presently she remarked:

"Sir Jocelyn was quite right about Mr. Fletcher. Miss Regina told me 'twas entirely his fault that they had to return to Jamaica, for he persuaded his step-mother —who is also their aunt—to inform Mr. Charnwood that Miss Olivia was on the point of turning papist."

"And is she?" Kit asked with a frown.

"Oh, no, I think not! It was simply a ruse to remove them from London. He hopes to marry one of them, because he has no money of his own!" A frown wrinkled her brow. "I think he must be very stupid, for although he hopes to marry the daughter, he does not try to please the father. Anyone can see that Mr. Charnwood despises him."

"Well he might!" Kit's voice was contemptuous. "He will be a fool if he allows his daughter to throw herself away upon that over-dressed jackanapes. Even in Port Royal he can find a better match for her than that."

Quite suddenly, and for the first time in her life, it occurred to Damaris that Kit might one day bring a bride to Fallowmead. She had never considered the possibility before, for though they knew several marriageable girls he had never been more than ordinarily courteous to any of them, but now she felt that she had been incredibly obtuse. One day, of course, he would marry. She tried to picture Olivia Charnwood taking her place as mistress of Fallowmead, and was conscious of a sinking heart and a curious feeling of loneliness and loss.

The thought would not be banished, and continued to tease her for the next two days, though she contrived to smother it with plans for the coming party. On the third day, however, which was that chosen for the gathering, everything was in readiness by noon, and she had nothing left to do but select the gown and jewels with which to honour the occasion. All too soon even this trivial problem was settled, and then, with nothing further to engage it, her mind returned again to the thought which had come, unbidden, to disturb its peace.

It was in vain that she tried to convince herself that she was mistaken, that Kit had shown no extraordinary interest in Miss Charnwood. The memory of Olivia's serene and perfect face, with its soft dark eyes and broad brow, was uncomfortably vivid, and, picking up a mirror, she studied her reflection for the first time with dissatisfaction.

"Rebecca," she said abruptly to the quadroon waiting-woman who was moving quietly about the room, "do you think I am beautiful?"

Rebecca smiled indulgently. She was a tall, lithe creature some ten years older than her mistress, whom she loved with a fierce, protective devotion. She had served Jane Brandon until her death, but her affections had always been centred upon the supposed daughter of the house.

"Yes, Miss 'Maris," she replied promptly. "The most beautiful young lady in Jamaica."

Damaris continued to stare critically into the mirror. It was true that for the past two years she had been the acknowledged beauty of a somewhat restricted society, and she wondered whether mere jealousy was the cause for this feeling of antagonism towards Olivia. She was not much given to introspection, and the feeling was too tenuous to put into words, so she remarked with a sigh:

"Mary Ritchie is a year younger than I, and she has been wed these six months."

Rebecca put down the shift she was folding and came to stand beside her mistress.

"What ails you, Miss 'Maris?" she asked bluntly. "Poor Miss Mary had but one suitor, but you could be married tomorrow if you chose."

"I do not wish to be married," Damaris replied pettishly, but the words had given her thoughts a fresh direction. Olivia was new to Jamaica, and her father's intimates were mostly his own contemporaries rather than the younger, eligible men, but with many of the latter Damaris herself was on the best of terms. She resolved to make Olivia known to them, and gave thanks for the foresight which had prompted her to include several among the evening's guests.

Slightly comforted by this decision, she left her room and went out into the garden, where Nicholas presently found her. She thought, with a stab of remorse, that she had not been very kind to him since his return to

Jamaica, and this guilty reflection lent an added warmth
to her greeting. For a while they made desultory conversation, while he watched her with adoring eyes, and
she, fully conscious of the regard though apparently
heedless of it, sought idly among the riot of blossoms
for one to pin at her breast. At length, some chance
mention of her brother's name calling to mind her earlier disquiet, she said abruptly:

"I have been thinking, Nick, that 'tis strange Kit
does not marry."

They were leaning now upon the wall of that small,
seaward-facing terrace where she had talked with Sir
Jocelyn. Nicholas was silent for a space, fingering a
small plant which grew between the stones, and then
he said with suppressed violence:

"I wish to God he would!"

She was startled by his vehemence.

"But why?"

"Because if he took a wife, he would be less posses-
sive towards you." Nick's strong, brown fingers were
wreaking havoc upon the hapless plant. "But 'tis useless
to talk! He will never find a woman to satisfy his in-
sane pride, just as he will never find a man whom
he thinks worthy to be your husband. Lucifer! By
Heaven! The devil himself could not be more damnably proud."

"Nick!" She was almost weeping in her distress. "You
must not say such things to me. He is my brother, and I
love him, and besides, it is not true. You know that he
won that name simply because he has never squan-
dered his gold in idle dissipation as so many do. The
men do not understand him and so they think him
proud, but you, at least, should know better than
that."

"How hotly you defend him!" he said bitterly. "Sometimes I think neither of you has room in your heart for any other affection. You are all in all to each other."

"That is not true, either." Realizing that she had hurt him, she hastened to make amends, and in her anxiety implied perhaps more than she intended. "If you meant nothing to me it would not matter what you said. 'Tis because I care that I cannot bear to see you and Kit quarrelling."

She heard him catch his breath, and turned to look up into his face. Next moment she found herself crushed in his arms while he poured out his feelings in a flood of hasty, impassioned words she was too inexperienced to check. She was startled and confused, for none of her admirers had ever dared so much, but not sufficiently alarmed to struggle against the embrace. After the scarcely acknowledged sense of insecurity which had been with her during the past few days, it was strangely comforting to feel Nick's strong young arms about her, and when he paused she lifted her face as trustfully as a child to meet his kiss.

Kit, meanwhile, had spent the morning riding with Sir Jocelyn around the plantation, where slaves were at work among the sugar-cane, and explaining to his guest the methods by which the sugar was produced. Returning to the house, they found Dr. Blair reading on the shady piazza, and Sir Jocelyn, observing that the book absorbing his attention was the works of Horace, reflected with inward amusement that these must surely be the most unusual buccaneers who had ever sailed the seas.

Kit called for wine, and inquired of the servant who brought it the whereabouts of his sister. When he was told that she was in the garden with Mr. Halthrop, a frown darkened his eyes, and though he pledged his guests courteously enough it was obvious that his thoughts were elsewhere. After a little he got up, saying abruptly that he would find Damaris, and Alex, with a shrewd glance at his face, rose at once to go with him. Sir Jocelyn followed suit, spurred by an uneasiness he could not define, but which subsequent events proved to be well-founded, for only a few minutes later they reached the tree-shadowed terrace to find the missing couple locked in each other's arms.

Jocelyn, after one startled glance, looked instinctively at Kit, and was appalled by the expression in his face. Anger he had expected, but not this murderous fury, and then, while surprise and dismay held him rooted to the spot, and Dr. Blair, it seemed, was similarly paralysed, Brandon strode forward, gripped Halthrop by the shoulder, and flung him away from the girl with such violence that he stumbled and fell.

Damaris uttered a little cry, and Jocelyn and Alex started forward together, expecting they knew not what. Nick scrambled to his feet, and at sight of his captain's face his hand flashed involuntarily to his sword. Through Jocelyn's mind drifted the words Blair had used when speaking of Kit's quarrel with Renard—"if ever I saw the devil looking out of a man's eyes, I saw it then"—and he understood suddenly what the Doctor had meant.

"Sir Jocelyn," Kit's voice was level and quiet, but his deadly gaze never shifted from Halthrop's face, "will you have the goodness to take my sister back to the house?"

Wade hesitated for a moment, but then, reflecting that Dr. Blair, with his cool common sense and established friendship with both Halthrop and Brandon, was better able to deal with the situation than a comparative stranger, and that whatever followed, Miss Brandon would be better away from it, he proffered his arm silently to her. She laid her hand on it, but her frightened gaze turned towards her brother.

"Kit!" she said pleadingly, but he was still watching Halthrop and did not look at her.

"Do as I bid you, Damaris," he said, and his tone admitted of no further argument. She let Sir Jocelyn lead her towards the house, and only he heard the small, stifled sob which escaped her lips as they went.

They passed out of sight, and in a silence broken only by the baleful slither of the steel, Kit drew his sword from its sheath. Nick's glance flickered for an instant, and then his own blade flashed in the sun, but before unspoken challenge and tacit acceptance could be translated into action, Alex stepped between them.

"Kit! Nicholas! For God's sake, think what you are doing!" he said sternly. "Put up your swords, and let us have no more of this folly. Put them up, I say."

Neither obeyed his command, but Nicholas fell back a pace and lowered his point to the ground.

"I have no wish to fight, God knows!" he said soberly. "But I'll not brand myself a craven at your bidding, Alex. If Kit thinks I have given him cause, I am willing to meet him."

"If I think it!" There was savage irony in Kit's low voice. "What need to think, you damned puppy, when I have the evidence of my eyes? Stand aside, Alex! This is no concern of yours."

"Give thanks, then, I've sense enough to make it my concern," Alex said sharply. "You young fools! Do you think I will stand by and let you brand the maid a wanton in the eyes of the world, for who will believe her innocent once 'tis known you fought over her?"

It was a shrewd stroke and he knew it. Nicholas bit his lip, and Kit, after an instant's furious reflection, slammed his sword back into the scabbard and strode to the low wall bordering the terrace, where he stood with his back to them and his hands gripped hard upon the stone.

"You are right, Alex, damn you!" he said over his shoulder. "We cannot fight. Get off my land, Nick, and stay off it in the future, and off my ships, too."

"That will not serve, Kit!" Nicholas, too, had put up his sword, and spoke with an attempt at calmness, though Alex could see with what difficulty he was curbing his temper. "You cannot turn me off as though I were a lackey who has displeased you. I love Damaris, and I want to marry her. God's light! Why should you suppose aught else?"

For a long moment the question hung, unanswered, upon the air, while Alex stood watchful and silent, ready to intervene at once should the need arise. Kit stared blindly out towards the sea, fighting with all the strength of his will to conquer the sickening waves of murderous jealousy which for the past few minutes had threatened to deprive him of reason. He knew that they were watching him, waiting for him to speak, wondering what madness had taken possession of him, and he could not bring himself to turn and meet their eyes.

"She is too young to marry," he said at last, without moving.

He heard Nicholas utter an exclamation of mingled anger and contempt, and then Alex said, swiftly and sternly:

"That is absurd, and you know it! Whatever your reason for resenting Nick's feelings for her, do him the justice of telling him the truth."

The truth! Kit's lips writhed in a smile of mockery and pain. Could any lie he might invent be more fantastic, less likely to command belief, than the simple facts? He said slowly:

"I cannot tell you my reason, but it is such as to make it impossible for me to consent to your marriage. That is all I can say."

"Is it, by God?" Nick took a hasty step forward, and was only checked by Blair's sudden grip on his arm. "Have done with pretence, and admit the truth! 'Tis your infernal pride, is it not? I am not worthy to wed the sister of the great Captain Lucifer!" He gave a short, angry laugh with no amusement in it. "I suppose you are hoping that this sprig from the Court will make her 'my lady'!"

"Sir Jocelyn has nothing to do with it," Kit replied coldly. He had himself in hand at last, and his voice was calm. "My answer would have been the same had I never heard of his existence. There are good and sufficient reasons why you cannot marry Damaris, but you must accept my word for it that they exist."

Nicholas sneered.

"Why should I?"

"Why should you not?" Kit turned abruptly to face him, and met his eyes squarely. "Have I ever given you cause to doubt my honesty?"

There was a hint of reproach in the quiet words. Nicholas flushed uncomfortably.

"No," he said in a low voice, "never. I ask your pardon for that, but if such reasons exist, I do not understand why you refuse to disclose them."

"That I cannot do," Kit replied firmly. "One day, perhaps, you may learn the truth, and then you may understand my silence. No," he raised his hand to check the words hovering on the boy's lips, "we will speak no more of the matter. You have my answer. Your future is for you to decide, but Damaris can have no part in it." He turned to go, but as he passed Halthrop he paused, and laid a hand on his shoulder. There was a curious expression in his face. "I am sorry, Nick. You think me without heart or sympathy, but you are wrong. Believe me, I can appreciate your feelings to an extent you cannot even guess."

He went on towards the house, leaving them to stare after him and wonder at the bitterness which had rung through his parting words. At last Alex said, with the air of one speaking his thoughts aloud:

"Yon's a man with some secret trouble, some burden he cannot or will not share. I've suspected it these many months." He sighed, and looked again at his companion. "Have a care how far you provoke him, Nicholas. When a man is on the rack, he is apt to be hasty of temper."

Chapter V

THE GOLDEN LURE

Kit went slowly towards the house, conscious suddenly of an overwhelming weariness. How long must it go on, this conflict which seemed to be rending him asunder? How long before the torment within him drove him into some act of violence which he would regret as soon as sanity returned? He knew that he had come within an ace of it today; that but for the intervention of Alex Blair he would have fought Nicholas and killed him, for once sword had crossed sword nothing less than the boy's death would have satisfied him. Yet Nicholas was his friend. The thought set a chill upon him which not even the tropic heat could dispel.

He found Sir Jocelyn in the hall, alone, and obviously uncertain what to do. When Kit appeared, he looked at him dubiously and volunteered the information that Miss Brandon had gone to her room. Kit thanked him briefly and left him, and Sir Jocelyn, having watched him mount the stairs, went, still with that air of uncertainty, into the garden again.

The door of Miss Brandon's bedchamber was locked, and a knock brought no response, but when Kit spoke her name, sharply, because of a swift stab of alarm, her footsteps came slowly across the room towards it. She opened the door and turned away at once, but not in time to conceal the fact that she had been weeping. He accepted the mute invitation and went in, but paused just within the door to regard her with troubled eyes.

It was a beautiful room, sumptuous as only great wealth and great love could make it. Richly carved woods, hangings of velvet and brocade, tapestries and pictures beyond price, were combined to make a bower fit for a princess. The long windows opened on to a balcony, its balustrade and pillars twined with flowering creepers, and between the clusters of gorgeous blossoms was visible a breath-taking view across the harbour to the fort and the open sea beyond. When Fallowmead was being built, Damaris had begged for a room from which she could watch her brother's ship entering or leaving the harbour, and he had given her what she asked, and more besides. It was a room as nearly perfect as mind and skill could make it, a setting worthy of its occupant.

Damaris had turned her back to him, and was fidgeting with the curtains of the window by which she stood. He had meant to be calm in his dealings with her, and had stood for a few moments outside her door considering what to say, but the measured phrases were forgotten now. When at length he spoke, it was the one question he had not meant to ask which broke from his lips, born of the anguish within him.

"Do you love him, Damaris?"

It seemed an interminable while before she answered. He could not be sure whether she did hesitate, or whether his own anxiety magnified the pause.

"I do not know," she whispered at length. "Oh, Kit, I do not know!"

He said with an effort:

"He wants to marry you. Did you know that?"

She nodded.

"He told me he meant to seek your consent, but that he feared you would not give it."

"He was right," Kit said grimly. "I will not."

"Kit!" She turned to face him, her composure belied by her wide, anxious eyes. "You did not quarrel?"

"No," he answered briefly, "we did not. He said that he desired to marry you, and I told him that it was not possible. That is all."

"But why?" she insisted. "What have you against Nick?"

"I have nothing against him, nor do I, as he supposes, withhold my consent out of empty pride, although he has little enough to offer you. He is a good friend and a loyal comrade, but a man who follows our calling makes a poor husband."

She looked at him gravely, a direct, questioning look with some unfathomable thought behind it.

"Is that why you have never married, Kit?"

The question took him by surprise. He felt that they were upon dangerous ground, and answered hurriedly, in words forgotten as soon as they were uttered.

"I am not yet, I trust, so stricken with years that I must resign myself to solitude, but it is not my marriage we are discussing. That is a question of no immediate importance."

She had the curious and unwelcome feeling that a door had been slammed in her face, and felt a sharp stab of pain. The raillery in his voice jarred upon her, for she felt sure that he was in no mood for jesting, and that the lightness was a cloak for some feeling into which she was not to probe. Tears stung her eyes again, and to conceal her hurt she said pettishly:

"Neither, it seems, is mine, nor will it ever be if you treat all my suitors as you have treated Nick. You have been trying to pick a quarrel with him ever since you came home, and today in the garden you looked as though you meant to kill him."

The reminder was unfortunate. As the memory of the scene he had witnessed recurred to him, he was shaken again by some measure of the fury which had possessed him then. Nicholas had dared to make love to her, and she had made no protest. It was that latter thought which whipped his smouldering anger into flame again.

"And if I had done so," he said between his teeth, "may I point out that you would have been largely to blame? I do not like to see my sister treated like a common doxy; I like even less to see her behaving like one."

He was conscious, even as he spoke, of the injustice of the words, and, irrationally, the knowledge increased his anger. For an instant Damaris looked stunned, but she had too much spirit to let that pass without protest.

"Is that how such women behave?" she retorted with breathless anger. "I do not know, but I will not presume to argue with you upon a subject in which you are no doubt widely experienced." She turned with a flounce of her wide skirts, and swept across to her dressing-table. "Now, if you will be good enough to leave me, I wish to change my dress. Our guests will be arriving soon."

He turned on his heel and went out without another word, but she made no immediate attempt to summon her woman. For the few minutes that her ill-humour lasted, she stood where she was, drumming her fingers on the table and staring unseeingly into the mirror in its broad frame of silver-gilt, but, as always, her anger burned too fiercely to be of long duration. Very soon it gave way to unhappiness, and she cast herself down on the day-bed near the open windows and wept more bitterly than before. It was the first time in her life that she had quarrelled with Kit, and it seemed a fitting culmination to the uncertainties of the past few days.

She was in no hurry to prepare for a party for which she had lost all enthusiasm, and the first guests had arrived before she made her appearance. Twice Kit had sent a servant with a curt message to her to hasten, and each time, out of sheer perversity, she had found a fresh cause to delay. When at length she went down, the Charnwoods and Mr. Fletcher had just entered the house, and so had an excellent view of her as she descended the stairs. They stood and stared, the demands of courtesy forgotten in sheer astonishment.

She had chosen to dress entirely in white, and against the stark simplicity of that background, the jewels she wore glowed with added fire. The great rope of pearls was about her neck, and a lesser string wreathed the shining masses of her hair; long earrings set with emeralds framed her face, while her sleeves, slashed to the shoulder to reveal the lace and cambric beneath, were fastened at intervals with jewelled clasps instead of ribbons. She wore several rings, and about her slender waist, after the fashion of a girdle, she had seen fit to fasten a heavy golden chain, in each link of which was set a precious stone.

Mr. Fletcher blinked as this jewelled vision came towards him, and a gleam of covetousness woke in his eyes. He had already been impressed by the size and style of the house, and now he began to wonder whether he could not do better for himself in the matter of marriage than his cousin Olivia. He had no desire to become a planter, and, apart from her father's

estate, Olivia's whole dowry could not equal the value
of the gems this girl was wearing so casually. To be
sure, the pirate brother was something of a stumbling-
block, but Mr. Fletcher decided that it would be wise
to practise tolerance in that respect. In the face of
such wealth, tolerance suddenly seemed to him an
admirable attribute.

As Damaris greeted them, she noted with satisfaction
that even Olivia's saint-like calm was not proof against
the assault of envy. She smiled cordially at her, and
led the way into the room where the guests were
assembling. Her attention being claimed just then by
the arrival of the guests of honour—the Governor, Sir
Thomas Modyford, and his lady—she missed the first
meeting between Jocelyn and Regina, but when she
again had leisure to observe them, Wade was in ami-
cable conversation with Mr. Charnwood and his
younger daughter, while Dr. Blair, who had guessed
how matters stood, good-naturedly held Mr. Fletcher
in talk. Kit, she noticed with mingled irritation and
uneasiness, had engaged Olivia's attention in a similar
fashion.

Damaris was exceedingly gay that evening, demure
and daring by turns, her cheeks faintly flushed, her eyes
more sparkling than her jewels. Throughout the long,
elaborate dinner she laughed and talked, dividing her
attention between the Governor upon the one hand,
and Sir Jocelyn upon the other, but finding time to steal
occasional glances at the elder Miss Charnwood. She
had contrived to seat Olivia between two of her own
erstwhile admirers, young Rob Ritchie and Colonel
Prestyn, and was pleased to observe that though Rob
was ungallant enough to gaze wistfully in her direction,
the Colonel, a dark, sardonic man in his late thirties,

seemed very well pleased with his present company.

When at last the meal was over, her guests begged her to sing for them, and she complied with a becoming modesty, though this did not prevent her from frequently smiling up beneath her lashes at Ingram Fletcher, who had stationed himself beside her as soon as opportunity offered. She seemed indifferent alike to Nicholas, glooming by himself in a distant corner, and to Kit, whose attention appeared to be wholly occupied by his guests. The Colonel, a determined man, was still at Olivia's elbow.

Towards the end of the evening, when the guests were beginning to think of departure, the hurried beat of galloping hoofs came up out of the hot darkness to the door of Fallowmead, and a minute or two later a servant entered the room and bent to speak softly in his master's ear. Kit rose and, excusing himself, went out of the room, with a swift glance at Alex which drew the Doctor in his wake. After a few moments, Nicholas got up also, and strolled unobtrusively after them.

They were gone for some while, and only returned in time to take leave of the departing guests. Damaris had had no chance of private conversation with Regina, but under cover of the farewells the other girl pressed her hand and whispered joyfully that everything was in a fair way to being settled. Miss Brandon expressed satisfaction, but her tone was absent. She had just seen Kit draw the Governor aside and speak swiftly and earnestly; they were too far away for her to hear what was said, but as he turned away she heard Modyford say:

"Come to me in the morning, then, and we will discuss it further," and a premonition of what those words portended seized her in a cold clutch of fear.

When the last of the company had departed, Kit
and his two lieutenants withdrew again to the library,
leaving Damaris and Sir Jocelyn alone. This suited the
gentleman very well, for it enabled him to relate to her
all that had passed between him and Mr. Charnwood,
whom he was to visit on the following day. She listened
attentively, but behind her interest and pleasure part
of her mind was wondering what news had come to
Fallowmead that night, and what was being discussed
behind the closed doors of the library.

He left her at last, and she went quickly to the library
and entered without knocking. One swift glance about
the room was enough to confirm her fears. On the
table, in the full light of the candles, a map was spread,
and Kit had apparently been explaining something to
his companions, for though he glanced up at the sound
of the opening door, one fine hand in its wealth of
costly lace rested still upon the map. Alex stood at his
shoulder, and Nicholas, at the table's end, leaned forward across it in order to see. Opposite him, a ragged
stranger with a shifty, rat-like countenance turned a
startled and astonished gaze upon the newcomer.

She closed the door and went slowly forward, her
anxious glance resting on each in turn, but returning at
last to her brother's face. She said in a low voice:

"So soon?"

It was Alex who answered her, for both Kit and
Nicholas were looking again at the map, though the
thoughts of neither were any longer concerned with it.

"Aye, lassie," he said gently. "There's news come
tonight we cannot ignore. We must sail within the
week."

"But you cannot!" Undisguised dismay rang in her
voice, and both Kit and Nicholas wondered instantly

if it were for him. "You have been in harbour only a few days. The *Loyalist* cannot be ready to put to sea again so soon."

"She must be made so," Kit said shortly, "and the *Jane,* thanks be to Heaven, is ready. Nick, you will take command of her."

"I?" The boy looked up in quick surprise, a frown between his brows. For a moment his eyes met those of his captain, and then a smile which was half a sneer touched his lips. "As you please. No doubt it will be better so."

"Better that we do not sail together again," said his tone, and for an instant the air was tense again with a suppressed violence of emotion. Damaris said quickly:

"What is the purpose of this venture? It must be a prize of great value to stir you to so much haste."

"It is!" Kit told her curtly. "A plate-ship, bound for Spain with a fortune in her hold. This man has just brought news of it."

She glanced fleetingly at the stranger. He was staring at her, just as he had stared from the moment she entered the room, his awed gaze moving constantly from the pearls to the emeralds in her ears and thence to the jewelled chain about her waist. The naked greed that gleamed in his eyes made her uneasy, and she drew back a little, and moved closer to Kit. He looked sharply from her to the man.

"The rest can wait," he said with some finality. "Nick, will you take this fellow and see that he is given food and a bed?"

Nicholas nodded and stood upright, signing to the man to follow him. Kit waited until they had left the room, and then said in a low voice to Blair:

"Go after them, Alex, and see to it that he is bestowed somewhere where he can do no mischief. I do not think he will be fool enough to attempt robbery, but we'll take precautions none the less. He may find those gems a temptation too great to resist."

Alex smiled grimly and went out. Kit slowly rolled up the map and returned it to its place, while Damaris, the memory of their quarrel uncomfortably vivid, sought for something to say to relieve the awkwardness of the moment.

"Sir Jocelyn tells me that his fears were groundless," she ventured at length. "Mr. Charnwood approves him, and he is to visit him tomorrow to discuss matters further."

"I am delighted to hear it." Kit's tone was dry. "Perhaps he can contrive to get himself invited to stay. You realize, of course, that it is out of the question for him to stay here in my absence?"

"I suppose so." She moved forward to the table, and began to trace patterns on its polished surface with one slim forefinger. "When must you go?"

"I shall leave Fallowmead in the morning. There will be much to do, and 'twill save time if I stay aboard the *Loyalist*."

Reason told her that this was true, but she could not quite cast out the fear that he was making of it an excuse to leave the house because of their quarrel. The thought hurt her unbearably, but she could not bring herself to put it into words. Twenty-four hours ago she would have flung herself into his arms and begged him to stay, but now, for the first time in her life, she was conscious of constraint between them.

"Will not a plate-ship be heavily guarded?" she asked, after a long pause. Kit shook his head.

"The Dons grow cunning," he replied. "They think

a single ship less likely to attract unwelcome attention than one under powerful escort. The secret has been well kept, but that fellow who came here tonight has but just escaped from imprisonment among them, and learned of it in that way. He hoped to find Morgan in Port Royal, and when he did not, he brought his news to me."

"But even if it is a single ship," she persisted, clinging to her original point, which had its root in fear, "it will surely be a very powerful one. They would not trust such a cargo to meagre defences."

"It will be powerful," Kit agreed with a faint smile. "A lumbering man-o'-war as unwieldy as a castle. The *Loyalist* and the *Jane* together will be more than a match for her."

She had learned too much, during the past few years, of ships and the sea, to be wholly convinced by this pose of easy confidence, but she knew that at no time would he welcome a show of fear. So she choked back her forebodings and said no more, reflecting miserably that with this new, inexplicable stiffness between them they were conversing like strangers.

"Come," he said after a moment, " 'tis time we were a-bed. It grows late, and I must be early aboard." Still without speaking, she moved reluctantly towards the door, while he paused to snuff the candles on the table. Suddenly he added: "It is needless, I believe, to tell you that no word of this venture must be allowed to leak out. Until we return, no one in Port Royal must know anything of any plate-ship."

"I will say nothing," she replied in a low voice, but this fresh reference to the plate-ship conjured up an all too vivid picture of the quarry he was proposing to hunt down. She had heard of such ships, floating cas-

tles, as Kit had contemptuously named them, with a
tremendous weight of metal and of men. Even if he
achieved the impossible, and captured the golden prize,
many must die in the battle. What if he were one of
them? A sudden conviction, unreasoning and unassail-
able, that they were about to be parted for ever, laid
hold upon her, and dignity and resolution alike were
swept aside.

"Kit!" She turned to face him, and in spite of the
modish gown and the preposterous array of jewels, it
was a child who spoke, a child lost and frightened,
crying in the dark for the comfort he had never failed
to give her. "Do not go! The danger is too great!"

"Why, what is this?" He came towards her through
the dimness, for the only light now in the room was
that which found its way through the half-open door.
"It is not like you, Damaris, to shrink from the thought
of a blow against Spain."

"I am afraid," she said, her voice catching on a sob,
"and you have been home so short a time. Oh, Kit, let
it go! What use is gold if it costs your life to win it?"
Her voice broke, and she laid hold upon his coat as
though to restrain him by main force. "Do not go!
Something tells me that this venture is ill-fated."

He caught her to him, crushing her in a merciless
grip so that she could scarcely breathe, and buried his
face against her shining hair.

"I will come back," he said fiercely in a whisper, and
his tone made a vow of the simple words. "I will come
back!"

A moment he held her so, and then abruptly he released her and stepped past her into the lighted room
beyond and stood there with his back towards her
while seconds slipped away. At last he turned, and

she saw that he was very pale.

"I will come back," he said for the third time, but lightly now, and with a twisted smile, "and you shall dip your pretty arms in gold to the elbow, and have yet more jewels with which to deck yourself. God's light, child! This venture is no more perilous than any other. Let me hear no more of forebodings, and such old wives' tales."

"I am sorry," she said unsteadily, and dashed a hand across her eyes. "It has been such a miserable evening, and this news is something of a shock." She came to him, and looked up timidly into his face. "Oh, Kit, say that you forgive me! I cannot bear to quarrel with you, and that is the truth."

"I think I have need to ask forgiveness of you," he replied, and put his arm about her shoulders again. "Did I indeed spoil your pleasure, child? I did not mean to, God knows!"

"It is over now," she said contentedly, and laid her head against his shoulder, "and at least my party did not fail of its real purpose, which was to help Regina and Sir Jocelyn."

"No," Kit's voice was rueful, almost bitter, "they, at all events, find their troubles at an end."

"But you do not?" She raised her head to look up at him again, and gently touched his cheek. "Dear Kit, will you not tell me what it is that troubles you so? I am no longer a child. Do not shut me out in this fashion."

He imprisoned the caressing hand in his own, and looked searchingly into her face.

"Are you not, Damaris?" he said in a low voice. "Could I be sure of that——" he broke off, shaking his head. "No, the time is not yet! When I return, perhaps!" He bent and kissed her cheek, and then let her go. "Good night, my dear, and let us have no more faint-heartedness. Captain Lucifer's sister must have some share of his pride."

She showed no lack of pride during the days that followed, but hid her fears behind a smiling face. Everyone knew that Captain Lucifer was making ready to put to sea again, and everyone wondered why, but no one, least of all the Captain's sister, showed any desire to gratify the general curiosity.

Sir Jocelyn, as Kit had suggested, removed to the Charnwood house. He was now formally betrothed to Regina, and both were disposed to hold Miss Brandon largely responsible for their happiness. Regina, who had learned from Jocelyn of the situation between Damaris and Nicholas, was eager to repay the debt in kind, but Miss Brandon refused to discuss the subject, and Sir Jocelyn, on being appealed to, said darkly that there was some mystery surrounding the Brandons and she would be well advised not to interfere.

Kit, after hours of torment and inward conflict, had realized at last that the present state of affairs could not go on, though he still shrank from the prospect of telling Damaris the truth. For the first time for many years he felt himself in need of advice, and finally he resolved that during the voyage he would take Dr. Blair into his confidence. Alex was his oldest as well as his closest friend, and whatever counsel he gave would be sound.

On the day of his departure, Damaris came aboard the *Loyalist* to bid him farewell. Jocelyn and Regina had been invited to accompany her, and since Olivia had expressed a desire to see the ship so graphically described by Sir Jocelyn, the invitation had been extended to her also. In those circumstances it was impossible to exclude Ingram Fletcher, and so it was quite a large party which assembled in the *Loyalist's* spacious cabin to drink success to a venture the exact nature of which was unknown to half of them.

Nicholas had come from the *Jane* to join in the general leave-taking, but though Regina's kindly efforts finally procured him a moment or two alone with Damaris, he did not feel to have gained much thereby. He had high hopes of great profit from the capture of the plate-ship, and proposed with his share to buy land, hoping that this would induce Kit to view his courtship with more favour, but though Damaris earnestly wished him well, and even allowed him to kiss her in parting, she steadfastly refused to plight troth with him without her brother's consent.

Her parting from Kit was almost casual, for she had long since resolved to plague him no more with foolish, idle fears, while he was afraid that his feelings might once again betray him, but in the minds of both was the unspoken thought that their real farewells had been made that night at Fallowmead. Now there was no more to be said.

Chapter VI

STORM CLOUDS GATHERING

Sir Jocelyn Wade dismounted from his horse at the door of the Governor's house in Port Royal, wondering curiously and a little uneasily why Modyford had sent for him. The message had come just as he was setting out for Fallowmead with the Charnwood sisters and Ingram Fletcher, and he had ridden with them as long as their roads had lain together, promising when they parted that he would join them at Fallowmead as soon as he was able.

He had noticed as he rode down into the town that a strange ship lay at anchor in the harbour, and wondered whether the summons were in any way connected with that. Since Kit Brandon's departure, a close friendship had grown up between his sister and Regina, and scarcely a day passed without intercourse of some kind between the two households; if misfortune had overtaken Kit, Sir Thomas, knowing this, might well have chosen this way of breaking the news to Damaris. With a sense of deep foreboding, Jocelyn followed the servant into the Governor's presence.

A moment later he knew his fears to be groundless. Modyford already had one guest with him, a slight man with a pale, sensitive face and dreamy grey eyes, who came forward eagerly to meet Sir Jocelyn. He walked with a pronounced limp, and looked delicate.

"Martin!" Jocelyn exclaimed, and started forward

with outstretched hand. "What in the name of fortune brings you here?"

Martin Farrancourt smiled. He had a charming smile, which irradiated his thin face with sudden warmth and humour.

"A quest similar to your own, I believe, Jocelyn," he replied, as their hands met. "Had you left England less hastily we might have made the journey together."

"I have been telling Mr. Farrancourt," Modyford remarked as Wade turned belatedly to greet him, "that had he travelled with you, his journey, at least in its latter part, would have been eventful. The ship which brought him was fortunate enough to escape hindrance of any kind."

For a few minutes longer he remained in conversation with them, but then excused himself on the score of business, and withdrew. The ship in which Mr. Farrancourt had travelled had brought official documents from England, and he must deal with them without delay. When he had gone, Martin said with a somewhat wry smile:

"I am to congratulate you, Jocelyn, it seems. Sir Thomas tells me that you are already contracted to Miss Regina. Upon my soul, you wasted no time!"

Jocelyn laughed.

"Say rather that fortune favoured me. The pirate who took me prisoner did me no disservice after all, since Captain Brandon came to my rescue, and invited me to stay in his house. He and his sister are close friends of Mr. Charnwood, and so I came to him with powerful allies."

Martin's smile was wistful.

"Could you prevail upon them to exert a like influence on my behalf?"

Jocelyn hesitated for a moment before he replied. He knew in his heart that Martin's wooing was foredoomed to failure, but he realized that since he had made the long and arduous journey from England, his hopes of winning Olivia must be high indeed. He could not bring himself to dash those hopes, so he said with forced cheerfulness:

"Brandon is not at present in Jamaica, but his sister, I am sure, would be willing to use her efforts on your behalf." He paused, and then added abruptly: "Does the name of Brandon mean anything to you, Martin?"

"Mean anything?" The other was puzzled. "No, why should it? I doubt I had heard it until today, when Sir Thomas was telling me of your adventures. The man is a buccaneer, is he not?"

"A buccaneer of no common sort," Jocelyn replied slowly, "and, however little his name may mean to you, he knows something of your family," and he recounted Brandon's curious reaction to his own reference to the Golden Panther.

" 'Tis a mystery I cannot explain," Farrancourt said when the tale was told, "but I will hazard a guess that Ralph might do so an he would. He is a man of many secrets, which not even I am allowed to share."

"That thought was in my mind also," Jocelyn admitted. "It is significant, is it not, that before they came to Jamaica, the Brandons lived in Devon?"

"True, but Chelsham lies far to the east of Plymouth, though, to be sure, Ralph has made his influence felt throughout the county. They are Royalists, you say? I could understand it better if they were not, for my brother made himself very thoroughly hated by every Parliamentarian in the west, and old enmities die hard."

"Martin," Jocelyn said slowly, "was Chelsham aware of your intention to come to Jamaica?"

Again the swift smile lit Farrancourt's face, this time with a glint of mockery.

"What manner of fool do you think me?" he retorted. "He learned of it by letter when I was already several days at sea, for had he known he would have tried to prevent me, and what Ralph attempts he generally achieves. I had no mind to be stopped. 'Slife, Jocelyn, I am not a schoolboy! If a man of four-and-thirty may not look where he chooses for a bride, 'tis a poor thing indeed."

"Nevertheless, there will be a reckoning to pay when you do return to England, for never tell me that you, of all men, mean to settle here."

Martin laughed.

"I would do even that gladly enough if I might have Olivia at my side." He leaned forward eagerly. "Jocelyn, how fares she? Does that foppish cousin still plague her with attentions?"

Sir Jocelyn thoughtfully rubbed his chin.

"Miss Olivia is as she ever was," he replied at length, "but Fletcher has transferred his attentions to Miss Brandon, no doubt because her brother is extremely rich, and the child herself flaunts jewels worth a king's ransom. What Fletcher has forgotten—or perhaps does not know—is that Kit Brandon seems to look with scant favour upon any suitor for his sister's hand. Regina swears that Miss Brandon merely amuses herself, but to my mind the tale is like to have a tragic ending when Brandon returns. I cannot believe Ingram Fletcher a match for Captain Lucifer."

"Captain Lucifer!" Martin repeated slowly, as though savouring the strangeness of it. " 'Tis an odd title! Do you know, Jocelyn, the more you tell me of these Brandons, the more eager I grow to meet them. Will you present me to the lady?"

"With the greatest pleasure," Sir Jocelyn agreed with a laugh. "I'll warrant you have never before met her like. Stay! An idea presents itself. Why not ride out with me now to Fallowmead? Regina is there, with her sister and Fletcher. We were bidden to dine, and Mody-ford's message reached me just as we were setting out. Are you his guest?"

Martin nodded.

"When I came ashore I sought an inn in the town, but Sir Thomas from the ship's captain, learned of my presence and sent a servant to bid me here. I would not wish to show him any discourtesy."

Jocelyn laughed.

"As to that, I dare swear he is fully occupied at present with the business of his office, and will have little time to spare for the entertainment of a guest. You may come to Fallowmead with a clear conscience."

Martin's inclinations overcoming his scruples, he allowed himself to be persuaded, and before long they were riding in the direction of Fallowmead. When they reached their destination Martin was clearly surprised by the style and beauty of the house and its flower-filled garden, and Jocelyn reflected with some amuse-ment that the mistress of the house was likely to prove a source of even greater astonishment. How right he was in this surmise he did not yet suspect.

The door stood hospitably wide, and, consigning their mounts to the care of a groom, they mounted the steps and passed into the house. After the brilliance of the sunlight they could see little in the cool dimness of the hall, but somewhere not far off Damaris was singing.

The glorious notes soared effortlessly through the house, and beside him Jocelyn heard Martin catch his breath. When he would have moved forward, the other's hand closed compellingly on his arm, and so they remained where they were until the song ended. There was a murmur of appreciation from the unseen audience, and then a girl's laugh rang out, clear and gay and vibrant with youthful happiness. The grip tightened painfully on Jocelyn's arm, and, glancing in surprise at his friend, he saw that Farrancourt was deathly pale.

"That voice!" he muttered. "That laugh!"

Light footsteps sounded on the polished floor, and Damaris herself came through the intervening room towards them. As she came within their range of vision, a stray gleam of sunshine fell across her face, and turned her hair to burning gold.

"Holy Virgin!" Jocelyn heard the low whisper beside him, the note of incredulity, of awe, almost of horror. "Do the dead then walk the earth?" and with the words Martin reeled and would have fallen but for his friend's supporting arm.

"Is it you, Sir Jocelyn?" Damaris was calling. "Faith! You are soon returned." The words ended in an exclamation of dismay as she came into the hall and saw Wade lowering his burden into a chair.

" 'Tis Martin Farrancourt," he explained as she hurried to his side. "He was with Sir Thomas, and we rode here together. The heat must have been too much for him, for he is not strong."

"Mr. Farrancourt!" she exclaimed, and flashed a glance over her shoulder. "Into the library, then! I will help you."

Between them they managed to get Martin into the library and lowered him into the big chair by the table.

His face was ashen, his eyes closed, and Jocelyn regarded him anxiously.

"I have a cordial which will restore him," Damaris said softly. "Stay with him, sir, while I fetch it."

She hurried from the room, and Jocelyn was left to stare at his friend and wonder at the strange words which had preceded his collapse. After a minute or two Martin's eyelids flickered, and he looked up dazedly at his companion. For a moment his expression was blank, and then with returning memory came also returning horror.

"Am I mad?" he murmured. "Or did I dream it? Hair like new-minted gold, and a face that has been dust these fifteen years! By all the saints! What witchcraft is here?"

"No witchcraft, Martin!" Jocelyn spoke briskly to cover the uneasiness he felt. " 'Twas Miss Brandon you saw, and whom we heard singing as we entered the house. The heat of the sun overcame you, and you were taken by a faintness, but it will soon pass."

"The heat?" Martin shook his head. "No, my friend, I think not."

He leaned his elbow on the arm of the chair and covered his eyes with his hand, and remained thus even when Damaris re-entered the room and came across to join them. It was as though he was afraid to look at her. Then, slowly and fearfully, he lowered his hand and raised his eyes to her face. She returned the look smilingly, and without bashfulness.

"Pray drink this, sir," she said gently, and proffered the glass she held. " 'Tis a cordial of my own making, and will help to restore you. Our tropic heat plays strange tricks on those unaccustomed to it."

He put out a shaking hand for the glass, his eyes

still fixed with painful intensity upon her face.

"I thank you, madam," he said haltingly. "You are most kind." He swallowed some of the cordial, and seemed to take a firmer grip upon himself. "I must ask your pardon for making your acquaintance in so unceremonious a fashion. Pray forgive me."

Damaris laughed.

"I'faith, sir, I forgive you most freely, for 'twas no fault of yours. Let us blame Sir Jocelyn, who has had time to grow accustomed to our climate, but not to foresee its effect upon strangers."

Before he could reply, or Wade make any protest, the door opened again to admit Regina, who came in saying:

"Was it not Jocelyn after all, Damaris? I wonder—" she broke off, staring. "Mr. Farrancourt!"

Martin started to rise from his chair, but was prevented by Miss Brandon, who replied briskly:

"Mr. Farrancourt was overcome by the heat, Regina, which is the reason for our delay in joining you. He will feel better directly, so we will leave him with Sir Jocelyn for a few minutes longer, and they may join us when he is fully recovered." She caught her friend by the hand and whisked her out of the room again, adding in a whisper, as soon as the door was shut behind them: " 'Tis your sister he has come to see, of course! Do you tell her of his arrival, while I take Mr. Fletcher to walk in the garden."

Within the library, Martin slowly drank the rest of the cordial and then sat turning the empty glass between his hands, while Jocelyn, perched on the edge of the table, watched him with bewilderment and some anxiety. At last Farrancourt said:

"I owe you an explanation, Jocelyn, I believe. I remember saying something a while since which must have perplexed you." He paused, as though finding it difficult to put his thoughts into words, and then continued hesitantly: "You will not be aware that I once had a sister, for she died long ago. We were much of an age, and since our brothers were all many years older than we, it is not surprising that she and I were much attached. Miss Brandon resembles her to a marked degree. When I first saw her, I thought 'twas Margaret herself—or her ghost!" Another pause, while he set the glass carefully upon the table. " 'Tis but a chance likeness, of course, as I realized when I saw her more clearly, but you may guess how great a shock was that first glimpse of her as she came to greet us. That is all the mystery, and you will grant 'tis simple enough. Now let us not speak of it again."

They did not, and Jocelyn was left to form conclusions which he confided later to his betrothed. He had already discussed with her the mystery of the Golden Panther, but now he fancied that the solution was in his hands.

"It is my belief," he told her, concluding his account of what Martin had disclosed to him, "that Damaris is Chelsham's daughter, and Brandon knows it. That would account for her likeness to Lady Margaret."

"But you say that only the mention of the Golden Panther disturbed Captain Brandon," Regina objected. "Would he not have recognized the Earl's name, if what you suppose is true?"

"He may never have known it," Jocelyn pointed out reasonably. " 'The Golden Panther' has been Chelsham's nickname for years, and Brandon could have been no more than a child himself when Damaris was born. I am sure I am right, Regina! It would account also for their departure from England when the King came into his own again, and Chelsham might be expected to return from exile. Damaris can have no suspicion of the truth, of course."

"If it is the truth!" Regina's voice was troubled. "Oh, Jocelyn, I wish Mr. Farrancourt had not come to Jamaica!"

"But I thought you liked him," he protested.

"I do like him, too much to wish to see him hurt. Olivia cares nothing for him, I am sure, and he thinks her perfect, which she is not. Oh, I love her dearly, but I am not blind to her faults! She may look like a saint from a stained-glass window, but she is as human as the rest of us, after all. She has no thought, either, of turning papist, and he is too devout a Catholic to wed what he would call a heretic. You may say what you choose, Jocelyn, but you will never convince me that no trouble is brewing here!"

But whatever storm clouds were gathering in the distance, only the faintest shadows were as yet discernible. Martin Farrancourt was accepted everywhere as the guest of the Governor, and though Ingram Fletcher took pains to see that he was known for a papist, Martin's own quiet charm of manner disarmed suspicion and disapproval alike. True, James Charnwood regarded him with a darkling eye, but since Farrancourt was the valued friend of his prospective son-in-law, the old man accepted him perforce, and took what comfort he could from the fact that Olivia gave her suitor no encouragement at all.

Everyone, even Regina, believed that this coldness was due to the difference of religion between Olivia and Martin, and no suspicion of the real cause had as yet entered anyone's mind. Olivia was a secretive girl,

and entirely without her sister's warm-heartedness. In
London it had flattered her vanity to have Martin Farrancourt at her feet, and to know that the arrogant,
cold-eyed Earl, his brother, considered her a force to
be reckoned with, but she was not in London now. In
Port Royal, Martin was nothing. She had never expected him to follow her to Jamaica, and found it exceedingly tiresome that he had done so, for such heart as
she possessed was set now upon a very different
object.

It had taken Olivia Charnwood precisely three days
to decide that she would like to marry Kit Brandon,
and be the mistress of Fallowmead. He was like no
other man she had ever met, as courtly as any of the
elegant triflers of Whitehall, yet with the glory of his
daring ventures against Spain to prove that here was
a man indeed. He was rich and handsome and, in his
own sphere, famous. He would do very well for a
husband.

It never occurred to Olivia that though she had made
up her mind to one course, others might be equally
determined against it. She was not particularly clever.
Her aloof beauty covered very little besides vanity and
selfishness, and though, once she had set her heart upon
a thing, she pursued it with a sublime disregard for the
feelings of others, these ruthless methods had so far
succeeded only because she had never yet been pitted
against a will as stubborn as her own. Even now,
though she looked daily for the return of Kit's ship,
and inquired frequently of his sister when he might be
expected, her impatience was due solely to the delay of
her plans, and not to any real anxiety for Kit himself.

Damaris was growing very anxious indeed. Days
had passed into weeks since Kit's departure, and though

he was often absent for months at a time, she knew instinctively that this particular venture was not of that kind. The foreboding she had felt when the enterprise was first planned returned with redoubled force, and this time refused to be shaken off. She began to sleep badly, either tossing in the grip of nightmares wherein the *Loyalist* and the *Jane* were at the mercy of the whole navy of Spain, or dreaming that she heard the triple salute with which Kit announced his home-coming, and waking again to darkness and silence. Night after night her pillow was wet with tears, and she could not tell for whom her fears were greatest, for Nicholas or for Kit.

So, slowly and relentlessly, the storm clouds which Regina had foreseen gathered invisibly over Fallowmead, until the day when a weather-beaten vessel whose voyage had begun among the grey mists of London's river glided at last into the haven of Port Royal, and furled her sails as a weary bird might fold its wings. It had been no easy voyage. The officers were haggard, the crew gaunt and hollow-eyed, their ranks thinned by scurvy, but the solitary passenger who presently emerged on to the deck showed as unperturbed, as immaculately modish, as he had done on the day he left England, as he had done throughout the long-drawn hell of the voyage. They eyed him with dull, resentful wonderment, for it seemed that storm and disease alike drew back affrighted from that cold arrogance, that supreme and terrible self-sufficiency.

A little while later, Martin Farrancourt, frowning over the composition of a letter to his lady-love in the seclusion of the Governor's library, was disturbed by the sound of the opening door. Annoyed by the interruption, he glanced up impatiently, and then with a

choked exclamation started to his feet, the pen falling
from his hand to scatter a lessening trail of blots across
the half-written page.

Upon the threshold of the room a man was standing,
a slight man of no great height, yet of bearing so commanding that he seemed a giant. He was dressed all in
silver-grey, and the pale curls of his periwig framed a
face straight-nosed, thin-lipped, with high cheek-bones
and eyes of a curious greenish blue—aquamarines set
in a mask of ivory. Silent he stood, and motionless, a
man whom some feared and many hated, but few, if
any, loved. Ralph Farrancourt, Earl of Chelsham. The
Golden Panther.

Chapter VII

THE BREAKING OF THE STORM

It was said by those who had known him longest that the Earl of Chelsham felt only one selfless emotion, and that was affection for the lame and delicate brother nearly twenty years his junior, but if such gossips spoke truth, that affection was for the present in abeyance. His face, as he closed the door and moved softly forward, was as little expressive of warmth or pleasure as the face of a statue, and Martin felt a familiar surge of fear at having incurred his displeasure. It was one thing to speak lightly of my lord when he was half the world away, but it was less simple to maintain such boldness in his actual presence.

"I am told," Chelsham said abruptly, and though his level voice was quiet, the words bit like acid, "that I am come in time to prevent you from committing the ultimate folly. You may give thanks for that."

Martin moistened his lips, despising himself for the effort needed to make a reply, and the weakness of the words themselves.

"I do not understand you, Ralph."

"You understand me very well." The Earl had halted beside the table, and now glanced down at the letter with its garland of blots. Deliberately, and as of right, he picked it up, ignored his brother's instinctive movement of protest, and read it through, his lip curling. Then he crushed it into a ball and dropped it again upon the table. "Very well," he repeated. "There is to be an end to this buffoonery, and that at once."

"You have no right!" This time the words broke from Martin's lips with no effort at all, almost, it seemed, of their own accord. "Your authority over me ended years ago, and if I have continued in obedience to you it is because nothing has ever mattered so much to me that I would sacrifice your good opinion to attain it. Now all that is past! I would forfeit the friendship of a dozen brothers if 'twould help me to my goal."

Chelsham laid his long cane across the table and began to draw off his fringed and embroidered gloves. In the same cold, passionless voice he said brutally:

"Permit me to tell you that you are ridiculous. Such romantic fervour would better become a younger and lustier man." A pause, while the gloves were laid beside the cane. "You came here with the avowed intention of making Olivia Charnwood your wife. What success has attended your wooing I shall not inquire, for it is of no importance. You will not marry her."

At the first, heartless taunt, colour had flamed briefly across Martin's white face, but now he was pallid again, pallid and wordless. He knew that his brother was right, that Olivia would never be his wife. Not because Chelsham forbade it, and had come in person to prevent it, but because Olivia herself willed it so. The false hopes on which he had lived for weeks vanished like a pricked bubble as soon as the thing was put into words, and spoken in that cold, arrogant voice that brooked no defiance, acknowledged no rights save its own.

"I will do you the honour of supposing," Chelsham continued, "that you would not have married Miss Charnwood unless she embraced the Catholic faith, but what would be the result, think you, of such an apostasy on her part? She would come to you dowerless, cast off by her own family and not accepted by yours, for the Farrancourts must marry in their own rank, or not at all."

"What does it matter whom I marry?" Martin had dropped into his chair again and bowed his head upon his hands; his voice was bitter. "The succession is in no danger. You have sons to follow you."

"You are still my brother. If you must marry, I will find you a bride of your own rank and faith, with a respectable portion to bring you, and not the daughter of some upstart planter. What has Olivia Charnwood to commend her save a fair face? You must forget this sickly infatuation, for I did not travel hither to brook defiance from you."

"You might have spared yourself the journey," Martin replied dully. "Olivia will have none of me for a husband."

"So you are a liar as well as a fool? That impudent letter you sent to me implied that you had but to present yourself to be accepted. Mother of God! Should I have come here else?"

"I wrote what I believed to be the truth," Martin retorted. "In London she did favour me, but now—"

"Now she has found someone more to her liking? We are both at the mercy of a woman's whims and fancies? By all the saints! Miss Olivia has much to answer for." He turned away and paced the length of the room, moving softly and with that feline stealth which was one reason for his nickname. "Do you know what this folly may have cost me? Never has my position at Court hung by so slight a thread, my influence been so undermined. The Castlemaine has turned

against me at last, and none has the King's ear as
she has. Seek as I will, I can find no effective weapon
to use against her, and the slut laughs in my face! And
at such a time, I am forced to leave England for
these God-forgotten islands, because my brother is
acting like a love-sick schoolboy. Then, to crown all,
you tell me that the wench will have none of you, that
she has changed her mind. What, are the Farrancourt
fortunes to be laid in the dust because of an empty-
headed slip of a girl?"

"If so much is at stake, why did you come?" Martin
spoke without looking up. "Better, surely, for me to
marry against your will than for you to risk ruin to
prevent it."

"Why?" Chelsham halted beside his chair and laid
a hand briefly on his shoulder. It was the only demon-
stration of affection he ever permitted himself. "Because you are my brother—my only brother, now—
and there is a bond between us which must transcend
worldly gain. Because where there are such differences
of rank and creed a marriage can end only in disaster,
and I want no more such in our family."

Martin looked up quickly, for that reference to past
defiance and old tragedy recalled to his mind a matter
which had hitherto been thrust aside by the shock of
his brother's arrival and the talk of Olivia. He reached
up and caught the Earl's sleeve as the hand was withdrawn from his shoulder.

"Ralph!" he exclaimed. "Leave my affairs a while,
for there is something I must tell you. I have found
Margaret's daughter, I am certain! She is here in Port
Royal, a woman grown, and Margaret's own self for
beauty. She goes by the name of Brandon, and believes

herself to be the sister of one of Sir Thomas's priva-
teers."

There was a long moment of silence. Chelsham stood
utterly still, eyes narrowed in the pale mask of his face,
and with what dark memories stirring like risen ghosts
in his mind? A wild pursuit through the moonlit stillness of a winter's night; the short bark of a pistol
speaking the final word in a tale of love and hate, but
the longer, more subtle vengeance still to seek; a fruitless quest, and the bitter knowledge that an enemy
had triumphed even in the hour of his death. The Earl
drew a long breath, and thrust the memories back into
the past to which they belonged.

"You rave!" he said shortly. "Margaret's daughter
here, when 'twas in England she vanished, fifteen
years ago? You have been deceived by some chance
likeness, a similarity of feature or colouring, and a too
vivid imagination has done the rest."

"This is no delusion!" Martin repeated stubbornly. "I
tell you, Ralph, the first time I saw her I thought 'twas
Margaret herself, risen from the grave! 'Tis not merely
her looks, but her walk, her laugh, her voice, like an
angel singing. Besides, there is more to it than that.
Jocelyn Wade had scented a mystery before ever I
arrived in Jamaica."

With unmoved countenance the Earl listened to his
brother's eager tale, but behind that impassive front
his mind moved swiftly. Each shred of evidence, insig-
nificant in itself, formed a total which admitted of
only one interpretation. Lady Margaret's daughter was
found, and he had no sooner accepted that fact than
he was seeking a way of using it for his own benefit.

"So," he remarked when Martin paused, "that is
why the search I made on my return to England met

with no success. This man Brandon had removed the
child to the Indies." He paused, and a faint frown
came. "But why? What reason lay behind his flight?"

"Perhaps," Martin suggested, "he and his mother
had by that time grown so fond of the child that they
feared to lose her, for she seems devoted to her supposed brother. What perplexes me is that Tremayne
should have bestowed his daughter in Royalist hands."

"With me hard upon his heels, I doubt he had time
to inquire into Brandon's politics. It is probable that
he hoped to lead me upon a false trail, and return for
the child when he had shaken off pursuit. However, he
did not live to return."

"And they kept the child, and raised her as their
own," Martin concluded slowly. "Perhaps it is not
wholly to be deplored that her father died. At least she
has been bred in loyalty to the King, if not in the true
Faith. In Tremayne's hands she would have learned
neither."

Chelsham, busy with his own thoughts, paid no heed
to this. It had been simple enough, where his own
exiled family was concerned, to cloak his murderous
deed in the specious tale of an accident, of a horse,
hard-ridden, coming down heavily on an ill-kept road,
breaking its own back and its rider's neck, and by the
time the Farrancourts returned to Devon, too many mo-
mentous happenings had come to pass for the murder
of an unknown man to be remembered. John Tremayne
lay in a nameless grave, and the man who had killed
him believed the secret to be locked in his own memory. Even now, no suspicion came to trouble him that
other eyes had looked upon that infamous deed.

Martin's voice broke in upon his thoughts.

"How must we go about this matter, Ralph? I have

confided in no one, for Brandon is away and I am sure that the child herself has no suspicion that she is not his sister."

Chelsham fingered a curl of his periwig, his thoughtful gaze fixed upon the opposite wall.

"First I must see the girl and talk with her," he said softly. "You say that she has all her mother's beauty?"

"Aye, and more! In feature, form and colouring she is Margaret over again, but there is something else, something that our sister lacked. A gaiety, a roguishness—'tis hard to define, but one is aware of it at once in her presence."

A faint smile of satisfaction touched Chelsham's lips. No need now to curse the chance which had brought him to this out-of-the-way corner of the world, since it brought him also the weapon which in England he had sought in vain. A young girl, beautiful and spirited, with a strange, romantic history to cast an aura of magic about her; a tool which would be his to use as he would; a Protestant, moreover, whose motive would not be suspect by those of like faith as his own must be. If Margaret's daughter had wit as well as beauty, it would lie in his power not only to regain his erstwhile influence, but also to revenge himself upon the Countess of Castlemaine, for the weaknesses of his King were as well known to my lord as those of lesser men. With his niece in her ladyship's place as first favourite, his power could be made absolute.

His anger forgotten, my lord sat silent, with narrowed eyes and secretly smiling lips, envisaging a day when the Golden Panther would stalk unchallenged throughout the length and breadth of England.

Chapter VIII

TEMPEST

Next morning my lord rode with his brother to Fallowmead. By that time the news of his arrival had spread through the town and out to the neighbouring plantations, and Jocelyn and Regina had hurried to Fallowmead to discuss the matter with Damaris in all its aspects save one. That one they had debated during the ride, and Jocelyn had given it as his frank opinion that if Chelsham were still in Port Royal when Kit Brandon returned, Regina's prophecy of trouble would be amply fulfilled.

Damaris had by this time heard enough about the Earl of Chelsham to be agog to meet him, and her wish was granted even sooner than she had expected. When the arrival of my lord and his brother was announced to her, Jocelyn and Regina exchanged a look at once startled and dubious, but Damaris was delighted, and bade the servant admit the visitors at once.

When they came she moved forward to greet them, with a warm smile and an outstretched hand for the younger of the two. He had sought her company often, and she felt strangely drawn towards him, though she had sometimes caught him watching her with a wistful affection which puzzled her.

Mr. Farrancourt presented his brother, and the Earl swept a magnificent bow while she sank in a deep curtsey. Rising, she looked up into eyes of a cold sea-blue, which seemed to sweep over her in one swift, comprehensive survey yet gave no hint of the thoughts behind them. Nettled, she tilted her chin and gave him back look for look.

As they stood thus facing each other, the likeness between them was unmistakable. The proud carriage of the head, the high cheek-bones and blue-green eyes, showed for all to see that here were two of the same blood. Regina caught her breath, and Jocelyn frowned with gloomy satisfaction at his own shrewdness.

Miss Brandon, unaware of the moment's tenseness, bethought herself of her duties as hostess, and applied herself to them with her usual grace. Lord Chelsham greeted Miss Charnwood and Sir Jocelyn, and spoke a few words of felicitation on their betrothal, and then the conversation became general. Martin took little part in it, but my lord encouraged Damaris to talk, and with each successive minute his satisfaction grew. One look at her had dispelled any lingering doubt of his brother's judgment, and he became more certain every moment that in his long-lost niece he had the answer to all his problems. He smiled his faint, secret smile, and watched her, biding his time.

Suddenly their talk was stilled by the distant boom of a gun, followed a moment later by a second, and then a third. A pause, and then the triple salute crashed out again, bringing Damaris to her feet with caught breath and shining eyes.

"Kit!" she whispered. "Kit—at last!" and before the muffled thunder of a third salvo had died away she was out of the room and halfway up the stairs, flying towards her own chamber and the balcony that overlooked the harbour.

Jocelyn said stupidly:

"It must be Brandon come home," and Regina, with a swift, startled look from one to the other, got up and with a murmur of excuse went after Damaris. Martin looked at his brother, dismay and anxiety shadowing suddenly his thin face, but Chelsham merely dropped his gaze thoughtfully to the massive signet ring on his right hand, where the golden panther stalked across an onyx field.

When Regina at length caught up with Damaris, the other girl was already on the balcony beyond her room, a telescope at her eye. As her friend joined her, she lowered the glass, and showed her a flushed, excited face.

"He has done it!" she exclaimed exultantly. "He has captured the plate-ship, just as he said he would. How could I ever have doubted it? Oh, Regina, was there ever another like him?"

She thrust the glass into Miss Charnwood's hands, and Regina raised it to her eye, seeking inexpertly for the incoming ships. At last she found them, gliding slowly across the harbour, the *Loyalist* and the *Jane,* and behind them the towering bulk of the Spanish prize. All three bore the scars of battle, evident even to her inexperienced eyes, but there was no doubt that this was yet another triumphant homecoming to Captain Lucifer.

She returned the telescope to its owner, and Damaris, after another prolonged study of the ships, punctuated by delighted comments on her brother's prowess and the nature of his prize, led the way downstairs again. Apparently the household had no need of orders once the triple salute had heralded the master's return, for already there was a stir of preparation throughout the house, and the butler had just carried wine into the room where the gentlemen were waiting. Damaris signed to him to pour it, and then turned to her guests, cheeks and eyes aglow.

"Here is a brave venture safely ended," she said. "My brother brings home as prize a Spanish man-o'-war, a plate-ship, gentlemen, laden with the spoils of Mexico and Peru. A shrewd blow against Spain, and more treasure for England." She turned to the Earl, and if he had thought her radiant before he saw her now transfigured, dazzling in her happiness and relief. "My lord, very soon now I shall have the honour of presenting my brother. You shall learn then how well served His Majesty is by the buccaneers of Jamaica."

Chelsham bowed slightly, a curious smile on his lips.

"Madam, it is a meeting I await with no common degree of eagerness."

All were now served with wine. Damaris lifted her glass and looked about her with shining eyes.

"A toast, my friends," she said unsteadily. "I give you—Captain Lucifer."

Amid varying emotions the toast was honoured, and then the Earl went quietly forward to where Damaris had seated herself by the table and set his glass down close beside her with a deliberate movement which drew her glance towards it. For a moment the white hand with the panther ring was directly before her eyes, and his own were intent upon her face. It was a test, a bow drawn at a venture, and it succeeded even beyond his hopes, for she leaned forward, staring, and then looked up quickly at his face.

"My lord," she said impulsively, "that ring—" she stopped, and a frown of perplexity came.

"Yes, Miss Brandon?" My lord's voice was soft, gently inquiring. "My ring—?"

"It—forgive me, but 'tis so unusual a design. I have seen such only once before."

"You astonish me, madam. This ring is the signet of my house, and I believed it to be unique."

"Oh, 'twas not a ring, but a brooch! It belonged to my mother."

Martin made a startled movement, as though he would have come forward, but Chelsham's upraised hand forbade it. The Earl said quietly:

"You interest me exceedingly, madam. May I ask whether the brooch is in your possession?"

Damaris shook her head.

"No, my lord, I saw it but once, four years ago when my mother died. Kit was away from home, and I took all the jewels he had given her to my room for safe keeping until he returned. The brooch was among them, though I had never seen it before. When I spoke of it to Kit he seemed displeased, and said it was a trinket our mother had had as a girl, and took it from me. The other jewels he let me keep, but the brooch I never saw again."

"There was one such brooch," Chelsham said slowly. "It belonged to my sister, Margaret, who had a great affection for it."

Miss Brandon's frown deepened.

"But if that is so, sir, how came it into my mother's hands?"

The Earl seemed to hesitate, considering his reply, but the pause was merely for effect. He had gambled upon Damaris recognizing the golden panther, and now that the gamble had succeeded he was in no doubt how to proceed. The untimely return of Captain Brandon had forced his hand, but his faith in his own powers never wavered.

"Permit me to tell you my sister's story," he said at length. "During the late wars, when I and my brothers —all save Martin, here, who was but a child—were with the King's army, the house of Chelsham was captured by Roundhead troops. The rebels hated us, for we are Catholics as well as Royalists, but though they sacked the house and turned it into a barracks, they offered no violence either to my wife and children, or to my young brother and sister—an unusual forbearance! The man in command of the rebels was the son of a merchant of Bideford, a young captain named John Tremayne." His voice grew cold as he spoke the name, as though even now it called forth memories which angered him.

Damaris was staring at him, her perplexity increasing, and mirrored now in the eyes of Jocelyn and Regina. None of them could guess the purpose of the story.

"Margaret was fifteen then," my lord resumed after a moment. "A wilful girl, and foolish. Tremayne was a smooth-tongued rogue, and she so far forgot herself as to lend an ear to his wooing. My wife discovered it, but she could do naught, for she was prisoner in her own house, with Tremayne as gaoler. Then, fortunately as it then seemed, the rebels found that they had no further use for the house of Chelsham, and Tremayne and his men were ordered elsewhere. Soon after that came Naseby, and, matters seeming ill for the Royal cause, I contrived to send my family to France, where I had many friends. That, I thought, would be the end of the matter."

"But it was not?" Damaris, with no suspicion yet of how closely these events concerned her, spoke eagerly. The story had enough in it of romance and adventure to appeal to her.

"No, madam, it was not. In France a nobleman of my acquaintance sought my sister's hand in marriage, and my wife, knowing that such a match would have my approval, consented in my name. Margaret, however, had learned enough of rebellion from her Roundhead lover to defy her natural protectors."

"Tell her the whole truth, Ralph! She has a right to know!" Martin, who had covered his eyes with his hand as though the tale roused memories too painful to bear, looked up at that. His voice was bitter. "The noble Marquis who sought Margaret as his bride was old enough to be her grandfather, with a reputation which reeked to Heaven. What wonder that she shrank from him in horror?"

The Earl directed towards him a look of cold rebuke, but made no comment. Instead he took up the tale again.

"Somehow, by means which were never discovered, she sent word to Tremayne of her approaching marriage, and he, so little did he know of honour, deserted his post and came to France. They fled together, and took refuge in one of the Lutheran states of Germany, where neither my influence nor that of the Marquis could reach them."

"Oh, 'twas bravely done!" Damaris declared impulsively. "To sacrifice all for each other! Oh, brave indeed!"

A curious and rather unpleasant amusement gleamed for a moment in my lord's cold eyes.

"That you should think so is, I suppose, only natural. There is little more to tell. Margaret renounced the Catholic faith upon her marriage, and with it, no doubt, her loyalty to the King. A year later a daughter was born to her."

Jocelyn looked up quickly, and the beginnings of dismayed comprehension glimmered in his eyes. He glanced at Regina, and saw from her expression that she, too, could see now whither the story was leading.

"When the child was almost three years old, Margaret died," the Earl went on, "and Tremayne, himself racked by sickness, resolved to take his daughter back to England and bestow her in the care of his own family, thinking, no doubt, that while Cromwell ruled I should not dare to set foot in England." He smiled faintly, disdainfully. "He was mistaken."

"You followed him?" Damaris asked breathlessly.

"I did. I had no mind that a niece of mine should be reared a Puritan and a rebel. Tremayne landed at Plymouth and rode north towards Bideford, and I followed hard upon his heels. Some miles beyond the town of Tavistock I came up with him." He smoothed the lace over his long, white fingers; his tone was reflective. "It was, I remember, in a little hollow by a brook. His horse had come down, throwing him from the saddle. His neck was broken."

There was a long pause after the cold voice ceased. At last Regina said, in a high, unnatural tone:

"And the child?"

My lord raised his eyes to meet hers.

"The child, Miss Regina, had disappeared. I made search for her, then, and again when I returned to England with the King, but found no trace of her. I concluded that Tremayne had bestowed her somewhere, hoping to return for her when he had shaken off pursuit." A moment's pause, and then he added deliberately: "It has always been my hope that she fell into kindly hands. Now I believe it to be so."

Damaris was still frowning.

" 'Tis a brave tale, my lord, albeit a tragic one, but it does not explain how your sister's brooch—if hers it was—came to be in my mother's jewel-box."

He regarded her inscrutably.

"My sister, I am told, was wearing the brooch on the night she fled. What more natural than that she should bequeath it to her daughter, or that during the flight to England it should be pinned to the child's clothing?"

Damaris stared at him, and behind the bewilderment in her eyes, fear began to stir. What had Martin Farrancourt said, not long ago? "Tell her the whole truth, Ralph! She has a right to know!" What right did he mean? Another memory, a much older one, of childhood days in Plymouth, flashed into her mind, and she heard Josiah Barrow speaking jovially to Kit of "the day we met in Tavistock". She said quickly, as though to repudiate that growing fear:

"The brooch belonged to my mother. She had it as a girl."

Chelsham said nothing, but silently bowed agreement. Her eyes dilated, and she seemed to shrink back in her chair, the colour fading from her cheeks. In the background, Regina groped suddenly for Jocelyn's hand and held it tightly, for events were moving at frightening speed, a speed as headlong and seemingly uncontrollable as the hoofbeats which were coming swiftly from somewhere in the distance.

Martin got up and came to stand beside Damaris. He laid his hand on her shoulder and spoke gently.

"My child, there is no room for doubt. I realized it long since, when at our first meeting I saw, in you, my sister Margaret live again."

She stared up at him, white-lipped, and in the silence those approaching hoofbeats sounded ever nearer, but now not even Regina heeded them, for she was watching the incredulity in her friend's face give way to horrified, unwilling belief. She, like all the rest, had forgotten those three ships coming into harbour to the triumphant thunder of their guns.

The hoofbeats ceased, and a moment later firm footsteps sounded, crossing the hall and the outer room. Damaris, her frightened gaze still locked to Martin's, suddenly thrust his hand away and sprang up out of her chair.

"No!" she cried. "No, it is not true! Kit would not lie to me! He would not!"

The footfalls checked for an instant and then came on more swiftly, and Kit himself appeared in the doorway. His face was pale and drawn, with deep trouble in the blue eyes; not at all the face of a returning conqueror, but rather of a tired and anxious man weighed down by some grave responsibility. He halted on the threshold and my lord's unfathomable gaze rested thoughtfully upon him. He had no need to ask who this tall stranger might be; only the master of the house would walk with such assurance into it.

"Captain Brandon, I believe?" he said softly, and at the first word Kit grew rigid. "Permit me to present myself, sir. I am Farrancourt of Chelsham."

The introduction was unnecessary. His voice, cold and clear and arrogant, had betrayed his identity as soon as he spoke, though Kit had heard it but once before in his life. He looked at Damaris, standing white and stricken between them, and knew that he had delayed too long in telling her the truth. His heart sank, but he forced himself to look away, and advanced slowly into the room.

"I am honoured, my lord," he said in a level voice,

and bowed slightly to Regina and Jocelyn, postponing as long as possible the moment when he must look again at Damaris. She had neither moved nor spoken since he entered the room, and he thought, with a wrench at his heart, that never before had she failed to come running to greet him. That fact, more than anything else, brought home to him the gulf which now yawned between them.

"Kit!" She spoke at last, desperately, as though she words were torn out of her against her will. "They say that I—that you—" she broke off, and my lord's voice cut smoothly in.

"I think you can guess, Captain Brandon, the discovery we have made. It is a matter which hinges largely upon a certain brooch, wrought in the semblance of a golden panther, which I believe is in your possession."

Kit heard him as though from a great way off, and made a fruitless effort to collect his wits. His mind felt numb, dazed by the suddenness of the blow, and he could think only of Damaris, of the terror and bewilderment in her eyes which it was beyond his power to comfort.

"A brooch," the pitiless voice went on, "which belonged to my sister, Lady Margaret Tremayne, and which was bequeathed by her to her infant daughter. An infant, Captain Brandon, who disappeared in England fifteen years ago, but who is now, I think, found again."

With the last words he looked up, and their eyes met. My lord's gleamed with cold triumph, and Kit realized then that the fight he had been preparing to make was lost before it had begun. Slowly, and without a word, he thrust his hand into the breast of his coat and drew out the panther brooch and laid it on the table before the Earl. It was a gesture of defeat.

A faint smile flickered about my lord's lips. For a second or two he contemplated the brooch, and then raised his eyes again to the haggard face of the man confronting him.

"The panther of Chelsham," he said softly, "and the final proof. I believe I must thank you, sir, for the care and protection which for fifteen years you have bestowed upon my niece."

A little, broken sound, half cry, half moan, seemed to echo his words. Damaris was swaying on her feet, but when Kit took a pace towards her she made a sudden gesture of denial and, turning, stumbled from the room. Regina pulled her hand from Jocelyn's and ran after her, but he was scarcely aware that she had gone. He had seen Kit's face as Damaris shrank from him, and suddenly all questions were answered.

"Poor devil!" he thought, appalled by his discovery. "My God, poor devil!"

He turned away to one of the long windows and stood there with his back to the room, staring across the piazza to the sunlit garden. He heard Chelsham say:

"A natural reaction, of course! She will need time to grow accustomed to the truth. Captain Brandon, there is much that we must discuss, but this is not, I think, an opportune moment. Perhaps, when you are less occupied with affairs, you will be good enough to wait upon me in Port Royal."

Jocelyn heard Kit's curt word of assent, and retreating footsteps, and then silence, but for some time he was still too busy with his thoughts to move. At length it occurred to him that if Brandon came back into the room his own presence would be unwelcome, and that he had best make himself scarce until Regina was ready to return home. He turned, and then checked again, staring in blank dismay.

Apparently his presence had been forgotten, for Kit had not, as he thought, left the room with Chelsham and Martin. He was there still, seated at the table, and his head was down upon his arms, and the fingers of one strong hand were clenched hard upon that fateful brooch. The man whose pride had earned him the name of Lucifer was humbled now, and Sir Jocelyn, an involuntary and horrified witness of his wordless agony, turned back to the open window and stepped softly out on the piazza, holding his breath lest any chance sound betray his presence. At a safe distance he paused and mopped his brow, and then betook himself discreetly to the furthest corner of the garden.

It was nearly two hours later that a second sweating horse pounded up the avenue to the door of Fallowmead, and Dr. Blair, its rider, flung himself out of the saddle and strode into the house. A frown at once anxious and impatient made his lean, dark face even grimmer than usual, and when, through an open door, he caught sight of Captain Brandon standing with his back to him, apparently lost in thought, he muttered an oath under his breath and went quickly forward.

"Why in the devil's name are you idling here?" he demanded irritably. "Did I not tell you that every moment is precious?"

Kit had started violently at the sound of his voice, but he did not turn. He said, in a tone so utterly unlike his usual crisp speech that Alex stared in astonishment:

"I forgot."

"Forgot?" The Doctor's surprise was lost in anger. "Forgot a matter of life and death?" He went forward as he spoke, and so caught a glimpse of the other man's face. His voice changed, and he gripped Kit's arm. "God in Heaven! what is wrong? What has been happening here?"

Kit's right hand was closed hard upon some small object. He stared at Alex as though he did not see him, and then very slowly unclasped his fingers and showed the panther brooch lying upon his palm. He said, still in that dull, hopeless voice:

"She knows, Alex! My Lord Chelsham was here when I reached home." Blair uttered a startled oath, but Kit seemed not to hear him. "By some devil's chance he had guessed the truth and told it to her. I came too late."

The Doctor opened his mouth to speak, and then with a helpless shake of the head closed it again. Those few, brief sentences told at once so little and so much. After a pause he asked in a low voice:

"What said she?"

"To me, nothing! As I came into the house I heard her cry out that it was false, that I would not lie to her, but afterwards, when she knew it for the truth and was nigh swooning with the shock of it, she would not even let me come near her." His voice broke, and he turned abruptly away. "My God, Alex! she shrank from me, and the look in her eyes a more bitter reproach than any words."

Another long silence followed that anguished outburst, but at length Blair moved, and went to set a hand on Kit's shoulder as he stood with bowed head and both hands gripping the edge of the table.

"Time heals all wounds, Kit," he said quietly, "and you have time enough to make your peace with her.

The business which brought me here in search of you will not wait."

"No!" Kit raised his head, shaking it a little as though to clear his wits. "God forgive me! I may have delayed too long already. Go to her, Alex, and tell her. I will see to the horses."

"Where is she?"

"Upstairs in her room. Regina Charnwood is with her." He caught Blair by the arm as he turned to go. "Be gentle with her, Alex! God knows what she must be suffering already."

When the Doctor tapped on the door of Damaris's room he heard a swift, low murmur of voices, and then footsteps, and it was opened a little way by Regina. She looked defensive, but at sight of him her expression changed to relief, and she stepped back, making way for him to enter.

"Dr. Blair!" she said in a low voice. "I am thankful you have come, sir. I know not what to do."

Alex went in. Damaris was sitting on the day-bed by the window, her hands clenched on the edge of the seat on either side of her, and her gaze fixed on the floor. She looked up as he approached, and showed a white, stricken face and bewildered eyes.

"Poor lassie!" he said gently, and laid his hand on her bright hair. "Poor lassie, this was no way to tell you."

"You know?" Her voice was a scarcely audible whisper.

"Aye, child, I know, but 'tis not that alone which brings me here." His eyes searched her face as he spoke. "Damaris, have you courage enough to face yet another blow?"

"Courage?" Her lips twisted mirthlessly. "Deal me

what blow you choose, Alex. I do not think I have the power to suffer more."

"Pray God you have not," he replied gravely. " 'Tis Nicholas, Damaris. He was wounded when we took the plate-ship. Will you come to him?"

For a moment longer she regarded him, and then she rose to her feet.

"I will come," she said tonelessly. "Regina, will you find me a cloak? How chanced it, Alex?"

Blair seemed to hesitate for a moment.

"Through recklessness," he said reluctantly at length. "He had Kit's orders, but it seems he had sworn to be the first to set foot on the Spaniard's deck, and he brought the *Jane* in too soon to grapple with her. He kept his word, but in doing so he was cut off from his men, and fell before they could go to his aid."

Regina came with a cloak of blue silk and put it about her friend's shoulders. Damaris said:

"Is he badly hurt?"

"He is dying, lassie," Blair replied quietly, and Damaris closed her eyes for a second and her hand tightened on the silken folds of the cloak. Beside her, Regina gave a gasp of pity and dismay. "It is a miracle that he has survived so long."

"Let us go at once," she said, and without another word went past them out of the door and down the stairs. Alex frowned, and glanced at Miss Charnwood.

"She is too calm," he said in a low voice. "Will you await our return, ma'am? I think she will need you then."

At the door three horses stood saddled, and Kit was already mounted. Damaris did not look at him, but let Alex help her into the saddle and then spurred her mount forward along the avenue. In silence the two men fell in behind her.

The *Jane* had sailed home under a new commander, and Nicholas lay now in his old quarters aboard the *Loyalist*. Still he lay, and quiet, his eyes closed, and the violet shadows like bruises beneath them the only trace of colour in his wasted countenance. Even his long, thick hair, which had once been as bright as Damaris's own, was lank now, and lustreless, drained of life and colour. When Alex led her into the cabin, Damaris caught her breath in a sob, and pressed the back of her hand against her lips. Then she went softly and swiftly forward and bent over the low bed where he lay.

"Nicholas!" she whispered. "Nick!"

Slowly, and with a tremendous effort, the heavy lids were raised, and his eyes focused hazily upon her face. He tried to speak, but had to make several efforts before he could summon up the strength even for a whisper.

"Damaris?" he murmured at last. " 'Tis not another dream?"

"No, it is I." She dropped to her knees beside him and laid her cheek to his. "You are come safe home, my dear."

"Home?" he repeated dreamily. "Where is home? There was a farm once, in a valley by the sea, but that was long ago. I meant to buy land, to build a house—" his voice trailed into silence, and his eyelids drooped again.

"We will build it together," she said gently, smoothing the hair back from his brow. The tears were running down her cheeks, but somehow she kept her voice steady. "In a green valley, as your farm was."

His head moved on the pillow in a slight gesture of denial.

"It is too late. This is farewell, my love." His eyes shifted from her face, and sought Dr. Blair, who had come to stand behind her, Kit remaining by the door. "Alex, where is that which you keep for me?"

The Doctor bent forward to take his hand, and clasped the weak fingers about some small object. With an effort Nicholas held it out to her, and she saw that it was a gold ring set with a great ruby like a drop of blood.

"I meant it for a troth-ring," Nick's failing voice was wistful. "Give me your hand." She did as he asked, and clumsily he slid the ring on to her finger. "I . . . cannot see very well," he whispered. "Will you kiss me once more, Damaris?"

She pressed her lips to his; his hand lifted, and touched her tear-wet cheek for a moment, and then fell back. Alex looked up, and across the cabin his eyes met Kit's. He made a small gesture of finality, and the other man bowed his head.

"Nick!" Damaris's frightened whisper seemed loud in the stillness. "Oh, Nick, I needed you so!" She dropped her head upon her arms, and was shaken by a storm of weeping, like a flower in the grip of tempest.

Kit looked up, his face as white as the dead man's. For a long moment he stared at her, at the bright hair tumbled across Nick's quiet breast, and then he turned and went silently away, knowing that he no longer had the right nor the power to comfort her. He could not know that she wept, not for Nicholas alone, but for herself, and for him, and for everything which that day had seen destroyed. He saw only a broken-hearted girl mourning the man she loved, and in the bitterness of his despair he thought that it might have been better for them both had he lain now in his dead comrade's place.

Chapter IX

AFTERMATH ·

Damaris sat on the piazza of the Charnwood house and gazed apathetically across the garden, her hands, with the ruby ring glowing upon one finger, lying idle in her lap. She was often idle now, and her listlessness was causing her friends a good deal of concern. Regina and Jocelyn tried in vain to interest her in the preparations for their approaching marriage; Dr. Blair told her sternly that no physician in the world could help her unless she made an effort to help herself; Ingram Fletcher sought ceaselessly for some means of diverting her; and her two uncles came daily from Port Royal to visit her, the one anxious, the other hiding a growing irritation behind an impassive face.

Only Kit held aloof. He had not once seen her alone since his return to Jamaica, for when he and Alex had brought her back to Fallowmead after Nick's death she had been in a state of collapse, and for several days had kept to her bed, with Regina and the Doctor to care for her. As soon as she was well enough, Miss Charnwood had carried her off to her own home, and there she had remained ever since. At first Kit had come every day, hoping always for an opportunity to talk to her alone, but always there were other people about her. At last, growing impatient, he had told Regina bluntly that he wished to talk privately with Damaris. Regina looked distressed, for she liked Kit and, guessing his feelings, pitied him profoundly.

"Do you not think; sir," she suggested hesitantly, "that it would be better if the first overture came from Damaris herself?"

"Miss Regina," he replied impatiently, "I have waited for weeks for some sign from her. Whenever I visit this house, either you or your sister are with her constantly. God's light! do you think she needs a chaperone in my presence?"

"Of course not, Captain Brandon, but in her present state of mind—"

"In her present state of mind she is incapable of making a decision."

Regina lifted troubled eyes to his face.

"You are mistaken, sir," she said in a low voice. "I had hoped to spare you this, but you give me no choice. It is by her own wish that she is never alone with you."

There was a dreadful pause. At last he said steadily, too steadily, she thought:

"I was indeed mistaken. I am grateful for your frankness, madam. Pray assure her that I shall not force my company upon her."

He left her with that, nor did he return again. She wondered whether Damaris noticed the sudden cessation of his visits, but she never spoke of it, and Regina did not dare to question her.

Damaris herself scarcely knew what her feelings were. She seemed to be living in a curious world where nothing was quite real. Life went on around her, but she had no part in it, and thought sometimes that it was as though she, too, had died that day. Beneath the double blow of Nick's death and the discovery of her true identity she had suffered terribly, but now she felt drained of all emotion, cold and empty as a shell tossed to and fro by the tides. It was like being only half-alive, but it was a refuge from pain, and of pain she felt she could endure no more.

If there was anyone for whose company she showed a preference, it was Martin Farrancourt. The Earl she feared, but in Martin she sensed the affection her bruised spirit craved, though she realized after a time that there must always be a barrier between them. He loved her simply because she was Margaret's daughter. He spent hours talking to her of her mother, and even cudgelled his memory for scraps of information about John Tremayne, but her parents remained to Damaris the shadowy hero and heroine of an old story, no more real than figures upon a stage.

"It is no use!" she said desperately to Regina upon one occasion. "Jane Brandon was the only mother I knew, and no one can ever take her place. How can one tear out of one's heart the affections of a lifetime? The bond of blood is not everything. I know I am not a Brandon, but I cannot think of myself as a Tremayne, or even as a Farrancourt. Oh, Regina! how will it all end?"

Regina could not tell her, but there was one person who believed that he saw the future plainly, because he meant to shape it to his liking. My lord allowed his niece a month and more to recover from the shock of his disclosure, but he was not idle during the interval. He knew that the best means of bending others to his will was a knowledge of their weaknesses, and he had cultivated over the years a talent for discovering such weaknesses, and a ruthlessness in using his knowledge, which had made him both hated and feared. He liked to picture himself usurping the function of destiny, and playing with men and women as with pieces on a chess-board. It was his greatest vanity.

By the end of a month, most of the secrets of those immediately about him were in his possession. He knew why Ingram Fletcher had come to Jamaica, and why he had transferred his attentions from Olivia to Damaris; he had learned of the high-handed manner in which Kit Brandon had rescued Sir Jocelyn from the pirates, and of the bitter enmity between Kit and Renard; he had discovered his niece's ardent desire to go to Court, and watched his brother consoling himself for the loss of Olivia by lavishing affection upon Damaris; and he had perceived what no one else had yet guessed—Olivia's infatuation for Brandon. Only where Kit himself was concerned was his judgment at fault, but for this lapse Chelsham was not entirely to blame. Kit had good reason to distrust him, and, once the first shock had passed, a self-command equal to the Earl's. Where Captain Lucifer was concerned, my lord had something yet to learn.

At last the Earl decided that he had been patient long enough. He was anxious to get back to England, for he had been a courtier for too many years to be blind to the danger of a long absence. A ship was due to leave soon for Bristol, and he meant to sail in her, taking his brother and his niece with him.

So when he came that day to sit beside Damaris on the piazza, he informed her of the plans he had made. She showed him a startled countenance, for it had never occurred to her that she might be expected to leave Jamaica.

"I have heard, my child," he told her kindly, "that you have some eagerness to see the Court, and it is my intention that you shall do so. It is in my mind to procure for you a place about the Queen. That would please you, would it not?"

She agreed, though with less enthusiasm than he had hoped, and he went on to describe in glowing terms the future which now lay before her. She listened with growing disquiet, for though she had dreamed often enough of such a future, there had always been a place in it for Kit; without him, the prospect seemed far less alluring.

"You are very kind, my lord," she said timidly when he paused, "and I am grateful indeed, but I do not think I would like to leave Jamaica. It has been my home for so long."

My lord frowned.

"You must understand, Damaris," he said with a hint of sternness, "that I am now your lawful guardian. I have tried to make allowance for your feelings, but I cannot and will not wait upon your pleasure for ever. This is your home no longer, and you cannot remain here when my brother and I return to England. Do not put me to the necessity of commanding you to accompany us." Thus he showed her a glimpse of steel beneath the velvet, and then added in a kindlier tone: "If, as I suspect, you are thinking of Brandon, I believe you need have no fear that he will be lonely for long." He smiled faintly into her startled, questioning eyes, and added meaningly: "Miss Olivia, I have no doubt, will know how to console him."

There was a pause while the significance of his words dawned upon her, and then she said breathlessly:

"But he never comes here!"

His brows lifted.

"That, surely, is by your wish. He understands the difficulties of your situation, and does not wish to add

to them, but do not imagine that because his visits
have ceased he spends no time in Miss Olivia's company."

Damaris sat silent, submerged in a cold tide of despair. Of late she had forgotten her forebodings concerning Olivia and Kit, but if he was indeed paying
court to her, then their marriage was inevitable. True,
she had other suitors, notably that Colonel Prestyn
whom Damaris herself had made known to her, but
how could he, or anyone, compete with Captain Lucifer? After a little, still keeping her gaze averted, she
said carefully:

"I should not have supposed it. No hint of such a
thing has ever reached my ears."

"My dear child," Chelsham's voice was tolerant,
"is it likely that such a matter would be discussed in
your hearing? In fact, I imagine that it is being kept
secret between the pair of them. No doubt Brandon
feels that while you are a guest in this house, to broach
the subject could only cause you embarrassment. His
regard for you will prompt him to use patience, however little inclination he has to do so."

Thus, subtly, did my lord hint that his niece's departure from Jamaica would not be unwelcome to
Captain Brandon. The suggestion fell upon fertile soil,
but Damaris said, with a flash of her old spirit:

"If 'tis kept so secret, sir, I marvel that you should
have discovered it."

He smiled, in no way discomposed by the retort.

"I, my child, am more observant than most, and
possibly more experienced in human weaknesses. However, if you doubt me, why not ask Miss Olivia herself?"

On that he abandoned the topic, judging that he had

said enough to give her food for thought, and presently took his leave of her. Before returning to Port Royal, however, he sought out Olivia, and drawing her aside, said abruptly:

"It will please you to know, madam, that I am planning to return soon to England, taking my niece with me."

"Please me?" Olivia was startled. "Indeed, my lord, I do not know why you should suppose it."

His lip curled.

"My dear Miss Charnwood, let us not waste time upon civilities which we both know to be false. Your hopes of becoming mistress of Fallowmead have a far greater chance of fulfilment if Damaris is no longer in Jamaica."

Olivia turned first red, and then white. He regarded her confusion with mocking indulgence.

"Be easy, madam, no one else has yet guessed your secret, least of all Brandon himself. Permit me to say that I wish you every success." Olivia tried to speak, but could find no words. Chelsham continued blandly: "We may, I believe, be of use to each other. I have already suggested the possibility of such a match to Damaris, in order to stifle any qualms she may feel at deserting one to whom she owes so much, and whether or not she broaches the subject, I advise you to tell her that there is an understanding, at present to be kept secret, between yourself and Brandon."

Olivia recovered the power of speech, and wasted no breath in denials. Instead she said:

"Why do you need my help? You are her uncle. Could you not make her obey you?"

"Certainly, but I prefer that she should go willingly. the least hint of coercion, and Brandon will oppose her departure by every means in his power. Or are you so blind that you suppose his affection for her to be purely fraternal?"

Olivia caught her lower lip between her teeth, and her hands clenched hard upon the feather fan she held. My lord laughed under his breath.

"Quite so," he said gently, "and passion begets passion, so 'tis said. I have nothing against Brandon, but for Damaris I have—other plans. Therefore she must go willingly to England, and he must know it. She has desired you never to leave her alone in his company, so there is no fear of this harmless deception being discovered." He smiled and bowed, preparing to withdraw. "I shall not be here to dance at your wedding, Miss Charnwood, but I shall hope most earnestly for your happiness."

It was not long before Olivia had an opportunity to act upon my lord's advice, for on the following day Damaris taxed her with the matter. Miss Charnwood at first denied the charge, in a manner which was in itself a betrayal, and finally confessed, with well-simulated confusion, that she was indeed promised to Kit.

"But do not, I beg of you, betray the fact that you know it," she added. "He has charged me most strictly to say nothing, not even to my father, while you are still in Jamaica, and he will be so angry if he knows that I have done so. He thinks that it would not look well to make known our betrothal so soon after—" she paused, and made a vague gesture with her hands.

"I think he is being over-scrupulous," Damaris replied indifferently, "but it is no concern of mine, after all. I am happy to know that there will be someone to take my place at Fallowmead. With Kit so much away, the place has need of a mistress."

With this slightly barbed retort she abandoned the topic, and began to speak of the life which awaited her in England, but it was pride alone which prompted this show of unconcern. My lord was right, it seemed, and Kit was indifferent to her departure. Indeed, he apparently expected it, since his betrothal was to be kept secret only while she was still in Jamaica. She told herself severely that it did not matter, that it was better to know that he would not feel her absence, but this did nothing to dispel the curious feeling of desolation within her.

When next she saw her uncle she told him that she would be very pleased to go with him to England. He received the assurance calmly, but Martin, who was present, was clearly delighted by the news, and later revealed to his brother one of the causes of his satisfaction. It was time, he said, that Damaris was instructed in the Catholic faith, and he had feared that as long as she was in Jamaica Captain Brandon would endeavour to prevent her conversion. My lord, who knew how easily all his careful plotting could be overset by the introduction of such a question, told him curtly not to be a fool. That matter could wait. A hint of it now, and Damaris might well refuse to accompany them to England, no matter how many Court appointments were dangled before her eyes. Martin was only half convinced, but in the end gave his brother his word that he would say nothing of religion, at least until they were at sea.

Having dealt with that matter, my lord looked about him, decided that his plans were prospering, and proceeded to enlarge them. His eye had long since alighted upon Ingram Fletcher, and marked him down as a use-

ful tool, for he had made a shrewd estimate of the
young man's character. He waited until a suitable opportunity offered, and then commanded Mr. Fletcher
into his presence.

He came a trifle uneasily, for though in London he
had lived only on the fringes of fashionable society,
he had heard enough of the Golden Panther to stand
in awe of him. However, he was a born sycophant, and
hoped that this summons might afford him an opportunity to ingratiate himself with the Earl.

"I have noticed, Mr. Fletcher," Chelsham began,
pleasantly enough, "that your attentions to my niece
are constant and particular. Do you, perhaps, aspire
her hand?"

Fletcher looked uncomfortable, and plunged into an
involved speech in which his vast admiration for Miss
Tremayne, and his own unworthiness, were hopelessly
entangled. Chelsham cut in upon his meanderings with
scant ceremony.

"I desire to hear no romantic vapourings, my friend.
When you believed Damaris to be Brandon's sister you
were enamoured only of her wealth. Now to that is
added awe of her noble blood. You desire to climb in
the world, and who is to blame you?"

Mr. Fletcher, afraid that my lord himself might
blame him, preserved a discreet silence. He was not
at all certain whether Chelsham was as friendly as he
seemed, but the Earl's next words did much to put him
at his ease.

"I believe, Mr. Fletcher, that under certain circumstances I might approve your suit. Under certain circumstances." He fell to smoothing the ruffles over his
hands; his voice was pensive. "Damaris is beautiful, and,
I believe, not without intelligence. With my influence

to guide her she might go far. So, also, might her husband." He paused, but his long, white fingers never ceased their measured movements; the panther ring, gold upon black, gleamed as it caught the light. "There are more ways than one of climbing to wealth and honours, Mr. Fletcher. Consider, for example, the man Palmer, who was as nothing and is now Earl of Castlemaine, and like to be a Duke before he dies. And what had Palmer to commend him to the Royal notice save —a wife?"

The cold, blue-green eyes lifted suddenly on the last words, and saw excitement and comprehension in the young man's face. My lord smiled faintly.

"It is my hope," he continued, "that Damaris may be chosen as maid-of-honour to the Queen. That would, of course, necessitate her frequent attendance at Whitehall. I trust, Mr. Fletcher, that you are not of a jealous disposition?"

"No," Fletcher's voice was a little unsteady; there was excitement in his eyes. "No, my lord, I am not— jealous! I take your meaning very well."

"Excellent!" My lord spoke mockingly. "How charming to discover such ready understanding. We will speak of this again, but for the present—silence!"

Mr. Fletcher assured him of his discretion, and withdrew with many protestations of gratitude. My lord yawned, and decided that for the present he had done enough. His expert fingers were upon the strings, and the puppets beginning to move at his command. It was an exhilarating sensation, and one which never failed to give him a sensuous pleasure.

Damaris and Kit did not meet again until the day of Regina's wedding to Sir Jocelyn, but as this was attended by the Governor, Lord Chelsham and his brother, and all the notables of Port Royal, it was not difficult for them to avoid each other. Damaris had dreaded the ordeal of appearing in company, for her strange story was by this time common knowledge, and throughout the ceremony and the festivities which followed it she stayed close, as though for protection, to Martin. She spoke little and smiled less, and people who had known her as Damaris Brandon shook their heads sadly, and remarked to each other in lowered voices upon the change in her.

It was seen that Captain Brandon did not approach her, and this provoked some shrugging of shoulders and raising of brows. Presently he stood up to dance with Olivia Charnwood, and Damaris, watching against her will, had to admit to herself that they made a handsome couple. She was quite shocked at the violence of her own feelings where Olivia was concerned. Hatred, black, venomous hatred, seemed to shake her whole being when she was in Miss Charnwood's presence, and she could barely bring herself to be civil to her. It was more than time, she thought wretchedly, that she left Jamaica for ever.

Kit as yet knew nothing of her projected departure. He was much occupied with the repair and re-fitting of his ships, for though the capture of the plate-ship had been one of his most spectacular triumphs, the cost had been heavy, and no one could tell when the need for well-armed, well-equipped vessels might arise. So he flung himself with feverish energy into the task, and spent more time aboard the *Loyalist* than at Fallowmead, for the silence and emptiness of the big house was more than he could bear. Never before had he known it without Damaris's laughing, vital presence, and it seemed symbolic of the desolation which had descended so suddenly upon his life.

He had talked with the Earl, and learned nothing of his future plans. He had betrayed nothing, either, and Chelsham was still in ignorance of the fact that the true circumstances of John Tremayne's death were known to any other than himself. That knowledge Kit kept to himself, seeing in it an unsuspected weapon of which he might one day be glad.

That day came even sooner than he had expected. He was standing on the deck of the *Loyalist,* staring thoughtfully at a ship which had just come to anchor, when Alex came aboard and joined him. Kit nodded towards the vessel which had been engaging his attention.

"The *Albatross,*" he remarked. "Renard does not lack effrontery, but I fancy he will find a welcome less cordial than he expects when Modyford learns of his presence."

"Aye!" Dr. Blair glanced fleetingly at the pirate ship, but seemed preoccupied with other matters. "Kit, I met Charnwood in the town. He tells me that Chelsham and his brother sail for England aboard the *Good Hope* three days hence. Damaris goes with them."

For a second or two Kit said nothing, but his hand went in an unconscious gesture to his sword, and closed hard on the gold-wrought hilt.

"She is forced to go?" he asked at length. Alex shook his head.

"Charnwood says she is all eagerness, and talks only of the Court. They are relieved to see her in such spirits." He shot a swift glance at Kit. "Our friend Fletcher travels with them."

"Fletcher?" Kit frowned. "What has become of my

lord's pride? I like it not." He drew a long breath, staring across the harbour at the white walls of the town. "I'll not let her go, Alex."

"You cannot prevent her," Blair replied drily. "They are her own kin, and she wishes to go," but Kit had already turned away and was shouting for a boat to take him ashore.

He was at the Charnwood house within the hour, and swept without ceremony into Miss Tremayne's presence, while Olivia, in alarm, came hurrying to play the part of duenna. Olivia had troubles of her own in these days, and her hopes of marrying Kit Brandon were fast disappearing, but she would not give in without a struggle.

He accorded her only the briefest salute, and then turned to Damaris, demanding, in a voice made harsh by anxiety, whether the news of her imminent departure was true. The tone was unfortunate, and so was Olivia's presence, since it reminded Damaris all too vividly of much that she had tried to forget.

"Yes, it is true," she said quickly. "My uncle has business awaiting him in England."

"And you go willingly?"

"Of course!" She smoothed the full skirt of her gown; her voice was airy. "I have always longed to go to Court—you know that! The Farrancourts have great influence in England, and I shall make many friends." She looked up, and their eyes met. Her hands moved in a little, despairing gesture. "Oh, Kit, how can I stay? There is nothing left for me here."

Olivia's heart seemed to leap into her throat, but Kit did not read into the words the meaning she feared. He took Damaris's hand and looked down at the ruby ring she wore so constantly.

"I know, child," he said quietly, "but you are very young. That wound will heal."

The gentleness of voice and touch, evoking as it did so many memories, was more hurtful than all the rest. How could anyone ever take his place? She caught Olivia's gaze upon her, and summoned pride to her aid.

" 'Twill heal more quickly in a new land," she said shortly, pulling her hand from his and turning away. "There will be much to divert me, no doubt. My uncle promises me a great future. I am to be maid-of-honour to the Queen."

A great light seemed to break suddenly upon Kit, and he marvelled at his own past blindness. He had thought more than once that it was strange for Chelsham to concern himself with a niece whom he had never seen before, and who could be only a responsibility to him, but now he perceived that there might be a way in which my lord could make use of her. He said slowly, as one speaking his thoughts aloud:

"An easy step, no doubt, for the Earl of Chelsham's niece to take, and from maid-of-honour to the Queen to mistress of the King an easier one still. God's light! Do you not realize what path you will have to tread to reach this great future he promises you?"

Both girls stared at him in the blankest surprise. Damaris was the first to recover.

"You have no right to say so!" she exclaimed. She was angry now, the more so because his words had struck a spark of fear in her heart. "Do you think my uncle a monster who would traffic in his own flesh and blood?"

"I think him capable of any infamy which would serve to increase his power," Kit retorted. He took a pace forward and caught her by the wrist, looking

down into her face. "Promise me that you will not put
yourself in his power without endeavouring to find out
if what I say is true."

"I will promise nothing! Let me go!" She struggled
furiously against a hold she could not break, then,
finding her efforts vain, struck out in words instead.
"If it is the truth, it is no concern of yours! I would
rather be a Royal favourite and move in the great world
than waste my life here as the wife of some colonial
planter."

He released her as abruptly as he had seized her,
and stepped back. His fingers had set a red mark
about her wrist.

"I understand!" he said in a low voice. "It has not
taken long for the noble blood of the Farrancourts to
assert itself. I cry your pardon."

He bowed briefly to Olivia and turned away. As he
reached the door, Damaris's voice, no longer defiant
but frightened, came again to check him.

"Kit, you cannot go like this! We may never meet
again."

He turned. He was very pale, with a curiously rigid
look about his mouth; his eyes were dark with anger
and something, too, of pain.

"Be easy, this is not farewell!" he said curtly. "I have
not done with you yet, Damaris. We shall most certainly meet again."

Chapter X

THE POWER OF THE PANTHER

From Damaris, Kit went straight to my lord at the Governor's house. His anger against the Earl was profound, but it was a cold anger, which would not betray him into any hasty or reckless action. He believed that he had the means to rescue Damaris from her uncle's power, for it was clear that she had already been too long under my lord's influence. Afterwards, it would be for her to choose the future course of her life.

He found Ingram Fletcher with the Earl, and wondered again what bond drew them together. Chelsham greeted him with a scarcely perceptible gleam of mockery in his eyes, for he had been expecting a visit from Captain Brandon, and had wondered a little that the news of Miss Tremayne's intended departure had not come sooner to his ears. Kit returned the greeting briefly, and requested the favour of a few minutes' conversation with the Earl.

My lord waved a graceful hand.

"My dear sir, my time is at your disposal. Pray be seated."

Kit stepped forward to a chair, but paused with his hand on its back to direct a straight glance at Ingram.

"Will you give us leave, Mr. Fletcher?" The words

were a request; the tone a command. "My business
with his lordship is private."

Fletcher bridled, and looked at the Earl for support,
but this Chelsham was clearly not disposed to give.
There was a faint smile curving his thin lips, as though
he relished the thought of the coming encounter.

"Mr. Fletcher and I can, of course, resume our
conversation later," he said ironically. "We are all
aware that Captain Lucifer's time is precious." He
waited until Fletcher had sulkily withdrawn from the
room before he went on: "Your business, sir, would
appear to be of an urgent nature. Is it, perhaps, connected with my imminent departure from Jamaica?"

"No, my lord, it is not," Kit replied shortly, adding,
as Chelsham's eyes lifted in involuntary surprise to
meet his: "It concerns the departure of your niece."

There was an infinitesimal pause.

"Of course," Chelsham said softly. "May I point out,
however, that my niece is no longer a concern of
yours?"

"She will always be my concern!" Not all Kit's resolution could entirely keep the feeling from his voice.
"God's light! my lord, do you think that the happenings of the past few weeks can wipe out all the years
that went before? That I will stand aside and let her
take the path that you design for her?"

"And what path may that be?" The Earl's eyes had
narrowed, his tone bit. "Enlighten me, if you please!"

"I think there is no need, my lord! You have filled
her head with thoughts of the Court, dazzled her with
false promises of a great future——"

"I must remind you, Captain Brandon, that I am a
person of some account in England. That Damaris is
my niece is enough, but when to the Farrancourt name

is added beauty and wit, her future is assured."

"And if she lacked both beauty and wit, my lord, would you still be ready to claim her as your niece? I think that, for all your talk of future greatness, 'tis but your own interests you hope to serve when you promise her a place about the Queen. Many ladies hold such places, I am told! Women such as the Countess of Castlemaine!"

There was a pause. Chelsham leaned back in his chair and looked up with some amusement at the angry young man confronting him. He felt that he could afford to be amused for whatever Brandon might suspect, however violent his protests, there was little he could do to harm my lord's plans. If Damaris Tremayne chose to return to England with her uncle, it was beyond Kit Brandon's power to stop her.

"The inference is obvious," he said contemptuously. "I find it offensive, and shall waste no time upon it. Instead I will point out, Captain Brandon, that Damaris herself is anxious to leave Jamaica. That is readily understood. There was, I am told, an unfortunate sentimental attachment between her and a young comrade of yours who lost his life in your recent brush with Spain."

The reference to Nicholas touched Kit upon the raw, as Chelsham meant it to, but he was unprepared for what followed. Kit's hand clenched on the back of the chair beside which he still stood, but he spoke levelly.

"Would she be as anxious to go with you, my lord, if she knew the true facts of her father's death?"

The Earl jerked upright in his chair, his amusement forgotten. In the sudden pallor of his face, his eyes were jewel-hard, narrowed and dangerous. The white hand which rested upon the table tightened into a fist.

"What in the devil's name do you mean by that?"

"Must I be plainer, sir?" It was Kit's turn now for mockery. "I mean that she would trust you less if she knew you for her father's murderer. You have taken too much for granted, my lord! John Tremayne never brought his daughter to my mother's house. I met with him on the road, when his horse had foundered and you were hard upon his heels. He thrust his child into my arms and bade me hide myself among the trees while he sought to send you upon a false trail. I was within a dozen yards of you when you shot him down."

Chelsham's face was livid, and below the heavy curls of his wig his brow was damp with sweat, but in no other way did he betray the dismay he must have felt. Even when he spoke, there was not the slightest tremor in his cold voice.

"I say that I found him lying dead of a broken neck. No doubt has ever been cast upon the story. It is your word against mine, Captain Brandon, and I venture to believe that in an English court, my word would carry the greater weight."

Kit's mouth curled contemptuously.

"I am not speaking of courts, my lord, but of Damaris. Whose word would weigh more with her, yours or mine?"

"Are you not forgetting something, my friend? Her trust in you was shattered when she learned how you had deceived her concerning her parentage."

"Not shattered, my lord!" Kit's voice was scornful. "She was hurt and frightened, but we have been too close, she and I, these fifteen years, for the bond between us to be broken so. I could convince her of the truth of what I say."

"Yet if you did convince her, I am still her uncle,

her closest surviving kinsman. I could command her obedience."

"I do not advise it!" Kit spoke as arrogantly as the Earl. "Understand this, my lord! One word more of compulsion, and not only Damaris, but all Port Royal —aye, and all England, too—shall know how John Tremayne died. I may have no proof, but, by God! I will raise a storm of scandal about your ears that not even you could hope to weather."

My lord's hand clenched again until the knuckles gleamed white. In all his adult life, no man had ever dared to address him in such terms, and impotent fury seethed within him. He choked it back, for just then Brandon undoubtedly had the whip hand.

"But if my niece were to remain in Jamaica," he said with assumed mildness, "what would become of her? She cannot continue to live under your roof now 'tis known that she is not your sister."

There was a pause, and then Kit said in a level voice:

"A solution to that difficulty might be found."

"A solution?" For a moment my lord affected bewilderment, then light appeared to break upon him. "Ah! I understand. Not as your sister, but as your wife." He appeared to ponder the question. "It is a thought which had not before occurred to me. It needs consideration, Captain Brandon."

The door opened, and a servant came in with a message from the Governor. When Captain Brandon's business with his lordship was completed, would he favour Sir Thomas with a few moments of his time? Kit nodded curtly.

"Tell Sir Thomas I will be with him directly." He

waited until the lackey had gone, and then turned again to the Earl. "Well, my lord?"

Chelsham had spread his hands palm downwards on the table before him and was apparently studying them with rapt interest. A moment or two passed before he replied.

"My chief concern," he said mendaciously, "is the welfare of my niece. Fifteen years ago I sought her because I desired to be revenged upon her father, but that desire is long since dead. Now that I have found her, my only care is to provide adequately for her future. I thought to do that by taking her to England. You think she will be happier here with you." He looked up suddenly; his eyes revealed nothing of the anger he felt. "Why not let Damaris choose for herself, Captain Brandon? She is not a child, and I am prepared to abide by her decision. Are you?"

Kit hesitated, suspecting a trick. The sea-blue eyes mocked him.

"No?" said my lord softly. "Do you fear to put it to the test, Captain Lucifer?"

"So little do I fear it," Kit's voice was hard, "that as soon as my business with Sir Thomas is completed, I will ride back to her and lay the choice before her. It is agreed, my lord."

He turned sharp on his heel and went out, and the Earl, rising, went softly to the door and opened it a little. He saw Kit disappear into the study where the Governor transacted his official business, and then went, secretly smiling, in search of Ingram Fletcher.

"Brandon is disposed to be troublesome," he informed the young man. "Get you back with all speed to your cousin's house and see to it that he has no word with Damaris. Miss Charnwood will help you. If

Brandon comes to the house Damaris must not know of it, and he be told that she will not see him. Any letter he sends her must be intercepted and brought to me. You understand?"

"Yes, my lord, I understand, but will Olivia——?"

"She will," Chelsham assured him cynically. "Now go, and do not fail me in this, or all those fine hopes you cherish will come to naught."

Fletcher went, and my lord turned his attention from his preparations for departure to other activities of a less commonplace nature. Next morning Ingram Fletcher came to him again, and laid before him a letter addressed to Miss Tremayne.

"Brandon came twice to the house yesterday," he told the Earl, "but finally Olivia persuaded him that Miss Tremayne would not see him. This morning, a servant from Fallowmead brought this letter."

My lord broke the seals and glanced rapidly through the lengthy missive, his face hardening. Then he put the letter away and turned his attention once more to Fletcher.

"Miss Charnwood understands that if Brandon comes again he must receive the same answer?"

"Yes, my lord, but he is not likely to come, I think. He quarrelled with Miss Tremayne yesterday, before he came here, so it is probable that he will at least await an answer to the letter."

"We must see that he receives one," my lord remarked smoothly. "Do you know why they quarrelled?"

Ingram did know why, for Olivia had given him a full account of the dispute. Chelsham listened in silence, and at the story's end he was smiling his satisfaction.

"It is very well," he said. "Now I see my way clearly.

Mr. Fletcher, I believe I will ride back with you to take my leave of your kinsman."

But leave-taking was not the true purpose of the visit. When civilities had been exchanged, my lord drew his niece aside and asked her if Captain Brandon had come to bid her farewell, expressing surprise when she said that he had not. So, reluctantly, she told him of Kit's visit the previous day, of what he had said, and the manner of their parting. My lord regarded her inscrutably.

"And did you believe his charge, my child?"

"No—no," she faltered, for though something in his manner made her uneasy, she did not dare to risk his anger. "Only I fear he does not like you, my lord, and sought by these means to persuade me to stay in Jamaica."

"And do you wish to stay, Damaris?"

"No!" She spoke emphatically, her face averted. "Not if—that is, I wish to go to England, but it hurts me to part from Kit like this."

"Then may I suggest, my child, that you write a letter to Captain Brandon to tell him so? There should be no ill feeling between you and the one to whom you owe so much. Come, here is pen and paper ready to hand."

She went slowly to the table and sat down, taking the pen he held out to her. For a minute or two she stared at the blank sheet of paper before her, and then raised troubled eyes to her uncle's face.

"It is difficult," she said in a low voice. "I do not know what to say."

"Then permit me to help you, my dear. I am perhaps more practised in such matters." He paused, considering, and then began to dictate the letter he had

already determined upon in his mind. She wrote obedi-
ently, but when it was done, and folded, and the
direction added, he stretched out his hand and took
it from her.

"I will see that it is despatched," he said easily, and
looked down at her with a faint smile. "There is no
need for anxiety, my child. Brandon, I am sure, has
no wish to part from you in any spirit of ill-will. He
will come to bid you farewell."

Damaris returned the smile perfunctorily. She supposed that her uncle meant to be kind, but now that
the time of departure was drawing near her courage
failed her. It did not seem possible that on the morrow
she must say good-bye to Kit for ever. Life without
him seemed unthinkable.

For my lord's own inscrutable reasons the letter did
not come into Kit's hands until after darkness had
fallen that night. He was alone at Fallowmead, for Dr.
Blair had been called away to tend a severely injured
man at a distant plantation, and Kit, in an agony of
impatience, was pacing restlessly back and forth
through the deserted rooms when the butler came to
him with the letter.

He seized it and ripped it open, but as he read, his
eagerness gave place to dismay, and then to perplexity.
This was not Damaris, these elegant, formal phrases
which informed him coldly that though she found it
impossible to believe the charges he had made against
her uncle, it was her earnest wish to part from him in
friendship, and to express her profound gratitude for
all the kindness he had shown her. It was my lord.
Every word bore the stamp of his personality, and Kit
could almost hear him dictating the polite, meaningless
sentences.

Suddenly he caught his breath and looked closer. Beneath the signature was another line of writing, so hastily scrawled that it seemed almost to come from a different hand; a pathetic, desperate appeal which gave the lie to all that went before. 'I believe you, but am forced to deny it. Come quickly, if you ever loved me.'

Kit's hands closed hard upon the letter, crushing it; there was a sudden light in his eyes. He strode out into the hall, shouting to the servants to bring him the swiftest horse in the stables, and within a matter of minutes he was in the saddle and riding recklessly in the direction of the Charnwood plantation. "Come quickly," she had written, and not a moment would he lose in answering her appeal.

Disaster, when it came, was sudden and complete. At a place where the road ran for some way between thick-growing trees, his galloping horse blundered against some unseen obstacle and fell heavily, flinging its rider from the saddle. Dazed and shaken, he struggled to his knees, dimly aware of footsteps and voices near at hand, and then something struck him a violent blow on the back of the head, a blinding light seemed to flash for a split second before his eyes, and he plunged headlong into an eternity of darkness.

Chapter XI

THE CUNNING OF THE FOX

The *Good Hope* sailed with the morning tide, and my lord stood with his brother and Ingram Fletcher upon the poop-deck, and watched the little town, deceptively peaceful in the early sunlight, fade gradually into the distance.

Damaris was not with them. She was below, behind the locked door of her cabin, weeping as though her heart would break. Right up to the last she had hoped for some word or sign from Kit; until the very moment when the *Good Hope* weighed anchor she had expected him to come, and had stood on the poop to watch for him, her attention divided between the boats about the mole and the place where his ships rode at anchor. He would come, of course. It was inconceivable that all should end thus, with not even an answer to the letter she had sent him. When at last the anchor came up out of the glittering water, and the ship began to move slowly but inexorably towards the harbour mouth, she was seized by a sense of panic, and a blind terror of the future to which she had committed herself. Unutterable loneliness assailed her, and she fled from them all to hide herself in her cabin and shed the tears she was too proud to let them see.

She stayed there for a long time, and when at last she emerged, a profound indifference had taken possession of her. Even when, later in the day, my lord called her into the great cabin and told her that it was his wish that she should marry Ingram Fletcher, she received the news unemotionally. The Earl regarded her with a faint frown, for he had expected dismay, protests, even open rebellion.

"Do you understand me, Damaris?" he said sharply.

"Yes, my lord," she answered calmly, "though I do not understand your reasons for it."

"You do not need to understand them. It is my will."

"Even though 'tis my future which is in question?" Indifference had cast out fear, and she spoke boldly. "Mr. Fletcher is naught but a fortune-hunter. I had suitors more worthy in Port Royal."

"And might look to find others in England?" My lord was not displeased with the rejoinder, and his voice was amused. "I will not deny it."

"I have no fortune."

His brows lifted.

"My child, you wear about your neck the equal of many a maid's marriage-portion."

Her hand flew to the great rope of pearls.

"They are mine! I will not part with them!"

"You need not, for I will dower you. I sought merely to explain one of Fletcher's reasons for seeking you as his bride."

"And his other reasons, my lord?" she asked quietly, looking him squarely in the eyes. Chelsham smiled faintly.

"You are my niece."

Damaris smiled also, but without amusement. It occurred to him suddenly that she seemed older, as though the ordeal through which she had passed had stripped her of the last traces of childishness.

"I am also of merchant stock, my lord, and my

father was a rebel and a deserter." She paused, gravely considering him, and then added: "I believe Kit spoke truth concerning the future you design for me."

There was a moment of silence. My lord was gazing reflectively at the panther ring on his right hand, his face inscrutable.

"If it were true," he said slowly at length, "you would have no cause to complain. At Court, the King's mistress is greater than the Queen."

There was another, longer pause. Damaris stared through the open casements astern, at the glittering, blue-green sea that stretched to an empty horizon. Jamaica had vanished as though it had never been, and Kit, though he knew the truth, had not cared sufficiently to make a second protest, or even to bid her farewell. The past, then, stood for nothing, and she had no place in his future; what matter then what her own future might hold? She gave a little shrug, and slowly her eyes turned again towards the Earl, to find that he was watching her intently.

"If it were true, my lord," she retorted, tossing his own words back at him with a trace of his own mockerry, "you would not find me—disobedient."

Satisfaction leapt like a cold flame in the eyes, so like her own, which were fixed upon hers, but all he said was:

"Have you the brooch which belonged to your mother?"

"Yes, my lord!" Her voice was puzzled. "It is in my cabin."

"Then wear it, my child." Chelsham had risen to his feet, and now laid his hand briefly on her shoulder; his cold smile was upon his lips. "The device of the Golden Panther would become you well."

It was not to be supposed that Martin would receive
with any degree of pleasure the news of the betrothal,
and at the first opportunity took his brother to task for
arranging such a marriage. As long as his objections
were upon the score of religion, my lord listened with
unwonted patience, for he was sufficiently fond of his
brother to be reluctant to argue with him upon such a
subject. He was himself strict enough in all the outward observances of his religion, but it was mere lip-
service, and his ultimate belief was in himself; to
Martin, his faith was a real and very precious thing. So
my lord evaded the question, with the skill of a born
dissembler, and Martin passed to the more worldly
aspects of the marriage. Who, he asked indignantly,
was Ingram Fletcher, that he should be considered a
fitting husband for the daughter of Margaret Farrancourt?

The Earl smiled faintly.

"At present," he replied, "he is a gentleman of no
fortune and little consequence. He is destined, however,
for greatness."

Martin stared.

"Fletcher is?" he said incredulously. "I perceive no
sign of it."

"But then, my dear Martin, you are less far-sighted
than I," his brother pointed out. "I know what I do,
believe me! Rest assured that if I did not, I would
not bestow my niece's hand upon him."

On that note the argument ended, but it left Martin
uneasy. He spoke to Damaris of the betrothal, and
though she declared herself quite satisfied, his mind
was not set at rest. With the departure from Jamaica
a change appeared to have come over her, and in
some curious way her physical resemblance to my

lord seemed heightened by a sort of understanding between them. It was his brother, and not his beloved sister, whom Martin saw looking at him now from Damaris's eyes, and the realization filled him with misgivings.

By the following morning, however, these problematical fears had been swamped by a greater and more concrete anxiety. Just before dark a distant sail had been sighted, and when dawn broke it was not only still within view, but appreciably nearer. As the sun climbed higher, it became apparent that the unknown craft was steering in pursuit, and also that her sailing power was considerably greater than that of the *Good Hope*. The captain, a prudent man, would have put about and run for Port Royal again, had it not been evident that such line of retreat would be cut by the stranger craft long before safety was reached. All he could do was to crowd on sail, and hope that the pirate—if pirate she was—would lose interest in the pursuit, or that help would arrive from some unexpected quarter.

Neither hope was fulfilled. The pursuer came tirelessly on, and no friendly sail lifted over the horizon. At last the unknown ship was close enough for the look-out to descry her identity, and there floated down from the mast-head the unwelcome news that this was the *Albatross*. Damaris, standing with her uncles and Ingram Fletcher on the poop-deck, gasped and turned pale, for the *Albatross* was Marayte's ship, and with Marayte sailed Renard, the pale, cruel Fox.

None of her companions immediately perceived her dismay, for Ingram was gaping in consternation at the pirate ship, and Martin watching his brother with frowning perplexity. At the first mention of the pursuer's identity, Chelsham had uttered a strangled oath, and now was staring across the sparkling water towards the other craft with his lower lip caught between his teeth and an expression of baffled fury upon his normally impassive countenance.

Slowly the pirate ship overhauled her prey, and then a gun boomed, and the shot whistled across the path of the *Good Hope* and splashed into the sea a short way off. There were a few minutes of seeming confusion, of shouting and hurrying to and fro, and a swarming of seamen into the rigging, and presently the *Good Hope* lay with idly flapping sails and the flag dipped from her mast-head in token of surrender.

The captain came up the companion to the poop-deck, and was met at the ladder's head by my lord. The Earl had recovered from whatever emotion had held him in its grip; he was calm now, but his eyes were narrowed and dangerous, and his thin lips set in an ominous line.

"Mother of God! what poltroonery is this?" he demanded arrogantly. "Will you surrender your ship to these cut-throats without a single shot fired in its defence?"

"My lord, the *Albatross* carries twenty-four guns to my ten," the captain replied bluntly. "Resistance would be worse than useless, and there is the lady to consider."

"Captain!" It was Damaris who spoke, with only the faintest tremor in her voice to betray her alarm. "Do you not know who commands that ship?"

He looked at her with trouble in his eyes. He was an honest man, and he sincerely desired to do what was best both for his passeneger and his crew in the perilous situation in which they found themselves, but the decision was not an easy one to make.

"I know, madam," he replied, "but it is not to be supposed that even Marayte will offer harm to a gentleman of his lordship's standing, or to his family. Besides, there is now another factor to be considered, which perhaps yonder villains have not yet perceived. We have sighted two other ships some way off, which have since altered course to approach us. Whether they be friend or foe I cannot yet tell, but we can scarcely be in worse case than we are at present."

"Can we not?" My lord spoke with some asperity. "What if they are more pirates hastening to the kill? In God's name, fight now, before the odds become too heavy for you!"

"By your leave, my lord, the odds are already too great, while in delay lies at least a hope of salvation. I will not engage the *Albatross*."

He sketched a bow to Damaris and turned away. With a glance at her uncle's set face, she said timidly:

"I think he is right, my lord. If these others are buccaneer ships, or those of any friendly nation, we are saved, while even with the Dons your name and rank must serve to ensure us courteous treatment."

As though she had not spoken, he moved away to the bulwarks and stood there drumming his fingers on the wood and watching the pirate ship. She came on steadily towards them, and it was obvious that Marayte intended to lay them alongside. Martin said quietly to Damaris:

"Would it not be better, my dear, for you to go below?"

She shook her head.

"I will stay here, if you please. He shall not think I fear him."

Rebecca, the waiting-woman, came quickly up the

companion to join them, and, reaching Damaris's side, began to remove the diamonds from the girl's ears.

"Give them to me, Miss 'Maris," she said urgently, "and the other jewels you have about you. I've hid the rest where they'll not soon be found."

Damaris let her take the gems, but when the woman pointed to the ruby ring she hesitated, for it had not left her finger since Nick's dying hands set it there. Rebecca clicked her tongue impatiently.

"Give it to me, or let them take it," she said, jerking her head towards the other ship, and reluctantly Damaris drew off the ring and dropped it into Rebecca's hand. She bestowed it with the other jewels in a pocket among the folds of her bright-coloured skirt, and then took up a position a yard or so behind her mistress.

With a shuddering impact the *Albatross* came alongside the *Good Hope* and grappled her fast, and then the pirates, elated by this bloodless victory, swarmed with shouts of triumph on to the deck of the captured ship. Marayte was in the forefront of that yelling horde, conspicuous by his bulk and the size of the axe he brandished above his head, but not until the first wave of boarders had spent itself did Renard make his appearance. Then he leapt lightly up on to the bulwarks of the pirate ship, and stood there, a hand on the shrouds, looking up at the little group on the *Good Hope's* high poop, and as though his pale gaze had some mesmeric quality, Damaris turned her head and looked at him across the milling crowd between.

He swung across on to the deck of the other ship and with never a glance to right or left shouldered his way aft through the press towards her, but Marayte was there before him. At the foot of the companion leading to the poop, the English captain tried to bar

his way. Marayte swung his axe, the captain went down
with a shattered skull, and his murderer stepped across
his body and continued on his way.

At the head of the ladder he was met by the Earl,
standing a little in advance of his companions. My lord
had observed the captain's fate, but since cowardice was
not among his faults, he had no hesitation in bearding
the swarthy ruffian who now confronted him. In the
shadow of his broad, plumed hat his face was a mask
of ineffable disdain, and he did not even trouble to
lay a hand on his sword.

"I am the Earl of Chelsham," he informed Marayte
haughtily. "Permit me to warn you of the danger you
incur if you offer violence to any member of my party."

The pirate looked down at him, his thick lips
wreathed in an evil grin, the bloodstained axe balanced
in his hand.

"We'll not harm you, my bully! Ye're of more value
to us alive than dead. We'll talk o' ransom presently."

He brushed past the Earl and advanced towards
Damaris, where she stood between her uncle and Ingram Fletcher. Martin's hand went to his sword, but
as quickly her own closed about his wrist to restrain
him, for she had seen the brutal murder of the captain,
and, faint and sick though she was with the horror of
it, she still had the wit to realize how Marayte would
deal with any offer of resistance. He tossed the axe
aside as he approached, but before he could touch her
there was a swirl of bright coloured skirts and Rebecca
was between them, a small, bright dagger glinting in
her hand.

She sprang upon him with all the fury of a tigress,
and while he was still struggling, between anger and
amusement, to subdue her, Renard came swiftly up

the steps on to the poop. His pale eyes took in the scene in one swift survey, and then he was bowing with ironical courtesy to the Earl.

"So we meet again, my lord, in spite of all," he said, in that precise voice which held now a note of mockery. "I regret this delay at the very start of your journey, but I believe we need not detain you for long. A week or two, a month, perhaps, and you may go on your way again."

"I will go on my way, you treacherous dog," retorted the Earl coldly, "when I have seen you and your scoundrelly friends hang. For that satisfaction I will most willingly stay."

There was no change of expression in Renard's pale, pock-marked face; he continued to smile with mild, ironical amusement. Marayte, still holding Rebecca by the arms, guffawed, and from the assembled pirates came laughter and some satirical applause. The men had crowded after their leaders on to the poop, until the prisoners were ringed about with picturesquely garbed ruffians, but they were in holiday mood after their easy victory and ready for some sport. The plundering of the prize could wait—they had all the time in the world.

"High words, my lord," Renard replied amiably, "but that satisfaction you are not likely to have. We shall convey you to Tortuga, and thence you will be free to go your ways. Of course, we shall require hostages to ensure that the ransom is duly paid, and for that purpose we shall keep with us your brother——" he paused, and his glance went once more to Damaris "—and your niece."

There was a brief, tense pause. Martin and Ingram

exchanged horrified glances; Renard continued to smile; the pirates waited expectantly.

"You damned, double-dealing scoundrel!" Chelsham said softly at length.

Renard laughed.

"They shall be well treated, my lord, I assure you," he said. He went past the Earl to where Damaris stood, slim and straight and defiant in her ivory-coloured gown, her golden head held high. "Miss Tremayne I will take under my own, personal protection."

She would not let him see the sick terror that gripped her. Though his very glance shamed her, though the men made audible comments which brought a flame of colour to her white face, she faced him every whit as arrogantly as her uncle had done. At that moment she was all Farrancourt.

"I put a bullet through your leg once, Renard," she said in a clear, carrying voice. "I perceive my mistake. It should have been through your heart."

This time the gust of laughter was at his expense, and beneath the goad of it, the evil that was in him, and never far below the surface, broke through the thin veneer of mocking courtesy. So swift was the change, and so sudden, that before she had a chance to draw back he had seized her with deliberate brutality and was kissing her again and again while she writhed helplessly in his arms. Then he gripped her by the wrists and forced her down on to her knees before him.

"Let that be an earnest," he said wickedly, "and a lesson in humility. I have tamed wilder pieces than you, my pretty."

Slowly Damaris lifted her head. Her hair was disordered and the lace on her gown torn, but her eyes still blazed defiance at her captor.

"There was a reckoning to pay before, Renard, and there will be another," she told him, "and this time I think it will not be a whip with which Captain Lucifer comes seeking you."

With a foul oath at that unwelcome reminder of his humiliation he flung her violently away from him, but the words had cast a sudden shadow upon those about her. The pirates began to exchange uneasy glances and to mutter among themselves, and even as Martin limped forward to help Damaris to her feet the swift-growing ripple of dissatisfaction became vocal through the mouth of the one-eyed, grey-bearded Ben Gribben, that inveterate pessimist.

"Maybe the wench is right, Renard!" he said. "We've troubles enough without bringing Lucifer down upon us."

"Lucifer will not know of it, you fool!" Renard retorted savagely.

"How will you prevent it, if you take her to Tortuga?" Gribben argued, planting his feet wide and hooking his thumbs in his belt while he thrust his grey beard truculently into Renard's face. "He'll hear of it, sooner or later! He's got two o' the fastest ships in the Caribbean—ah, and a Spanish man-o'-war now if he likes to use her—and if you try to tackle them wi' the old *Albatross,* you'll find yourself with a mutiny on your hands."

A growl of approval from his comrades followed this speech. They all knew Captain Lucifer, and though they might scoff at him among themselves they all regarded him with a degree of awe. The discipline he enforced upon his crews was a by-word; he took no part in the wild carousals with which they all celebrated their victories, but held aloof, and moved on an equal plane with the Governor and the gentry around Port Royal; he was as completely different from themselves as it was possible for a man to be, and because they could not understand him they feared him a little.

"Ye've been mighty free wi' promises, Renard," Gribben pursued, encouraged by the approval of his shipmates, "but what have we gained by heeding you? There's Port Royal closed to us, and where'll today's work lead us in the end? There are doxies enough in the islands besides Lucifer's sister, so let the maid be."

"She is not his sister," Renard told him furiously. "She is the niece of his lordship there! You were in Port Royal long enough to hear that story, were you not?"

"Sister or doxy, she belongs to Lucifer," Gribben insisted stubbornly, "and we're not minded to have him on our heels so that you may take your pleasure. Let her be, or we'll find a way o' making you!"

This time approval was signified, not by a murmur but by a full-throated roar. Marayte was scowling with mingled anger and alarm, for his men, in true pirate tradition, acknowledged no leader save when in action, and were quite capable of slitting his throat as well as Renard's if he opposed their will. But because he feared the quiet-voiced Frenchman as much as he feared his crew, he did not dare to side openly with them. Renard had a way of surviving crises of this nature which past captains of the *Albatross* had not shared.

Damaris, with Martin's arm still about her, was pale and quiet, with only her quickened breathing and wide, anxious eyes to betray her fears. My lord stood straight and still, a silent, quick-eyed spectator of a sense in which he had ceased to play a part.

"So it is Lucifer you fear, you cowardly, whining curs!" Renard said at length, and there was evil mockery in his voice. "Let me prove to you that such fears are vain."

His glance shifted to Marayte, and he jerked his head in the direction of their own ship. The mulatto grinned with sudden comprehension, thrust the spasmodically struggling Rebecca into the hands of his nearest comrade, and turned to push his way through the men about him.

There fell a puzzled silence. Pirates and prisoners alike exchanged glances of blank bewilderment; my lord fell to his favourite trick of smoothing the delicate lace which almost covered his hands; and Renard, lounging against the poop-rail, watched Damaris with evil, gloating eyes. The two ships, fast locked together, rocked gently to the slight swell of a calm sea, with little, creaking, straining sounds which seemed loud in the stillness, while a light breeze stirred the plumes in the gentlemen's hats and the bright tendrils of hair about the girl's forehead.

At last Marayte reappeared from below-decks aboard the *Albatross,* thrusting before him at pistol's point another man, whose arms were pinioned to his sides. At sight of this prisoner, of whose presence aboard their ship most of the pirates had been unaware, a murmur of astonishment passed through their ranks, like the ripple of the wind through a field of grain, and there was a sudden surge of movement as those in the rear pressed forward for a clearer view.

At the bulwarks Marayte paused to thrust the pistol into his sash, and then, exerting his huge strength, he

heaved the captive up, and across on to the bulwarks
of the *Good Hope*. For a moment he held him there
for all to see and then pushed him forward so that he
crashed helplessly to the deck.

"There, my bullies!" he bawled triumphantly. "There
lies your fine Captain Lucifer, for all his pride!"

Sudden uproar broke out, cut through by Damaris's
scream of horror. She started forward as though she
would go to Kit, but Renard caught her by the arm.

"Bring him here, Marayte!" he shouted above the
din. "Here to the poop, where all may see him."

Somehow Kit had managed to get to his feet without
assistance, and now Marayte shoved him aft between
the grinning, jeering pirates in the waist of the ship,
and so brought him to the poop, and to Damaris. "We
shall meet again" he had said when they parted, but
neither had dreamed then what manner of meeting
it would be.

For a long moment they stared at each other, and
then with a sob she covered her face with her hands.
Kit's own countenance was inscrutable. His person bore
evidence of the rough handling he had received, his
clothes still dusty from the road, the fine, laced coat
ripped from shoulder to waist; there was a fresh cut
above one eyebrow, from which a slow trickle of blood
was creeping down the side of his face, but he stood
erect despite his bonds and was not noticeably humbled
by his present ignominious position. His gaze passed
contemptuously over the rascally crowd about him,
and came to rest at last upon the Earl; the compressed
lips curved slightly to a smile of grim amusement.

" 'Tis an unpleasant sensation, is it not, my lord, to
be hoist with one's own petard?" he said quietly.

Damaris looked up quickly, her eyes startled and

questioning, but Kit was not looking at her. He was still watching Chelsham.

"I make your lordship my compliments," he went on. "That letter, with its pathetic postscript, was a stroke of genius which brought me blundering into your trap, but your confederates were ill-chosen. Renard has never yet been known to keep faith with anyone."

The Earl shrugged slightly, making no attempt to deny the charge.

"I use the tools which lie most readily to hand, Captain Brandon," he said languidly. "It was inevitable that in the course of time one of them would prove faulty."

"You did this, my lord?" Damaris spoke sharply, her fears forgotten now in a greater horror. "You delivered him into his enemy's hands? Merciful God! Why?"

It was Kit who answered her.

"Because I had the means to keep you from England, child, and a dead man can betray no secrets. I've no doubt his lordship imagined my throat to have been slit these twenty-four hours past."

Renard laughed unpleasantly.

"There was no mention of throat-slitting in our bargain," he said. "You are bound for a Spanish prison, my prideful friend! The Dons have offered a generous price for Captain Lucifer."

Damaris cried out at that, for she knew that Kit would find no mercy in Spanish hands. Again she tried to go to him, and again Renard prevented her, pulling her back against him and holding her captive, with his arms about her and his hands grasping her wrists. Over her shoulder he looked mockingly at Kit.

"You for the Dons, and this pretty plaything for me," he taunted him. "I have waited a long while, Lucifer, but there are some debts I do not forget."

She struggled valiantly to free herself, but in vain; a low moan broke from her lips, and her eyes turned in piteous entreaty towards Kit. He, too, had made one instinctive effort towards freedom, straining with all his strength against the cords that bound him, but after a moment he realized the futility of the attempt, and desisted.

"Nor I," he said in a low, terrible voice. "Be warned, Renard, for I swear that this debt shall be paid in full."

There was an instant's silence, for, bound and helpless though he was, at that moment Captain Lucifer dominated them all, and to the profoundly superstitious pirates his quiet words seemed like a curse, a warning of doom. Then, before Renard could speak again, a shout rang out from one of the men who had climbed into the rigging the better to see what was going on.

There was a note of dismay in his voice which drew all eyes towards him; he was pointing away to starboard, and in a moment they all perceived what had alarmed him. Hitherto unperceived, so busy had they been with their own concerns, two powerful ships were bearing down upon them. Steadily they came, dipping through the blue-green water under a great spread of canvas, their gilded beakheads flashing in the morning sunshine. They were still some way off, but near enough for those aboard the *Good Hope* to discern the gold and crimson banner of Spain stirring lazily in their mastheads. In the sudden, stricken silence, Captain Lucifer laughed softly.

Chapter XII

LUCIFER TRIUMPHANT

Panic ensued, in which the prisoners were for the moment forgotten. Even Renard loosed his hold upon Damaris and thrust through the staring, cursing pirates to a point whence he could see clearly the approaching danger. Finding herself free, she stumbled forward to where Rebecca's dagger, forced from her hand by Marayte, lay gleaming on the deck. An instant later she was at Kit's side and hacking at his bonds.

They parted at last, and with a shattering sob she let fall the knife and clung to him, brokenly murmuring his name. Martin Farrancourt limped up to them; he was very pale, and seemed to have aged years in the past few minutes; he said, in a low, urgent voice:

"Brandon, I did not know what he had done. Believe me, I did not know!"

"I believe you, Mr. Farrancourt," Kit said quietly, and looked towards the Earl. "I learned long ago that your brother keeps his own counsel."

The pirates had taken the measure of the foe, and decided that the only safety lay in immediate flight. They shouted this conclusion to each other, and were already hurrying to translate words into action when Kit's voice rang out above the din.

"Whither away, my friends? Port Royal is closed to you!"

That served to check their haste, and while they

hesitated, Kit put Damaris gently aside and advanced to the poop-rail. There was a certain grim amusement in his face as he glanced round at the crestfallen pirates.

"Modyford turned you out of Port Royal, and warned you that you ventured there again on pain of death," he reminded them. "If you return to Jamaica with these prisoners, there is not one of you will escape the gallows."

"Better an English hangman than Spanish torturers," Gribben retorted, flinging out an arm towards the approaching ships. "We can't tackle them!"

"Why not?" Kit countered swiftly. "Your ship is fast and handy. With a fighting seaman in command of her, instead of a pair of cut-throats whose place is the gutter where they were bred, you might so maul those lumbering Spaniards that they would be in no case to harm you."

"In short," my lord's cold voice cut in, "if Lucifer were your captain—" he did not complete the sentence, but left the implied suggestion to take hold upon their minds, which it did with astonishing rapidity. Whereas, a short while before, they had rejoiced in their prisoner's humiliation and intended fate, they now began to see in him their only hope of salvation.

Kit had no difficulty in following the trend of their thoughts. He knew that they were governed solely by self-interest, and that if they saw a benefit to themselves in making him their leader for as long as the present danger lasted, they would do so, and still have no hesitation in selling him to Spain as soon as his usefulness was past. As with the pirates, so with my lord the Earl; he supported Captain Lucifer because, for the moment, he had need of him.

The men were muttering among themselves. Gribben

fingered the pistols in his belt and regarded Kit dubiously out of his single eye.

"Ye'd cripple them two hulks wi' the old *Albatross?*" he said, in a tone of mingled disbelief and hope.

Kit shrugged. He was by no means as confident as he pretended, but the advent of the Spanish ships offered a faint ray of hope where before there had been none, and he would fight with every means he could devise to turn the situation to good account.

"I would try," he said calmly. "I have never fled from a Spaniard yet."

They were impressed by his air of quiet authority, and further influenced by the memory of his past brilliant successes, but before their growing indecision could resolve itself into action, Marayte thrust himself to the front of the crowd.

"Ye mutinous dogs! will ye let Lucifer cozen you wi' his lying boasts?" he demanded furiously. "The Dons will blast us out o' the water if they come within range, and well he knows it! By God! I'll show you who is master here——"

The crash of a pistol-shot cut short the denunciation. An expression of blank astonishment wiped the rage from the big mulatto's face, he pawed for an instant at the crimson patch which had appeared so suddenly on the front of his shirt, and then he pitched to the deck and was still, save for the spasmodic twitching of his limbs. Renard stepped forward, thrusting the still smoking pistol into his belt.

"Of course," Kit said mockingly into the startled silence, " 'tis Renard, is it not, who makes and breaks captains aboard the *Albatross?*"

"He had outlived his usefulness," Renard replied

callously. "Well, Lucifer, can you make good your boast?"

Kit's eyes held his.

"On my own terms," he said quietly.

"Terms!" The Frenchman laughed unpleasantly. "You think you are in a position to bargain with us?"

"If much more time is wasted, none of us will be in a position to bargain," Kit reminded him. "On my own terms, Renard. Otherwise——" he shrugged, and his glance flickered swiftly over the staring crew—"if I am destined for a Spanish prison I'd as lief have company there."

It was enough. Voices were raised, assuring him of their desire to clinch the bargain, and several demanded:

"What terms, Lucifer?"

"The prisoners to be released, and this ship allowed to go on her way unmolested," he replied, raising his voice so that all might hear. "There will be plunder enough yonder to make good the loss."

The few dissentient voices were drowned in a roar of agreement, and without more ado, led by Gribben, they swarmed back on to the deck of their own ship. Renard had hesitated, his eyes turning towards the girl, but he realized the futility of argument and turned away with a shrug.

Kit had caught one of the pirates by the arm as they surged past him, and plucked a pistol from his belt. Now, with the weapon in his hand, he moved quickly to the Earl's side.

"You, my lord, will come with me aboard the *Albatross*," he said briskly.

Surprise, suspicion and a hint of dismay flashed

across Chelsham's face for one unguarded moment.
Then he raised his brows.

"May I ask why, Captain Brandon?"

Kit regarded him steadily.

"Because it is my will," he replied. "Do you come,
my lord, or will you forfeit your dignity and go in
bonds? At present, these rogues will obey my commands implicitly."

For a few, tense seconds the dark blue eyes met
those of cold sea-green, and then the Earl's lips curved
to his faint, unpleasant smile.

"I will come," he said. "You command the situation,
Captain Brandon—at present."

He turned, and with no lessening of his dignity descended the companion. Kit looked after him for a
moment, frowning, and then, sweeping aside Martin's
indignant protests, he, too, made his way to the waist
of the ship.

The crew of the *Good Hope*, scarcely able to credit
their luck, greeted him with a cheer. He silenced them
impatiently and demanded the captain.

"He is dead, sir, slain by Marayte," a brown-faced
young seaman told him promptly. "I am John Ransome, the mate."

"Then you must take command. Do not linger here,
but as soon as we have cast off, set a course for Port
Royal, and make all speed you can. You understand?"

"Aye, sir, but what of you?" Ransome protested, with
an uneasy glance towards the pirate ship. "You'll not
trust them to keep faith with you, surely?"

"I put my trust in fortune and my own wits, my
friend," Kit replied with a faint smile. "Your duty is
to place Miss Tremayne and her companions in safety.
No more, no less."

He turned away, and was already at the bulwarks when a hand caught his arm, and he found Damaris at his side. She spoke his name in a fluttering whisper, but, conscious of the eyes all about them, and the precious minutes that were slipping by, he forced himself to ignore the appeal of voice and eyes.

"When you reach Port Royal," he said quickly, in a voice which reached her ears alone, "ask Alex to tell you all he knows concerning my lord your uncle. For the rest, I think you may trust Martin Farrancourt, and Wade and Modyford will stand your friends." He took the hand that still clutched his sleeve, and held it to his lips for a moment. "God keep you, child," he added unsteadily, and then, turning, he sprang up on to the bulwarks and across on to the pirate ship.

The grapnels had already been loosed, and a moment later a strip of water was widening between the two vessels. She saw Kit raise his hand in a gesture of farewell, smiling at her in the dear, familiar way for a moment before he turned aside to direct the preparations for the coming battle. Tears blinded her eyes, and she leaned sobbing against the bullwarks until Rebecca came hurrying to clasp her in loving arms and murmur words of comfort.

She composed herself presently, and began to look about her again. By that time the *Albatross* was some way off, advancing audaciously upon the enemy, and the *Good Hope* preparing to make her escape. The crew went reluctantly about their tasks, for though they had all heard Kit's orders they disliked the craven part he had thrust upon them. John Ransome felt this as strongly as his men, and when Miss Tremayne came hastening to him to protest, he lent a willing ear to her words, merely pointing out, in a half-hearted way, that Captain Brandon had ordered him to make her safety his first concern.

"Do you think I care for my safety when he is in such danger?" she retorted passionately. "Even if he defeats the Dons, do you suppose he can ever be safe aboard that ship? In God's name, do not desert him!"

Ransome hesitated, torn between his duty, which was obviously to obey the commands he had been given, and his reluctance to leave to his fate the brave man to whom he and his comrades owed so great a debt. Damaris caught his arm with both hands and lifted an imploring face to his.

"Please, please!" she begged him. "You cannot sail away and leave him to my uncle and Renard! You have seen how they both hate him."

She was very lovely in her distress, too lovely altogether for a soft-hearted young sailor who was only too eager to do as she asked. He smiled reassuringly into her anxious eyes.

"We'll not desert him, ma'am," he promised her. "As long as there is a chance that we can aid him, we'll stay."

He turned away to give fresh orders, which the men greeted with a cheer, and Damaris, finding her thanks brushed aside with some embarrassment, withdrew once more to the poop.

The sound of gunfire was already echoing across the water, for as the *Albatross,* with the advantage of such wind as there was, bore down upon the Spaniards, she opened fire with the small cannon in her prow, and both Spanish ships replied. The *Albatross* was Dutch-built, low and swift, but looking pathetically small in comparison with the two tall galleons with their tower-ing poops and wealth of gilded carving. They had shortened sail now and their advance was slower; almost they seemed contemptuous of this puny adversary, whom it was clear they expected to dispose of without difficulty before turning their attention to her companion vessel.

On the poop of the *Good Hope*, Damaris stood at the bulwarks, her lower lip caught between her teeth and her eyes fixed with painful intensity upon the three ships. Martin and Ingram were beside her, and Rebecca, too, but she was unaware of their presence; with every fibre of her being she was intent upon the struggle beginning there across the sunlit water, her whole spirit breathing a wordless prayer for Kit's success and safety.

The *Albatross* had almost reached the Spaniards now, holding steadily to a course which must take her straight between them. Damaris heard Ingram utter a strangled curse.

"Brandon must be mad!" he exclaimed. "He will be crushed between the two. 'Tis certain suicide!"

Clearly the Spaniards agreed with him, for they were holding their fire, waiting for this foolhardy foe to place himself wholly at their mercy. For one horrifying instant Damaris wondered if Kit had chosen this way to destroy both my lord and Renard, and then from the quarter-deck came a triumphant shout to tell her the purpose of his seeming madness.

"Those Spanish fools have delayed too long!" It was Ransome's voice, hoarse with excitement. "If they fire now, 'twill be upon each other!"

They saw at once that he was right. The two Spanish ships, towering high above the water, would do more damage to each other than to the low-built pirate ship, if they fired upon her while she was in her present position, and at that moment the *Albatross* loosed a double broadside as she swept between them, emptying all her guns at point-blank range into the hulls of the Spanish ships. A dense cloud of smoke rolled up on the still air, hiding all three vessels from view.

In the light breeze it was maddeningly slow to disperse, but at last, through the cloud's thinning fringes, one of the galleons became visible. She came staggering blindly from the fight, clearly sore hit by that murderous broadside, and offering a target which Ransome could not resist. The *Good Hope* bore down upon the crippled Spaniard, and discharged five of her guns at her without incurring any answering fire. By the time they had gone about to deliver another broadside, they perceived that the need for it was past, for the galleon was listing heavily and her decks were already awash. It could be a matter of minutes only before she went down.

Meanwhile, the lifting smoke-cloud had revealed the remaining Spaniard at close grips with the *Albatross,* for Kit had boarded her before her crew had had time to recover from that first, stunning blow, and now his men were at the kind of fierce, hand-to-hand fighting they best understood. It was plain that the *Good Hope* could render no immediate assistance, so Ransome gave orders to heave-to, and boats were lowered to pick up survivors from the sinking ship.

He came himself to join the four watchers on the poop, and was loud in his praise of the brilliance and daring of Captain Lucifer. He bore a telescope beneath his arm, and this he presently trained upon the two ships in an endeavour to learn how the pirates were faring, though the two opposing forces were so inextricably mingled that it was difficult to form an accurate opinion.

For what seemed a very long time the battle raged to and fro, but at last Damaris uttered a cry of excitement and flung out a pointing hand. The gold and crimson banner was being lowered, and the fight was over.

"Surrender, by God!" Ransome exclaimed, his telescope still at his eye. "One ship sunk and the other taken, and one man alone to thank for it!" He broke off suddenly, was silent for a moment, and then loosed a furious oath. "Ah, the curs! The thankless, treacherous swine!"

"What is it?" Damaris clutched his arm; her voice was frightened. "What is happening?"

He lowered the glass and stared at her, white-faced, as though seeking words with which to reply, but in an agony of impatience she snatched the telescope from him and applied it to her own eye, raking the Spanish ship in search of whatever sight had provoked his outburst.

Suddenly a cry broke from her lips. On the high poop of the captured vessel three men were at close grips, their swords flashing in the sun. One of them was Kit, and his two opponents, pressing him hard were Renard and my lord the Earl. None of the other men appeared to be taking any part, or indeed, any interest in the fight, being already engaged in despatching the prisoners and learning the value of their prize, and the desperate conflict continued with unabated fury.

It did not seem possible that Kit could for long defend himself against both his adversaries, but in their eagerness to destroy him they hampered each other. Before either could break through his guard, Renard slipped and, stumbling against my lord, sent him staggering aside. Kit took advantage of the moment's respite to spring back out of reach, then, tossing his sword aside, he leapt up on to the bulwarks and dived overboard. By the time his assailants reached the spot whence he had vanished he was swimming strongly towards the nearest boat. He reached it a few minutes later and was hauled aboard.

They were all in the waist to greet him when he came aboard the *Good Hope* again, and Damaris, heedless of his sodden condition, tumbled headlong into his arms, laughing and crying at once. He caught her in a hard embrace, but above her head his eye sought out John Ransome.

"Call in your boats and set a course for Port Royal," he told him crisply. "At present those rogues yonder are occupied with their plunder, but we'll not linger here to tempt them with more."

His orders were promptly obeyed, and later, sitting with Damaris and Martin in the great cabin, clad in borrowed raiment, he told them quietly the full story of his capture, and of how John Tremayne had met his death fifteen years earlier. When the tale was done, there was a long silence, broken at last by Martin. Soon after Kit began to speak he had rested one elbow on the table and covered his eyes with his hand, and he spoke now without looking up.

"That he is ruthless I knew," he said in a low voice, "and that he will brook no opposition to his will, but I have always believed him to be honest in his dealings."

"I can give no proof of what I say, Mr. Farrancourt," Kit replied quietly. "It is my word against his, and he is your brother."

"There is no need of proof, Captain Brandon!"

Martin raised his head at last; his face was ashen. "My mind may shrink from the thought of all that your tale implies, but in my heart there is no doubt that you speak the truth."

Damaris said nothing. She sat with her hands clasped in her lap and her eyes fixed unseeingly upon them. Her thoughts were chaotic, her emotions in a tumult of confusion. She knew that she should feel horror at the manner in which her father had died, but it was all too remote in time and place, and neither for him nor for his tragic bride had she ever been able to feel more than a vague pity.

To her, from the grim story she had just heard, it was not the figure of John Tremayne which stood out most clearly, not even that of his murderer, but of the boy who had shielded and saved a nameless waif; and as on that long past night, so through all the years between. Throughout her childhood and girlhood, though she was often parted from him for long periods, Kit had been the most important person in her life, commanding her deepest devotion. Then my lord had come, his cold, merciless voice shattering that precious bond for ever, leaving her lost and bewildered, a prey to such loneliness as she had never known, and from which there was no escape. To return to the old life was impossible; it was gone beyond recall. Yet, would she wish to turn back time, even if it were in her power to do so?

Unbidden, stabbing like a sword through the dark confusion of her thoughts, the question flashed into her mind. Seeking an answer to it, her startled gaze flew to Kit's face, and stayed there, as though she were seeing him for the first time. He was looking towards Martin, saying something to which she did not attend, and as she stared at the strong intrepid features, so familiar and yet suddenly so strange, realization of the truth brought a flood of colour to her cheeks.

She rose blindly to her feet, and, making what excuse she knew not, fled from the cabin. She climbed to the poop, leaned there, watching the water slide lazily past while the freshening breeze fanned her hot cheeks, and Nick's ruby, restored now to its place on her finger, glowed mockingly in the sunlight. She stared at it, realizing how she had deceived herself through all the long weeks since his death; Nicholas was a dear friend for whom she mourned deeply and sincerely, but Kit was a part of herself, and without him life must ever be empty and meaningless.

She thought of Olivia Charnwood, and was shaken anew by the emotion she recognized now as sheer, primitive jealousy. Olivia was to be his wife; would move as mistress through the fair rooms of Fallowmead, and stand upon the flower-hung balcony to watch for a ship homeward-bound, while for her, what defence, what refuge remained? She closed her eyes, swept by a storm of misery beside which all that she had suffered before was as nothing.

A footfall on the deck brought her swinging round, but it was only Ingram Fletcher who stood there. His long countenance was peevish, for he resented his exclusion from whatever discussion had been taking place, and was by no means certain of his position now that my lord's support had been so summarily withdrawn. Finding Damaris alone, however, he chose to be high-handed with her.

"I trust, madam, that I do not intrude!" he said waspishly. "You have, I presume, been discussing the present situation with Mr. Farrancourt and Captain Brandon. May I say that as your future husband I consider that I have a right to a part in such discussions?"

Damaris regarded him blankly. In the stress of recent events, she had forgotten their betrothal, but now, as he spoke, she saw with desolate clarity where her future must lie, the glittering, shameful future to which her uncle had yesterday pointed the way. Sooner or later my lord would be ransomed or rescued from the pirates, and after the terrible proof of his ruthlessness which had that day been given her, she knew that only by complete obedience to his will could she ensure Kit's immunity from further harm. Fletcher was Chelsham's creature, and because his fortunes were bound up in the Earl's he would be quick to betray her to her uncle if he suspected the truth. She must speak him fair, but there was one thing she felt impelled to ask, caution notwithstanding.

"Mr. Fletcher," she said abruptly, "did you know that my uncle had betrayed Kit into Renard's hands?"

Ingram regarded her warily. He could truthfully deny the accusation, but there was that awkward business of the intercepted letter, which must be disclosed eventually, even if it had not yet been discovered. He replied cautiously:

"I knew that Brandon sought to prevent your departure, and since his success in that would have jeopardized my own hopes I used every effort to stop him seeing you. I was aware that his lordship feared Brandon's influence over you to be great enough to persuade you to stay in Jamaica, but I had no suspicion that he would seek to harm him. Brandon's presence

aboard the *Albatross* was as great a shock to me as
to you, that I swear."

For a moment or two she continued to regard him,
but he met her searching gaze steadily enough, and
she decided that he was speaking the truth. It was
unlikely, after all, that my lord would confide in anyone more than was absolutely necessary.

"That is fortunate," she said drily at last. "Had you
had a hand in that betrayal, no power on earth could
have made me marry you."

He perceived that he had been wise to deal frankly
with her, and was sufficiently emboldened by the impli-
cation of her words to ask:

"Am I to infer from that, madam, that his lordship
overestimated Captain Brandon's powers of persuasion?"

Damaris turned away so that he should not see the
pain in her eyes, and looked down once more at the
lazily gliding water.

"My only desire now is to leave Jamaica," she said
in a low voice. "Have no fear, Mr. Fletcher! There is
no persuasion with the power to keep me here in the
Indies."

"No persuasion save one," said a small, wistful voice
within her, but she knew, with forlorn certainty, that
that persuasion would never be used.

Chapter XIII

AT THE SIGN OF
THE "BROKEN SWORD"

Within the cabin, after Damaris had left them, Kit came slowly back to the table and stood looking down at Martin, who still sat with bowed head, and one thin hand veiling his eyes. It was clear that the disclosure of his brother's villainy had stricken him hard, and there was profound pity in Kit's regard, for he liked and respected Martin Farrancourt as much as he distrusted and hated the Earl.

"Now that we are alone, Mr. Farrancourt," he said after a pause, "there is a question I wish to put to you. Have you any reason to suppose that your brother's power at Court is not as great as he might wish?"

Martin raised his head; there was surprise in his haggard face.

"How in the name of Heaven did you know that?" he demanded. "Ralph spoke of it to me on the day he arrived in Jamaica, but I have told no one, and I would stake my life that he has not."

"It is true, then?"

Martin nodded.

"Yes, it is true. He has made an enemy of Lady Castlemaine, and she has poisoned the King's mind against him. Ralph told me himself that he could find no effective weapon with which to counteract her spite."

"He has found one now!" Kit's voice was grim.

"God's light! if aught were needed to turn suspicion into certainty, that news supplies it." He saw that Martin looked bewildered, and added a curt explanation. "Damaris! He means to set her up as a rival to Lady Castlemaine."

"Damaris?" Martin repeated incredulously. "Oh, you are mistaken, sir! You must be! Why, he has arranged ——" he broke off, the disbelief in his eyes giving way to horror as he stared at Kit. Then he bowed his head again upon his hands; his voice was muffled. "His own sister's child! Holy Virgin! Is there no depth of infamy to which he will not sink?"

"What has his lordship arranged?" Kit asked sharply. "Come, sir, what new villainy does he intend?"

"He has promised her in marriage to Ingram Fletcher!" Martin spoke without looking up, and so did not see the expression in Kit's face. "When I questioned the wisdom of his choice, he laughed, and said that Fletcher was destined for greatness."

"For such greatness as the Earl of Castlemaine enjoys," Kit said bitterly. "The reward of compliance! God's light! Has the fellow no pride?" His narrowed glance returned to Martin's bowed head; he added sharply: "By what means did my lord compel Damaris to this betrothal?"

"He used no compulsion," Farrancourt replied wearily. "She told me herself that she was well satisfied with the match." He lifted troubled eyes to meet Kit's. "Ralph can be persuasive when he chooses. I fear he has turned her head with promises of grandeur, for they seem to understand each other only too well."

Kit shook his head.

"Damaris is no Castlemaine," he said with conviction. "Depend upon it, she believes him honest in this!

When I warned her before she would pay no heed, but, by God! she shall heed me now."

With that he left Martin to his unhappy thoughts, and went in search of Damaris, whom he found presently with Fletcher upon the poop-deck. When she saw him approaching, she laid a hand imploringly on her companion's arm, for she dreaded being left alone with Kit, but her anxiety was needless. Mr. Fletcher had had enough of slights and inattention, and was determined to assert himself. When Kit told him curtly that he wished to be private with Miss Tremayne, he made no move to leave them, but said, with that air of condescension he so loved to assume:

"You are perhaps unaware, sir, that Miss Tremayne is betrothed to me. Whatever you wish to say to her may be said in my hearing with perfect propriety."

"Of that, sir," Kit retorted, keeping his temper with difficulty, "you must allow me to be the judge. I pray you, have the goodness to leave us."

"I have some say in the matter, I suppose," Damaris broke in, in a high, unnatural tone, "and I desire Mr. Fletcher to remain. What is it that you wish to say to me, Kit?"

Ingram's brows lifted, and he looked at Captain Brandon with a supercilious smile which made Kit long to pitch him into the sea. He resisted the temptation with an effort.

"So be it," he said, cold as ice. "If Mr. Fletcher finds what I have to say offensive, the blame is not mine. Damaris, when I warned you against your uncle, you would not listen, and I had no evidence to offer in support of my suspicions. Now Mr. Farrancourt tells me that his lordship's influence at Court is waning, thanks to the enmity of the Countess of Castlemaine.

Do you need further proof that you are to be used to supplant her ladyship? If you do, look for it in the marriage he has arranged to lend some semblance of decency to your future."

Fletcher interrupted him with an inarticulate sound of indignation and dismay, and clapped a hand ostentatiously to the hilt of his sword. Kit's glance flicked him with undisguised contempt.

"I warned you, Fletcher, that you would find my words unpalatable. You must learn to swallow such insults if you are to become my lord's minion."

Damaris made haste to intervene. Now, if ever, was her opportunity to end Kit's efforts to dissuade her from going to England, but how cruel a price she must pay to do it. Deliberately she must destroy all his faith in her, for only thus could she be certain that no danger would ever again threaten him at the hands of the Golden Panther. Wondering if she had the strength of will convincingly to play her loathsome part, she said composedly:

"You bring me no new tidings, Kit. My uncle has told me of his plans for my future, and I have no fault to find with them."

Both men stared at her in amazement, but whereas Ingram preserved a discreet silence, Kit repeated incredulously:

"No fault to find with them? Then either he has not been frank with you, or you have not properly understood him."

"I am not a child, Kit!" Somehow she contrived to keep her voice light, even faintly amused. "I know precisely what part I am to play, and it suits my taste very well." She cast a fleeting glance at his face, and achieved a little trill of laughter. "For pity's sake, do not look so grim! There is no dishonour in being the mistress of a King."

For a moment or two he pondered her in silence, as she leaned gracefully against the bulwarks, with her bright hair stirring in the breeze, and for a background the burning sky and glittering, blue-green sea. There was bitterness in his eyes, and pain, and profound disillusionment.

"My lord has found an apt pupil," he said in a low voice at last, "and yet I thought I knew you, Damaris, if I knew any living soul. I would have staked my life upon your innocence and integrity. God! What a fool I was."

His tone, even more than the actual words, was like a knife twisting savagely in her heart, and from pain, anger was born. Was he so easy to convince, so ready to believe her worthless and wanton? With no suspicion of the anguish which had prompted those bitter words, she sought defiantly to confirm his opinion of her.

"By what right do you censure me?" she demanded. "The only life I knew ended on the day my uncle came to Fallowmead, but now I have a chance to build a new life, in a world outside your knowledge. I do not lack ambition, nor do I care what means I use to gratify it."

A sneer touched Kit's firm lips, twisting them in contemptuous irony.

"Then you are well matched with your future husband," he said scornfully, "since you are both so eager to sell your honour for worldly gain."

Fletcher started to bluster, but again Damaris gripped him by the arm. She spoke imperiously.

"Let us have no brawling, gentlemen. Kit, if you mean only to insult us, it were better to say no more."

Ingram, who had no real desire to force an issue, patted her hand and said magnanimously that he was willing to overlook what had been said. Damaris, withdrawing the hand somewhat hastily, turned her back upon them both and stared blindly across the sparkling water. How much longer, she thought desperately, was this nightmare to continue? How much self-inflicted torment was it possible to bear?

"Damaris!" Kit's voice had changed; there was a note in it now which made her pose doubly hard to maintain. "I cannot believe that you speak thus of your own free will. Are you afraid of your uncle? Has he threatened you?" She made no reply, and he gripped her by the shoulders, swinging her round to face him. "Child, you have trusted me often enough in the past! Will you not tell me your trouble now?"

"There is nothing to tell," she lied breathlessly. It needed an actual, physical effort to remain rigid and unyielding in his grasp, when she was aching to feel his arms about her, holding her safe and sheltered from all the world. With a supreme effort, drawing upon her last reserves of courage, she looked up into his face, and forced her lips to assume an amused, indulgent smile.

"I do not fear my uncle," she said in a level voice, "and nothing you have told me today has the power to turn me from my purpose. You should not seek to do so, Kit! Have you not thought what it would mean to have your sister a power at Court—for though there is no bond of blood between us, I shall never cease to regard you as my brother?"

His grip tightened so that she caught her breath with the pain of it, and he said grimly:

"Were you indeed my sister, there would be no question of your going to Court, and you know it!"

"Were I your sister, I would lack the means to go," she retorted, "but I will not quarrel with you, Kit, for my debt to you is too great. I shall repay it, never fear! When I am secure in the King's favour, what earnest of my regard shall I obtain for you? A title? The Governorship of Jamaica? You have but to name the favour you desire."

His hands dropped from her shoulders, and a look of disgust dawned in his eyes. For an instant longer they stood face to face, and then with an odd gesture, as though he cast from him something offensive, he swung round and strode across the deck and down the companion. Damaris put out a hand blindly to grasp the bulwarks behind her, for the ship seemed to be heaving beneath her with a movement not of the sea, and a curious darkness blotted out the sunshine.

"Madam, you are unwell!" Ingram's voice spoke in her ear; his arm lent her a support from which she shrank instinctively. "It is intolerable that you should be brow-beaten thus after all you have endured today. Let me take you below."

"It is nothing," she replied, despising herself for a weakness she could not control. "I shall be better directly. Pray have the goodness to help me to my cabin, sir, and send my woman to me."

For the rest of the day she remained in her cabin, submitting indifferently to Rebecca's anxious cosseting, and trying to forget the look in Kit's face as he turned and left her with Ingram Fletcher. Meanwhile, between the three gentlemen, the atmosphere grew hourly more strained, for Martin and Ingram cherished a mutual dislike, and Kit nursed his bitter disappointment in a mood of sombre abstraction which neither of his companions ventured to pierce.

Long after darkness had fallen, and his fellow-passengers had retired, he paced the deck beneath the tropic stars, his thoughts circling with weary monotony around that incredible conversation with Damaris. In the face of the morning's danger it had seemed as though the bond between them was as strong as ever, and the subsequent disenchantment was doubly hard to bear. The men on watch, staring at his restlessly moving figure, wondered among themselves what kept the famous captain pacing there.

The *Good Hope* came back into the shelter of Port Royal less than three days after she had left it, to find a fleet at anchor in the harbour, and the whole town drunk with excitement. Harry Morgan was home from Maracaibo, with the laurels of victory on his brow, and its more tangible fruits cramming the holds of his ships. The *Good Hope* slipped in almost unnoticed, though in one quarter at least her arrival was remarked, for she had barely dropped anchor when a boat came alongside, bearing Dr. Alexander Blair. Kit was in the waist when he came aboard, and at sight of him, the Doctor's lean, dark face lost something of its look of haggard care.

"Praise be to God!" he said fervently, seizing Kit's outstretched hand in a crushing grip. "I guessed some villainy was afoot as soon as I found I'd been lured away by a false message, though when I learned that the *Albatross* had sailed the night you disappeared, I thought Renard had some hand in whatever devilry had taken place."

"He did!" Kit replied grimly. "He and my lord to-

gether! You shall have the whole tale, Alex, but it is
not one to be noised abroad."

"I'll warrant it's not!" Blair's glance shifted to the
poop-rail, where Damaris stood with her uncle and
Ingram Fletcher. "So you have brought the lassie home
again, Kit? That's as it should be, the more so since I
don't see his smooth-spoken lordship with her. Is it
too much to hope that you have fed his carcase to
the fishes?"

"Far too much!" Kit said shortly, and turned abruptly
aside to speak to John Ransome. Blair's brows lifted
a trifle, and he glanced sharply from Kit to Damaris,
but made no comment. Whatever had happened since
they left Port Royal, it was clear that all was not yet
well between them.

The full truth of the brief, disastrous voyage of the
Good Hope was finally disclosed in the study of the
Governor of Jamaica, and shared only with Sir Thomas
himself, Alex, and Sir Jocelyn Wade, whom they
chanced to find with Modyford. Captain Lucifer's dis-
appearance had, of course, become common knowledge,
since his men, led by Dr. Blair, had set the whole town
in an uproar in search of some clue to his whereabouts, but at Kit's own request no mention was to be
made of my lord's part in the affair. That, said Kit
grimly, was a matter resting solely between himself and
the Earl, and none of the men who heard him speak
pretended to misunderstand him. Chelsham would find
himself with a reckoning to pay, if and when he returned to Port Royal.

For the rest, public curiosity could be satisfied by
laying the whole blame upon Renard, for no one who
knew the Frenchman, and the depths of his hatred for
Captain Lucifer, would doubt that he had sought in

this way to avenge the flogging he had once suffered
at Kit's hands. The absence of my lord was less easily
explained, but a casual word dropped here and there
by the Governor soon created an impression that
Chelsham was, through no fault of his own, a prisoner
in the hands of the pirates. Sir Thomas had no wish
to bring discredit upon his lordship. So far as he knew,
the Earl was still a power at Court, and Modyford's
own position was not so secure that he could afford to
make an enemy of such a man.

Kit returned with Alex to Fallowmead, but Martin,
Ingram and Damaris remained in Port Royal as guests
of the Governor. The *Good Hope* would resume her
interrupted journey within a few days, and they would
once more sail aboard her. If it was thought in some
quarters that Mr. Farrancourt showed extraordinary
callousness in leaving Jamaica while his brother's fate
presumably hung in the balance, Martin himself neither
knew nor cared. Chelsham's ruthlessness, the crimes he
had committed, and, most of all, his cold-blooded
schemes concerning Damaris, had shattered his last
vestige of kindly feeling towards the Earl. For the sake
of the family name he had obtained from Kit a promise
that the truth of John Tremayne's death should remain
a secret between them, but for the rest Ralph could
extricate himself without assistance from the predica-
ment into which his villainy had led him.

During the days which elapsed between the return
to Port Royal and the projected departure of the *Good
Hope*, Damaris stayed close within the Governor's
house, refusing to stir beyond the confines of its garden.
Dr. Blair, who had given Kit no peace until he told
him the nature of the rift between them, came to argue
the matter with her, but she clung obstinately to the

line she had taken aboard the *Good Hope,* and Alex departed baffled and disappointed. Regina came, with Jocelyn, and they tried, jointly and severally, to persuade her to stay at least until they could all make the journey to England together, but in vain. She was all eagerness to be off, and though she confessed that her dear Regina's company would do much to relieve the tedium of the voyage, she refused to delay her own departure.

"And we cannot possibly leave Jamaica yet," Regina said worriedly. "For one thing, there is Olivia's wedding—oh, perhaps you did not know——"

"Of course I know of it!" Damaris turned quickly to a nearby mirror and pretended to rearrange the pearls about her neck; her voice was hard. "But I am to be married, too, and my wedding must wait, my uncle says, until we reach England. Do you know, Regina, I can scarcely believe, even yet, that I am really to go to London? Are the ladies of the Court very grand? But at least my jewels are above reproach, and my uncle and cousins will advise me how to dress, and how to conduct myself."

She rattled on in this style until Jocelyn and Regina took their leave, even more puzzled than Alex had been. They knew nothing of the career my lord designed for his niece, but they were both acutely aware of the change in Damaris. She was no longer the merry, impetuous, confiding girl they had known when they first came to Jamaica, but the brittle gaiety she had lately assumed was an armour that neither could pierce.

On the afternoon before the day set for her departure, Damaris sat alone in the Governor's garden. Ingram and Martin had ridden out to the Charnwood plantation to take their leave of Mr. Charnwood and his elder daughter, but though Damaris knew that in common civility she should have gone with them, she could not face another meeting with Olivia. So she had charged the gentlemen with a message of farewell, and now sat in a shady corner, staring at a clump of azaleas and trying to bring herself to face the thought that after tomorrow there was no chance that she would ever see Kit again.

Her privacy was presently invaded by a servant, escorting a visitor whose presence in the Governor's garden was surprising enough to stir a spark of interest even in Miss Tremayne. She had lived long enough in the vicinity of Port Royal to be in no doubt of the profession of the gaudily clad, heavily painted young woman now confronting her, but she could not imagine what such a person might want with her.

The servant informed her austerely that the woman was the bearer of a message for her, and withdrew, as though washing his hands of the whole lamentable affair. The girl dropped without ceremony on to the seat beside Damaris; she was panting, and seemed to be in some distress.

"You're needed at once, ma'am, down in the town," she said breathlessly. "I came as fast as I could! 'Tis Captain Lucifer!"

"Kit?" Damaris came to her feet, her voice sharp with anxiety. "Why, what of him?"

"He was set upon by half-a-dozen ruffians in the street, and sore wounded. Some of Morgan's men drove the fellows off and carried the Captain to my father's tavern, and as soon as he came to his senses he asked for you. Dr. Blair is with him, and he bade me tell you to come at once, if—if you are to be in time."

Damaris shut her eyes for a moment as sunlight and shadow spun dizzily about her, but with an effort she conquered the weakness. She was trembling violently, but she clutched the girl by the arm and dragged her to her feet.

"Show me the way, quickly!" she gasped. "Oh, hasten, please! Dear God! What if I am too late?"

"Be easy, ma'am, 'tis only a step," the other assured her, and so, impetuously, never pausing to question the likelihood of the story or to leave word of her intention, Damaris went with her out of the garden and through the streets towards the waterfront.

The town was noisy and crowded, every tavern and drinking-den full to overflowing, and spilling drunken patrons of both sexes into the narrow streets, for the men who had taken Maracaibo had come home with well-filled pockets, which they were now emptying as fast as they could. Pleasantries and invitations of embarrassing frankness attended the progress of the two women, but Damaris was too absorbed in her own frightened thoughts to hear them, and her companion either paid no heed or replied in a similar vein.

The tavern to which they presently came was a squalid place, dilapidated and filthy, displaying over its door a faded sign depicting a broken sword. From its gloomy interior came the discordant uproar which filled every place of its kind as long as the Brethren of the Coast had money to spend, and for an instant Damaris hesitated, glancing to right and left along the narrow street. Then the memory of her errand stifled the brief impulse of caution, and she followed her guide through the uninviting doorway.

They skirted the low-pitched, shadowy, crowded room to a ramshackle stair at its far end, and so came to the comparative quiet of the upper floor. The woman led the way along a dark, evil-smelling passage and opened a door, and Damaris went quickly in, more than a little afraid of what she might find.

In point of fact she found nothing, nothing at all save an empty, dirty, poorly furnished room, inadequately lit by one small, grimy window. Then she perceived another door facing that by which she had entered, and had actually started towards it when the unmistakable sound of a key grating in a lock brought her swinging round.

The woman who had brought her was still there, but the door had been shut by a man who had followed them into the room and was even then in the act of dropping the key into his pocket. He was a lean fellow with a sharp, cunning face which was vaguely familiar, but before she could trace the elusive memory it evoked, the door behind her opened, and a precise voice said softly:

"The game, madam, is not yet played out! This hand, I think, goes to me."

With a gasp of disbelief and horror she turned, and saw confronting her the sallow, pock-marked face and pale, cruel eyes of Renard. She shrank back as he advanced into the room, until she fetched up against the wall and could retreat no further, and he studied her for a moment with a smile of wicked satisfaction before turning to his two confederates.

"All goes well!" he remarked. "The dove is in the trap, and will serve as bait for the hawk. Peg, be off with you to Fallowmead! You know the story you have to tell?"

"Aye," the girl replied with a grin. "You've taken the wench prisoner and sent to this uncle of hers at the

Governor's house to bring you her jewels as ransom. I've had word with her and she's bribed me to carry the news to Lucifer. I'm to guide him here, saying you are away seeing to arrangements for your escape."

"Excellent!" Renard turned to the shrinking Damaris and laid hold of the jewelled cross she wore about her neck. With a brutal wrench he snapped the slender chain that held it, and tossed the glittering thing to Peg. "There is the bribe you received, and the proof of your story. Lucifer will know that gaud."

She caught the cross with greedy fingers and bestowed it in her bosom, while Renard signed to the other man to open the door. With a taunting glance at Damaris, and a broad wink at the men, Peg sidled out, and Renard held out a commanding hand.

"The key!" he said shortly.

There was the barest hesitation, and then with obvious reluctance the other man surrendered it. There was a pause, while Damaris looked from one to the other with frightened eyes, and then the fellow said with an evil leer:

" 'Twill take Peg the best part of an hour to reach Fallowmead, and you'll not be wanting my company, Renard. I'll be off to the Governor's house with the message for Farrancourt."

"You will go below and keep watch for Lucifer," the Frenchman informed him brusquely. "You fool! Do you think I want Farrancourt blundering here before he has been dealt with?"

An ugly expression flickered in the other's beady eyes.

"You keep to your side of the bargain, Renard, and I'll keep to mine. You've got the wench you wanted, and unless Peg fails you you'll settle your score wi'

Lucifer, but it's the jewels I want, and I'll not be easy till I've set my hands on them. Weren't they the only reason I sailed with you at all?"

At these words, Damaris realized suddenly why the man's face had seemed familiar to her. He it was who had brought Kit the news of the Spanish plate-ship, on the occasion of the party at Fallowmead, and who had stared with such greedy eyes at the jewels she had worn that night. No doubt he had hoped to secure the gems when the *Good Hope* fell victim to the pirates, but the advent of the two Spanish ships had brought the scheme to naught.

"You will get the jewels, never fear," Renard was saying contemptuously. "Once Lucifer has been disposed of, the message shall go to Farrancourt, and I've no doubt he will obey it. Be guided by me, my friend! The slow road is the surest."

"Ye're a smooth-tongued rogue, Renard," the man said suspiciously. "If you think to cozen me——"

"How should I profit by that? Are we not to share the jewels? Now get below, and as soon as Lucifer appears bring word to me."

There was another palpable hesitation, but though the fellow was obviously in awe of his confederate, his greed, and his fear of again letting the jewels slip through his fingers, prompted him to further protests. For what seemed an eternity to the terrified girl the argument continued, Renard growing more coldly sinister as his henchman's bluster increased in violence. At last, obviously unconvinced, but overborne by the stronger will of the Frenchman, the pirate turned and went slowly from the room. As his footsteps faded along the passage, Renard turned his head to look at

Damaris, standing white and trembling against the far wall.

"So once more, my dear, you find yourself in my hands," he said mockingly, "and this time there are no cowardly fools to be wrought upon by the name of the great Lucifer. When he does come it will be to his death, and whether or not I gain possession of the jewels, I shall be well content."

"He will not come," she retorted, with a pitiful attempt at defiance. "He will not believe that you would dare to come to Port Royal."

Renard took a pistol from his belt, weighed it thoughtfully in his hand, and laid it deliberately upon the table beside him.

"He will come," he said quietly, "for he will realize that as long as I hold a hostage for my safety I have nothing to fear in Port Royal. Much as Sir Thomas Modyford would like to see me hang, he would not dare to move against me while I had the power to slip a knife between his noble lordship's ribs."

A tiny glimmer of hope sprang to life within her.

"My uncle is here, in Port Royal?"

Renard nodded, and laid a second pistol beside the first. There was a curious smile hovering about his lips.

"He is here. It was he who had the happy thought of luring Lucifer to his death with news of your desperate plight, for he is as urgent to be rid of him as I." He unbuckled his cutlass, and placed it by the pistols. "His lordship, however, intended the story of your danger to be no more than a ruse."

The glimmer of hope grew stronger. She asked, with an eagerness she tried hard to dissemble:

"Where is my uncle, then? I think you are lying, Renard."

"He is within!" Renard jerked his head towards the inner door, and made no move to stop her when she sprang forward to fling it open.

The room beyond was a bedchamber, as frowsy and dirty as the rest, but Damaris had eyes only for the man who sat there. His back was towards her, but the coat of grey brocaded silk, and the pale golden curls of his great periwig, left no doubt of his identity. He neither moved nor spoke at her tempestuous entrance, and his dreadful immobility struck a sharp fear into her heart even as her hand clutched his arm.

Beneath her touch, the seated figure moved at last. It toppled slowly sideways out of the chair and sprawled grotesquely to the floor, and a cry of mingled horror and despair broke from her lips at sight of the dagger-hilt protruding from the midst of the great crimson stain which disfigured its breast. The most noble Earl of Chelsham, the man whose influence had been felt by Kings and Queens, the Golden Panther who had stalked unscathed through a lifetime of Court intrigue, had died ingloriously at the hands of an outlawed pirate, in a squalid room in a disreputable West Indian tavern. There was a certain grim irony in the fate which had overtaken him.

Some such thought was in Damaris's mind as she stood staring in dreadful fascination at the dead man, scarcely aware, until he spoke, that Renard had followed her into the room.

"My lord was as damnably proud as Lucifer himself," he said in a tone of suppressed fury, "but he learned, as Lucifer shall learn ere long, that I am not with impunity defied. As for you, my dear, neither the one nor the other can aid you now."

As he spoke, he raised his eyes from the grinning

corpse at his feet and took a pace towards her. She looked up, but, reading her fate in his glittering eyes, she was seized by a terror so great that it deprived her of speech and movement. Not until he touched her did the bonds of dumb horror snap, and she began to struggle frantically. Then, finding her struggles vain, and although in that evil place there was little hope that anyone would hear, or, hearing, heed the cry, she screamed despairingly for the aid she had no hope of gaining.

Chapter XIV

THE RECKONING

In the main cabin of the *Loyalist,* Captain Lucifer bent over the map which he had spread upon the table. He had laid his sword across one end of it to keep it flat, and the slim blade with its hilt of intricately wrought gold gleamed in a patch of afternoon sunlight which fell through the tall windows astern. The horn casements stood wide, and on the cushioned locker below them Alex Blair was sitting, smoking a long clay pipe and frowning in grim abstraction.

"I cannot believe it," he said suddenly into the silence. " 'Tis against all sense and reason. Plague take it, Kit! The lassie has a will of her own, as well we know. Chelsham must have found some way of compelling her to obey him."

There was a perceptible pause before Kit replied, but at last he said:

"You assume that her will runs counter to his. It does not, and so he has no need to compel her. They are of the same blood. Is it wonderful that they should think alike?"

"Blood has naught to do with it!" Alex replied impatiently. "She was reared by your mother, whose memory, I'll warrant, means more to Damaris even yet than all the Farrancourts in the world. I'll not deny that to learn the truth as she did was a shock not easy to recover from, but can you, knowing the lassie as you do—aye, and loving her as you do—believe that she goes willingly to the future her uncle designs for her?"

"Do either of us know her, I wonder?" Kit said sadly. "I think you have forgotten the one thing, Alex, which supplies the key to the whole. She suffered another blow that day, more cruel, I fancy, than the first."

"You mean Nicholas?" Dr. Blair shook his head. "There was no depth of feeling there, Kit, on her side at least. You cannot be fool enough to believe that the reason for the change in her?"

"I prefer to believe it!" Kit was still leaning upon the table, his eyes fixed unseeingly on the map between his hands. "God's light, man! Do you not see that it is easier to believe her so sore stricken by his death that she cares nothing for the future, than to admit her to be incapable of aught save worldliness? To admit that were to lose all, even the memory of those years when there was true affection between us."

"That is what I cannot accept!" Dr. Blair got up and began to pace the cabin. "She did love you, Kit! Oh, not as you love her, perhaps, but she would never willingly have caused you pain. You held a place in her heart which no lover, were he King or buccaneer, could ever fill."

Kit raised his head; his face was very pale.

"If I did, Alex, I lost it when she learned the truth of her birth. Oh, I blame myself as much as Damaris, make no doubt of that! Had I not been too great a coward to tell her the truth, matters might have fallen out very differently. Think for a moment of what she suffered that day! Her whole world shaken to its foundations, and no one to whom she could turn for comfort. No one save my lord." A faint, mirthless smile touched his lips for an instant. "It is strange how a man can mismanage his life, even when fortune favours him. Since I joined the Brethren, every venture to which I have set my hand has prospered, and yet what use now is that success? I would have given my life for her, and yet——" he broke off, and through the open casements his eyes sought the *Good Hope* where she rode at anchor. "So it must end. She goes to England to sell herself to the King."

"And you, Kit?" Alex asked quietly after a moment. "Whither do you go?"

Kit's gaze came slowly back to him. There was an inscrutable expression in the dark blue eyes.

"There!" he said, and turned the sword so that its point rested upon a certain spot on the map. Alex came to the table to look, and then raised startled eyes to his captain's face.

"Panama!" he said blankly. "You're mad, Kit! Stark, staring mad!"

"Am I?" Kit picked up the sword and returned it to its scabbard. The map slowly rolled itself up again. "Yet I have heard Harry Morgan speak of such a raid."

"In his cups, perhaps! Why, you would need an army to take Panama, and a fleet to carry it there."

"I know it. There will be ships enough, and men."

"You are to join with Morgan? Is that what you mean?"

Kit shook his head.

"He will not be ready to put to sea again for months, and I do not mean to wait upon his pleasure. Oh, devil take it, Alex! Do you not see that I must have work to do, if I am to save my reason?"

Dr. Blair was silent for a space. He had feared something of this kind, for he realized that the intolerable pain which was driving Kit so hard must eventually find an outlet in action, no matter how reckless, how remote the chances of success. Just how reckless it would be he had not foreseen, but he knew that argument would be worse than useless. After a little he said mildly:

"How do you propose to obtain the necessary ships? To capture them is a chancy business, but any other way would cost a fortune."

Kit was replacing the map among others in a rack, and answered without turning his head.

"I am going to sell Fallowmead."

"Sell——!" Blair's jaw dropped; there was disbelief in his voice. "Man, you are not serious? I know what the place means to you!"

"I wonder if you do?" Kit said in a low voice, turning slowly to face him. "To me, Fallowmead was the attaining of an ambition. I was born in a house of that name, as was my father, and all the Brandons for five generations back, a house which I saw the Roundheads burn. That is my earliest memory! As I grew older, I resolved that one day I would build a new Fallowmead, to be the home of Brandons in generations to come." He paused, and once more his eyes sought the ship which on the morrow would sail for England. When he spoke again there was bitterness and self-mockery in his voice. "Let it go, like all the rest! There will be no son of mine to inherit it."

Alex stared at him beneath knit brows, a small, ugly fear gnawing, rat-like, at his thoughts. There was an ominous finality in Kit's words, in his decision to dispose of the estate into which had been poured all the fruits of his depredations against Spain. It was the action of a man deliberately setting his affairs in order under sentence of death.

In the gangway outside, footsteps sounded, swift and urgency, and the door was thrust hastily open. Into the cabin came young John Ransome, the master of the *Good Hope*, with no apology for his intrusion, and words on his lips which disposed of the need for one.

"There's mischief brewing ashore, sir," he told Kit bluntly. "I saw a hangdog fellow who was in Marayte's crew skulking at the door of the Broken Sword, and while I was wondering how he came to be in Port Royal, who should come down the street but Miss Tremayne, with some doxy or other to guide her, and went into the tavern." He paused, his honest, troubled gaze on Kit's face. " 'Tis a den of rogues there, sir, and no safe place for a woman."

Alex blinked at him, taken aback by the suddenness of his arrival and his news, but to Kit the words were in themselves explanation enough. He still stood with his hand resting lightly on the rack which held the maps and charts, and though he did not move, his face hardened into lines of anger and dismay and a growing dread.

"Renard!" he said, in a quiet, terrible voice. "I should have thought of that."

He moved then, and without another word went to take down a leather stole with a pistol at each end, and set it about his neck. Then he went quickly out of the cabin, and the others followed at his heels in silence, Blair pausing only to snatch up his sword from the corner where it stood.

The boat which had brought Ransome was rocking gently at the foot of the *Loyalist's* ladder, and in the space of moments they were speeding with a flash of oars towards the mole. Coming ashore, Ransome moved by tacit consent to lead the way, and they plunged into the tangle of narrow streets beyond the waterfront, three grim, purposeful men who went swiftly, with no need of words.

At the door of the tavern Ransome drew back, and it was Kit who stepped first into the gloom beyond. A moment he paused, his glance sweeping the squalid, noisy room, singling out the uncouth figure of the landlord, and then he went forward with long, arrogant strides which took no account of those between them.

The tavern-keeper, propped at loquacious ease against a stained and battered table, was startled to find himself confronted by one of Port Royal's most redoubtable captains. One strong, shapely hand gripped him by the front of his grimy shirt, the other thrust the long barrel of a pistol against his stomach, and in astonishment and alarm he looked up into a handsome, resolute face which was like a mask of pale bronze, from which merciless blue eyes met his in a look of cold ferocity.

"Where is she?" Captain Lucifer wasted no words. "Where is the lady who came into this foul den of yours a short while since?"

"A—a lady?" The fellow's eyes shifted desperately from side to side while his lips formed a stammering denial. "You—you're mistaken, cap'n. There's no lady here."

Lucifer's lips tightened; the pistol was thrust harder against the cringing body.

"No?" he said dangerously. "Remember, my friend, those who shelter Renard may well go with him to the gallows."

The fear deepened in the landlord's eyes, but before he could make any reply, from somewhere above came a woman's scream, on a note of terror and despair, to cut like a thrusting sword through the hush which had succeeded Lucifer's arrival. The sound of it was quivering still upon the air as Kit flung his prisoner aside and sprang towards the stairs.

He went up them two at a time, Blair and Ransome at his heels, and paused at the top to shout the name of her he sought. To Damaris, half fainting with terror in Renard's brutal hold, the sound of his voice seemed born of her own desperate need, and it was only when the Frenchman's grip slackened and he turned his head incredulously towards the outer room, that she realized it was no delusion. She cried out again, and heard the swift, approaching footsteps which heralded deliverance.

A furious oath broke from Renard's lips. He, too, had recognized that voice, and knew that Lucifer had come upon him without the expected warning, and an hour and more earlier than he had looked to see him— and his sword and pistols lay on the table in the outer room. He started towards them, but Damaris also had remembered the discarded weapons, and now it was she who clung to him, and he who tried to free himself from the hampering arms.

He struck at her savagely with his clenched fist, and, throwing her off, had actually reached the table by the time the door crashed open. Just for an instant he saw Lucifer framed in the aperture, saw with awful clarity the implacable eyes and the long-barrelled pistol, and then with a flash and a roar and a searing agony the whole world exploded into darkness.

The noise of the shot was deafening in that confined

space. Renard pitched forward across the table and slid slowly to the floor, the pistol he had tried to grasp slipping from his slackened fingers. For a second or two Kit looked down at him through the drifting smoke, and then strode past him to the doorway where Damaris was huddled.

He put up his pistol and knelt to raise her in his arms. She had been stunned by Renard's vicious blow, and her head fell back against his shoulder, her face chalk-white below the crown of bright, disordered hair. Alex, too, moved quickly forward, but he went past Kit, and, with his drawn sword in his hand, stepped into the inner room, while Ransome, after a moment's hesitation, turned to bar the way of those whom curiosity had drawn from below, and who were now staring and thrusting in the passage outside.

Alex came back to the doorway, thrusting his sword back into its sheath. His dark face was grim.

"Kit," he said abruptly, "Chelsham lies within, with a dagger in his heart."

Slowly Kit raised his head. From the moment of Ransome's arrival aboard the *Loyalist*, he had thought only of Damaris; his whole attention was still centered upon her, and it was a second or two before the full implications of Blair's words pierced his preoccupation, but when they did a frown gathered in his eyes. He rose, with her in his arms, and carried her to the bed in the inner room, and laid her gently upon it. Then he turned, and looked dispassionately at the mortal remains of my lord the Earl.

"This alters the situation, Kit," Blair said gravely beside him. "Renard is of no account, but the murder of a peer of the realm is a serious matter."

"It is Renard's work, no doubt of that," Kit replied

slowly. "Did my lord seek to protect Damaris from him?"

Alex shook his head.

"He has been dead for hours," he said. "'Tis an ugly business, Kit. You will need to go warily."

"Do I not know it? There is Farrancourt to be thought of, for he will not wish the truth of his brother's dealings with Renard to be discovered, and questions will be asked in England when this news is known." He paused, frowning down at the dead man, and after a little said abruptly: "I had best go to Modyford without delay. He is the man to handle this." He looked again towards the bed; Damaris had not moved, and the darkening bruise on her forehead told its own tale. "Stay with her, Alex, and let her speak with no one," he added, and was gone before Dr. Blair could make either comment or protest.

Captain Lucifer's authority was great enough to disperse the gaping crowd about the outer door, and bidding Ransome stay where he was and let no one enter, Kit made his way quickly to the Governor's house. Sir Thomas, on hearing his story, realized at once the need for discretion, and while a groom went hurrying to summon Mr. Farrancourt from the Charnwood house, the Governor's own coach was despatched to fetch Miss Tremayne from the tavern.

Kit went with it, but remained in the town to question the tavern-keeper, and discover, if possible, the identity and present whereabouts of Renard's confederates—for Modyford's servants had reported that a man of disreputable appearance had already been to the house asking for Mr. Farrancourt. An immediate search was made, but it met with no success, the crowded and riotous state of the town, which had so completely cloaked Renard's stealthy return, serving now to aid his henchman's escape.

It seemed likely that the fellow, learning of Renard's death, had taken fright and slipped away to rejoin the *Albatross* at some secluded rendezvous along the coast, but Sir Thomas considered it both unwise and unnecessary to pursue him. Deprived of their leader, the pirates were of little account, and it was unlikely that any of them would venture near Port Royal again.

When, on her return to his house, Sir Thomas questioned Damaris on events of the afternoon, she answered him frankly enough, with one notable exception. Asked what ruse had been used to lure her into the trap, she declared outrageously that she had forgotten, and was unable to give any clear description of the woman who had brought the message. Sir Thomas raised his brows a trifle sceptically but refrained from comment, for it was of little importance. Damaris, whose one desire was to keep the nature of the message secret from Kit, was thankful for his forbearance, and hoped devoutly that Peg would have the good sense to avoid the tavern of the Broken Sword until the hue and cry had died down.

It was this same anxiety to avoid disclosing the truth which prompted her to retire to her room immediately after her interview with Sir Thomas, thus escaping a meeting with Kit. Dazed and shaken by her ordeal, not knowing how her future would be affected by the Earl's death, she shrank from the thought of facing him; others she could deceive, but not Kit. He knew her too well.

Martin Farrancourt, who arrived back in Port Royal in the cool of the evening, she did consent to see, for by that time she had had leisure to collect her wits, and

had a request to make which surprised and did not
altogether please him. Her obvious distress wrung from
him at last a reluctant consent, but it was in a lament-
ably puzzled and uneasy frame of mind that he eventually bade her good night, and went back to Sir
Thomas.

While he was with Damaris, Kit had returned, and
had been discussing with the Governor the events of the
day. Modyford had already devised a version of the
tale to be made public, and now suggested that, if Mr.
Farrancourt were agreeable, it should be given out that
Renard, having captured the Earl aboard the *Good
Hope,* had brought him back to Jamaica as hostage
for his own safety, subsequently killing him when my
lord tried to protect his niece from the pirate.

"And that, my friend," Sir Thomas had said drily
to Kit before Martin joined them, "is as neat a vengeance as you could desire. My own estimate of his
lordship's character does not lead me to suppose that
he would be grateful for any charitable glossing-over of
his misdeeds."

Kit agreed with a somewhat grim smile. He was
tolerably certain that the Golden Panther would have
preferred his full infamy to be known rather than to be
remembered only as the well-meaning but ineffectual
victim of Renard's superior cunning. Any satisfaction
he might have taken in that thought, however, was soon
shattered, for as soon as Modyford left the room,
Martin said abruptly:

"I must tell you, Captain Brandon, that Damaris will
leave Jamaica tomorrow aboard the *Good Hope.* If you
wish to bid her farewell——" he paused, glanced fleetingly at the other man's face, and then averted his

eyes, adding helplessly: "It is by her own wish. I thought it right that you should know."

Kit, staring blankly at him, realized for the first time that until this moment he had never, in spite of what he had told Alex, wholly ceased to believe that my lord was in some way compelling Damaris to obey him. Martin's words gave the lie to that scarcely acknowledged hope. The Earl's death must have freed her from any such compulsion, but rather than avail herself of her escape she would not wait even to see her uncle buried, but must be off to England as though nothing had occurred to hinder her departure. Even though he was dead, she would follow the road my lord had chosen for her, and the vengeance of which Sir Thomas had spoken was an empty mockery.

"It does not please me that she should make the journey with no one but Fletcher to escort her," Martin was saying in a troubled voice, "but she seems in such agitation at the prospect of further delay that I hesitate to refuse her. It is natural, I suppose, that she should be anxious to leave the scene of so much recent unhappiness, and yet——! Can you not advise me, Captain Brandon? You know her so much better than I——" he broke off, staring, for without a word Kit turned sharp on his heel and strode from the room, with the look in his face of one who could endure no more.

He borrowed a horse from the Governor's stables and rode, like a man possessed, to Fallowmead, to the home which had meant so much to him and so little, it seemed, to her. All night he paced the garden walks in an agony of indecision and heartbreak. How could he let her go? Heartless and mercenary as she had proved herself to be, he loved her still, with an intensity which made unbearable the thought of losing her. Would she stay if he told her the truth; if he laid bare his heart's anguish and begged her not to leave him? Perhaps, out of pity, or a mistaken sense of gratitude, she might remain, but he knew that no happiness could lie that way for either of them. She must stay of her own free will, or not at all.

The sun had risen in splendour long before he came to a decision, but when at last he went slowly towards the house, he had summoned pride to his aid where all else had failed him. At the door he met Alex, booted and spurred, while at the foot of the steps a groom was waiting with the Doctor's horse. Blair gave him good morning, and then added with an odd look:

"The *Good Hope* sails with the tide, Kit."

"Well?" Kit prompted as he paused. Both voice and look were cold, and Alex hesitated a moment before he continued.

"Shall I wait for you, or will you follow me to Port Royal?"

"Neither," Kit said curtly, and went past him into the house. Alex turned quickly and caught him by the arm.

"You'll never let her go with no word of farewell? Man, 'tis wanton cruelty!"

"Cruelty!" Kit turned more fully to face him. He was white to the lips; his voice shook. "My God, Alex! Of what do you suppose I am made? I thought that with my lord dead—but I was mistaken! Nothing, not even her uncle's murder, will serve to delay her plans. Do not delude yourself, then, that I shall endeavour to do so."

"I said naught of delaying her, lad," Blair replied drily. "That thought was yours."

Kit drew a sharp, audible breath.

"You hit hard, do you not?" he said bitterly. "Yes, I am fool enough to want her at any price, upon any terms, but I have pride enough not to let her know it. I'll not go with you to Port Royal."

"Pride!" Alex repeated quietly, and shook his head. "Must you still be Lucifer, even now?"

For a second or two Kit regarded him in silence. In his face the strain and weariness were overlaid now with a kind of perilous calm; only his eyes betrayed him, and at them Alex found he could not look a second time.

"Leave me my pride, my friend," Kit said at length in a tone of infinite bitterness. " 'Tis all I have left."

He laid his hand on the Doctor's shoulder, gripping it hard for a moment, and then went past him across the hall and into the library. As the door closed behind him, Alex swore vehemently under his breath with mingled rage and grief, and then he went slowly down the steps and mounted his horse. He knew that there was no more to be said.

He rode slowly, conscious of a curious reluctance to see Damaris again, for he was as much grieved as puzzled by the change which my lord's influence had wrought in her. More than once he was on the point of turning back, and when at last he reached the town, the hour was so far advanced that he half hoped, half expected that she would already have gone aboard the *Good Hope*. This, however, was not the case, and when he arrived at the Governor's house he found her there with her uncle, Jocelyn and Regina Wade, and a palpably impatient Mr. Fletcher.

Damaris had, in fact, annoyed her betrothed by lingering ashore until the last possible moment, for this time, surely, Kit would come. She must see him

just once more, must show him, somehow, that in spite
of all she had not forgotten, and never would forget, the
happiness he had given her in the past. As time went
on she grew frightened, and when at last she heard
Dr. Blair's familiar voice, her relief was so great that
weakness flooded over her, and she found herself
trembling.

Alex came in, and the words of greeting froze on
her lips as she realized that he was alone. It was incredible, a nightmare repetition of that other occasion
when she had waited and watched in vain, and though
she did not know what she would have said to Kit
had he come, his absence was a blow which struck her
with stunning force.

A strained silence succeeded the murmur of greeting
provoked by Dr. Blair's arrival. At length Mr. Fletcher
broke it, to ask the question which was in all their
minds, but which only he was insensitive enough to
voice.

"May we know, sir, whether Captain Brandon is
with you, or intends to follow you?"

Damaris flashed him a glance almost of gratitude,
but the Doctor's voice was carefully dispassionate as
he replied.

"No, Mr. Fletcher, neither the one nor the other."

"And he sent no message?"

"He did not."

Ingram turned to Damaris; almost he seemed to
sneer at her.

"You hear, madam? Now perhaps you will consent
to bring this farce of leave-taking to a close, and come
aboard ship. Time grows short."

Slowly Damaris rose from her chair to comply with
that querulously voiced demand, the tone of which

brought a frown of anxiety and misgiving to Martin's brow. Thus, then, she must go, with no word of forgiveness or farewell, leaving Kit to remember her in the hateful guise which, for his sake, she had assumed. She took a pace towards Ingram, who was regarding her with ill-concealed triumph, and then she halted, impelled by something stronger than pride or jealousy, stronger even than her will.

"I cannot," she said desperately. "I cannot go without seeing him."

There was an instant of pregnant silence, and then Alex said harshly:

"To what purpose, Damaris? Have you not made him suffer enough?"

She stared at him without comprehension, and put a hand to her head.

"To tell him the truth!" she said wildly. "I cannot let him think so badly of me! Did you not guess that I pretended to fall in with my uncle's schemes only so that Kit should not incur his enmity again?"

"God in Heaven!" Alex said blankly. He stepped up to her and gripped her by the shoulders, staring down into her face. "Damaris, is this the truth?"

"Of course, of course!" she replied vehemently. "I made Kit believe it—'twas the only thing I could do for him. I thought I had courage enough to carry it through, but, oh, Alex! I cannot bear it. I would rather he pitied me than despised me."

Martin moved forward, blank bewilderment in his face.

"But Ralph is dead now, child, and can harm no one. Why were you in such haste to be gone?"

Colour swept into her wan face, and when she replied her voice was scarcely audible.

"Because of my jealousy of Olivia. I wanted to be gone before they were married."

The explanation did nothing to clarify matters. Regina said, in the tone of one groping blindly after the truth:

"Olivia is to marry Colonel Prestyn next month."

"Colonel Prestyn!" Damaris looked up sharply, her colour fading as swiftly as it had come. "But she is promised to Kit. She told me so herself."

Dr. Blair uttered an exclamation which, out of deference to Olivia's sister, he succeeded in strangling at birth; Martin turned sharply away to the window and stood with his back to the company; and Regina, after a troubled glance at her husband, which he met with a helpless shrug, said in a low voice:

"Be that as it may, 'tis Colonel Prestyn she is to wed. At our father's command, it is true, but I am sure that Captain Brandon never sought her hand, whatever Olivia's feelings for him may have been."

"Of course he did not!" Alex broke in explosively. "There is only one maid he ever thought to wed, and 'tis not Miss Olivia, that I know." He turned again to Damaris and spoke very gravely, with the utmost earnestness. "Believe me, my child, so far is he from thinking of marriage with any save yourself, that he plans to sell Fallowmead, and pour the gold into the maddest venture that ever I heard of, which he has not one chance in a hundred of surviving. Go back to him, lassie! 'Tis where you belong."

Damaris sank down into her chair again, covering her face with her hands, and in the pause which followed Dr. Blair's words, Mr. Fletcher, who since her first outburst had been growing steadily more angry and more alarmed, chose once more to make his presence felt.

"You forget, I think, that Miss Tremayne is betrothed to me," he said indignantly, and turned to Damaris. "Enough of this folly, madam! Make your farewells, and let us be gone."

Martin Farrancourt turned slowly from the window. His worn, sensitive face was ravaged by some deep emotion, but there was an authority in his manner which had never been apparent while my lord lived.

"I mislike your tone, sir," he informed Fletcher coldly, "and since I am aware of the bargain you made with my brother, it will not surprise you to know that your betrothal to my niece is at an end. It should never have been entered upon." He moved to Damaris's side and laid a hand on her shoulder, but his stern glance remained upon Ingram. "There is a ship about to sail, sir, as you have been so eager to remind us. I suggest you avail yourself of it."

Fletcher's face went white and spiteful. He started to argue, then, realizing that it availed him nothing, passed instead to blustering threats. Jocelyn strolled forward and took him persuasively by the arm.

"That's sound advice, my friend, if you want to keep a whole skin," he said pensively. "You seem to have overlooked the fact that if you try to assert a claim to Miss Tremayne's hand, you will have Captain Lucifer to reckon with." He saw the sudden alarm in Fletcher's eyes, and smiled contemptuously. "That puts a different complexion on the matter, does it not?"

For a moment longer Ingram hesitated, glaring from one to the other, and then with an inarticulate exclamation he flung out of the room. Jocelyn looked thoughtfully after him.

"There will be a word of explanation needed aboard the *Good Hope,*" he remarked, "but I've a notion Fletcher is not the man to give it. I'll just go with him to wish him Godspeed."

So when the *Good Hope* weighed anchor a short while later, she bore away from Jamaica not two passengers, but one, while Miss Tremayne's gear and her waiting-woman were conveyed ashore again in the charge of Sir Jocelyn Wade. From Fallowmead, however, all that could be seen was the ship putting out to sea, and Kit, standing upon that balcony where so often in the past Damaris had stood, watched it with yearning, hopeless eyes.

He had been drawn as though by a lodestone to that point of vantage. At his back was the beautiful room, empty now for so many weeks, and never again to know the beloved presence for whom it had been created. The whole house was wrapped in the stillness and silence of a tomb, for the slaves, mourning this final departure of the young mistress they loved, had withdrawn to their own quarters. Only, somewhere in the distance, a woman's voice was raised in a chant of lamentation, and the wild notes, rising and falling, seemed to pierce his heart with their burden of immemorial pain.

Suddenly he grew tense, his hands closing hard on the balustrade before him and the breath checked in his throat, for a light footfall was coming through the quiet house. It sounded upon the stairs and then in the corridor outside the room, and as he turned, doubting the evidence of his senses, Damaris herself appeared at the open door.

Kit stared at her, wondering whether this was some delusion born of weariness and despair and the night-long conflict between his longing and his pride. But no, it was Damaris in very truth, with her bright curls disordered as though from a hasty ride, and the bruise where Renard had struck her dark against her white brow. He flashed one incredulous glance over his shoulder at the departing ship, and then went slowly forward, into the room.

She had halted on the threshold, watching him wistfully and with a trace of uncertainty. At last she said, in a small, unsteady voice:

"I have come back, Kit. Will you let me stay?"

For answer, not trusting himself to speak, he held out his arms, and with a little sob of gladness she went into them, as she had so often done in the past, and felt them close about her. All the way from Port Royal she had been thinking what to say to him, how best to explain the web of lies and intrigue which had been spun about them both, but now that they were together there was somehow no need to say anything. Later, perhaps, they would talk of it, but for the present they were content to be quiet in each other's arms, with no word spoken, and none needed, secure in a sense of peace and homecoming.

Only, after a little, Kit took her hand and looked down at the ruby ring upon it. Sensing the thought behind the act, Damaris shook her head.

"There was never anyone else, Kit," she said gently. "I know that now." A sudden memory woke a smile in her eyes, and she drew his hand to her cheek and held it there. "On the day that Renard held us prisoner, one of his men warned him that I belonged to Lucifer. He spoke more truly than he knew. I always have, and I always will."

They looked at each other, smiling, past sorrow

forgotten in present happiness. Beyond the windows, between the flower-hung pillars of the balcony, the sails of the *Good Hope* faded, unheeded and unregretted, across the sunlit sea.

THE END